Lament

NICOLE KELLY

HAWKEYE
PUBLISHING

First published in Australia in 2020 by
Hawkeye Publishing.

Cover Design by Hawkeye Publishing.

Front Cover Photo by Matthew Deller, reprinted
courtesy of IronOutlaw.com

Historical photos courtesy of Trove, National Library
of Australia.

ISBN 978-0-6483661-4-0

www.hawkeyepublishing.com.au
www.hawkeyebooks.com.au

DEDICATION

For my greatest creations, Jack and Elsie.

The Kelly Gang

(L-R: Ned Kelly, Joe Byrne, Dan Kelly
& Steve Hart)

The Kelly Gang live today in Australian folklore, but before this, they were men. The gang was made up of Edward (Ned) Kelly, his younger brother, Dan Kelly, and their friends, Joe Byrne and Steve Hart. The Gang were wanted men from 1878 - 1880. They ran rampant through the north-east of Victoria—wanted for robbery and murder.

Ned Kelly was 25 at his death, and the eldest of the four. Joe Byrne was 23, Steve Hart 21 and Dan Kelly, only 19 years of age. One hundred and forty years since their deaths, they still capture the imagination of Australians, because things are never as simple as they seem.

LAMENT

I'm jolted. One way, then the next.

My back lays upon something hard, with not the slightest give in it. Unrelenting against flesh. It's uncomfortable, but I feel no pain.

What's pain anyway? Now, everything will always be this. What I feel is not enough.

It isn't the jolting that's the worst. It's the sound that drones on and on around my head. I can't tell if the constant noise is within, or a source outside my own broken mind. Coming from somewhere and pulling my mind to something that I can't quite reach out and grasp—not yet.

All I can remember is that I am me. I am Ned.

LAMENT

PART 1

THE CRASH

Saturday

I bang heavily on the door three times, and wait.

The moon is distant in the dark blanket overhead, signalling the early hours of the morning. The mare stands off to the side, reins dangling beneath her head, waiting patiently with Steve. She's a big, bay girl with a sure foot and gentle nature. The perfect companion for tonight, a lucky pick for me that I've borrowed from a property the other side of Wangaratta.

I knock again. The door is flimsy and could easily be pushed in, but that isn't the motive. I hear movement within and give two more sturdy bangs on the door;

impatient. I need her to get a move on. There are things to be done. An answering voice, muffled within the walls of the Inn signals that she's heard and is on her way.

'About bleedin' time,' I growl to myself.

It's the first time my face has been seen in Glenrowan town in many months. I won't be expected. The door swings open and it takes her a few seconds to size up who's standing in her doorway.

'Jesus, Ned. You scarit the life outta me. I thought it were the coppers again.'

'Annie Jones. How th' hell are ye?'

Ann Jones looks relieved—an irony, considering who I am and where I stand. The proprietor of the Glenrowan Inn looks the worse for wear since I last laid eyes upon her. The death of her daughter the year before shows in every line on her face and the hard set of her mouth.

I wouldn't call her a trusted ally. She's tried to keep everyone on side, the coppers included, and it means that she walks a tightrope. She's friendly with the Hart family though, and knows my Ma and the kids. Right now, I have to take a gamble on even the slimmest of friendships.

The Glenrowan Inn, which she opened only 18 months ago, lies across the railway tracks from McDonnell's Railway Tavern, the main watering hole of the men who support us: our sympathisers. The tavern is where I'd normally show myself. But not tonight.

The Jones' Inn is a neat little building of white-washed weatherboard and corrugated iron roof, with bark-slab kitchen sitting behind it. The verandah in front is made for standing under, catching up over an ale. It looks a damn good place to sit and watch for coming trains.

If I look out towards the station from where I stand, there's a huddle of pitched tents amongst the sapling gums: housing for the railway labourers who work these tracks. The Jones' Inn isn't the obvious place for us to hole up with a pile of hostages while we wait for the police train. But it's this unpredictability that makes it the right call.

Though she hasn't laid eyes on me for many months, Ann's smile is quick after her initial shock. Her face breaks into a wide grin and her body relaxes.

'I'm no' even in me decents, Ned.' She turns to call into the blackness behind her. 'Jane, get y'self dressed and come down 'ere. Hurry up, girl, you don't know who you're keepin' waiting.'

I ask how things have been, and about the coppers' visits. She tells me what I already know. They turn up on the doorstep regularly, despite the Gang not having shown our faces in the area for months. Mostly they hassle the Irish across at McDonells. Like me, many of the men on the land might be born or raised here, but there's Tipperary green running through their veins. The coppers know who's in our corner and they barge in, questioning and pushing them around. Ann's clientele, despite her own Irish roots, are generally a quieter lot— townsfolk and railway workers.

The men in the tavern have had no more knowledge of our whereabouts than the coppers themselves these past months. But it hasn't stopped them from being thrown into prisons, under the guise of the law. We take care of our own though. No loyal man's family goes hungry when he's shut away.

I swing my attention to the woman in front of me. At near 40 years old, no-one calls her Annie anymore. She likes my flattery and her face lights up, before turning to mock sternness.

'You might no' have seen me, but I've seen a few more of your mob in the last few weeks, Ned Kelly. They've suddenly taken a likin' to my grog over 'ere. There any reason for the change?' She crosses her arms across her ample chest. 'No' that any trade is unwelcome.' She's a businesswoman through and through.

I give her nothing but a small shrug. 'Jus' keepin' things interestin', Annie.'

In truth, Kelly supporters have been drinking regularly and rowdily at the Glenrowan Inn over the past month—an attempt to throw the police off. I don't want them suspicious of activity this side of the tracks. We've made sure to steal a few horses from the local area too— confuse the law about where we are and what we've been up to.

'Now, Ned Kelly, this'll be no social call at this time of the night, no matter your blarney. So out wi' it, what do ye want?' The Irish accent is strong, despite her twenty years in the new colony.

Jane arrives next to her mother, bleary eyed. Half-dressed as they are, Jane is the more appealing sight of the two Jones women. Only a lass of fourteen, she's a pretty thing, which is no-doubt running through Ann Jones' mind. She's canny. Her daughter is another business commodity at her disposal.

I've little time for thoughts of a pretty daughter. I'm at her doorstep for a reason. I tell her and Jane to hurry and dress warmly as they're coming with me to wake some quarry workers. Ann looks at me hard. She nods, once, then leans against the door to size me up. She understands this visit isn't any friendly get-together.

'How long'll we be away?'

I ignore the question and tell her to hurry. I reassure her that I'll leave her boys sleeping in the outbuilding of the Inn. They still sleep like the dead, despite my banging, and this settles her. She may have a head for business but her heart belongs to her children. The boys will be out of harms way and she has no fear for herself and Jane from the Kelly boys. Neither should she. I'm no killer or tormentor of innocents. No matter what the papers claim.

I wait in the shadows of the doorway as they dress. I'm hesitant to waste any more time than I have to when there's still so much to come in the night. I shift my weight away from the roughness of the slab bark wall, uncomfortable and acutely aware of the steel armour under my oilskin coat. Steve is dressed the same—clothed in the plough mouldboards that we've stolen and bought from around the area. His seems to wear him though, slight as he is. They're roughly fashioned but they'll offer some protection for what's coming.

Jane is out first, followed by her mother who makes an entrance in a flouncy red affair, which would have the eyes of every man in the colony of Victoria, no matter her age. I doubt she's worn it in years, but it still fits and squashes her ample shape into something quite becoming. I raise my brows at her, my beard hiding the small grin.

'Just found it lyin' under the bed did ye, Annie?'

'If bein' woken in the middle of the damn night,

by the most wanted man in the colony, to God-knows what end, isn't enough to don me finery, Ned, I don' know what is.'

A low chuckle escapes me. She has a point. At any length, it will add to the night and the feeling of celebration, which lies in my heart.

Ann looks me up and down in the light of the candle that Jane holds in front of her young face. 'I see it's true then,' she nods at me. 'I'd heard a whisper that ye were all outfittin' yourselves with armour—somethin' out of the crusades, ain't ye?' She was mocking in her tone, but I hadn't missed her comment that 'she had heard'.

'Where'd ye hear that?' I bark the words and she stalls. I stand taller and lean in towards her, my arm braced against the doorway, blocking her exit. 'Who'd ye hear it from, Annie?'

'Christ, Ned. How'm I s'posed to remember where I've heard every piece of drunken gossip from?' Her eyes dart from me to the floor but I refuse to move. I tower over the two women. She sighs. 'Apparently Daniel Kennedy—the ol' school teacher from Greta—he told someone, who told someone. You know how these tales spread.'

I nod at her and remain wordless, but I drop my arm to let her pass.

The news makes me considerably less at ease than I was just moments ago. If this is common knowledge, what else is? The body armour, fashioned in our bush forge on the banks of a creek that barely flowed, represents more than just fortification against the bullets of enemies—it is an emblem. Farmers are being denied land; now this tool of the land will help all of her sons loosen the oppression of the British. I had thought of our freedom with every strike of the iron as I moulded it into shape on that shady bank. Imbuing the steel with my strength of purpose. It must be unbreakable.

Now's not the time for these thoughts. The women are ready and I lead them into the night, with Steve following not far behind.

***

The stationmaster's house is only a few minutes from the Jones' Inn. That's where we're headed. Along the way, I'll collect some of the quarry workers who are tucked up in tents nearby. I need someone with a knowledge of getting up the train tracks efficiently, and the men camped out near the railway line fit the bill. I don't expect their reaction to me to be as friendly as the Jones women.

Ann and Jane have their heads close together, whispering to each other in the dark ahead of us. They know every step of this town especially this close to their Inn, so the dark cover around us doesn't seem to worry them. In front of me, alongside Jane and Ann, Steve looks as if he could be another of her children. Even at 21, his chin has barely started sprouting any stubbly growth— something we've ribbed him about no end. But I know, despite his smooth-faced appearance, he's a man. Dealing with the violence that comes from being a hunted man will do that. He's resigned himself to the life better than Dan, who wastes his time wishing away the wanted posters. Despite Daniel being my blood kin, sometimes I barely recognise him.

Out of the dark, the clump of hessian tents appear

abruptly, pegged haphazardly into the damp soil, just back from the small station building. I see no movement. The night is quiet with the snores, farts and moans that come with deep sleep. I wave Steve over to say as much when one of the moans becomes louder and more insistent. We look at each other with mirrored grins and raised brows. I wave my pistol in the direction of the tent furthest away from the track and take half a dozen steps towards it, listening. Another moan. I clear my throat loudly. 'Me name is Ned Kelly and I'm tellin' ye to come out o' your tent, wit' your hands in the air.'

The moaning and movement stops. I hear whispering before a voice breaks the night's silence. In broken English it yells, 'Piss off, ya mon-grel, Aussie bastards.' Steve's face breaks into a smile and there is quiet laughter from the Jones women behind me. The tent flap stays closed and another deep groan and whispering starts up again.

My patience is thin. I yell louder and cock my pistol, aiming it just above the top of the tent. 'I tell ye, I'm Ned Kelly, and I'm no bastard. Get out o' the tent wit' your hands in the air.' I let off a shot, a warning of my seriousness, and reload. A woman screams from inside the tent and there is a flurry of movement before a head pokes out, arms stretched in front.

'Okay, okay. Don't shoot. I'se here.' His accent is thick with fear and adrenaline. Movement starts from the nearby tents and there is a minute of confusion as people poke heads out or jump out into the open. I hear one cock his own pistol, which causes the women behind me to shriek. Steve and I are a twin image, pistols aimed straight at the tents, and I think again of the armour I wear.

'Put down yer arms and no-one'll come to harm. Raise 'em and me mate, Steve, here'll blow a hole through ye.' The soft thud of guns hitting the dirt is followed by hands being raised. I tell Jane to collect them up, which she does without hesitation and drops them at my feet.

The romancer, standing there naked with his hands in the air, looks at me closely and I hear his intake of breath. 'Figlio di puttana! It's bloody Ned Kelly.'

I wave my pistol back at his tent, 'Get ye strides on lover-boy. I need ye.'

I let him get his pants on, which he does in a hurry, and then explain my need to remove a part of the track. The Italian understands, but shakes his head.

'We have-a no tools Mr Ned. They is locked away and the boss has-a the keys.' I'm pissed off and kick at the ground. It's an inconvenience that we don't bloody need, another waste of time. Plus Dan and Joe still aren't back. I won't feel at ease until I see them ride in together.

I leave Steve with the railway workers and Jane standing by the tents. Now that the initial fear has died away, there's talk and laughter amongst the men, mostly at the expense of their foreman. I take Ann and head towards the stationmaster's house, to rouse him from his bed. He'll need to find us the tools that we require. Unlike the tents, as we approach I hear nothing but the sounds of the night. The dark amplifies the animal calls and our feet scuffing on the gravelled road. The house is silent. Apparently my gunfire hasn't disturbed them enough to force them from their beds. I rap my knuckles on the door, hard and fast. Not waiting for them to answer, I burst through and call out. My strides are long and it takes only a few before I find myself in the stationmaster's bedroom. Stanistreet is out of bed in an instant, pulling on the pants that hang over the end of the bed. His wife in the bed beside him shrieks. Ann moves from behind me, sits on the bed to comfort her briefly, hushing her cries. Their almost-grown girls come flooding in at the noise and look taken aback, before Ann tells them to huddle in with their mother. Stanistreet dresses quickly and stands beside the bed breathing heavily, watching me closely. I direct my words to his wife.

'I mean ye no harm, missus. I need t' talk wit' ye husband. If ye tell me ye'll do nothin' that'll risk yer husband's safety, you and yer girls can stay put.' Sheets pulled tight to her chin, her daughters in the bed next to her, she readily agrees.

Outside, the clouds clear, leaving the moon to light the town. The stationmaster seems unconcerned at me standing there, pistol in hand, once I've introduced myself and my need for his tools.

'I can't do anything for you, Mr. Kelly. The workers'll be no good to you, even with their tools. You need the plate layers. Reardon and Sullivan. They'll know what to do. They live just down this street. White house on the left.' He points into the darkness of the street ahead.

Things are not going to plan. 'Fuckin' hell,' escapes me, which makes Stanistreet look uncomfortable. Frustration bubbles under my every movement and I stand, hands on hips, staring down the Glenrowan street. This had better not be a sign of how the rest of this night will go. I look at Ann and see the shadow of a smile pass over her features, which deepens my irritation. She has no idea how important tonight is. But she soon will.

I take a deep breath in, steadying the thoughts

racing through my mind. 'Right, you're both comin' with me. Let's find the damn plate layers.' The look I throw to Ann wipes the smile from her face.

The job, which should have taken thirty minutes at most, has clocked up more than an hour, and we haven't even begun removing the track yet. The time passing isn't my only worry. Where the hell are Dan and Joe?

***

Aaron will be dead by now. The thought flashes through my mind as I turn from Ann. The boys will have finished the job. I've never doubted they would.

I don't feel the weight of Aaron's death on my shoulders like Joe will. Joe was almost his brother. I could never do to Joe, what he's done to Aaron this night—put a bullet through his skull. I've sent Joe and Dan to kill the man who, at one time, was almost amongst our gang. It weighs on my conscience, but it's been necessary.

Joe knew that he had to be the one to stand in front of Aaron and take his life. Had told me so. He wanted to be a comfort to Aaron. The last person that Aaron saw in this life. I don't care what he saw. The man was a traitor. Selling his brothers to the dogs, the Victorian Police Force, and for what reason? There was none, other than him lining his pockets with blood money from the coppers. He was firmly in Hare's pocket – the man who would do anything to have the capture of the Kelly Gang on his record. Including turning friend against friend. So it was a traitor's death for Aaron, with no regrets from me.

I'm no man of bloodlust. I've never killed a man that I didn't regret; even when it was a choice between his life or mine. The posters don't say that. They paint my eyes with the coldness of a killer and a mouth that's hard. I don't see that person. But that renegade informer deserved his death, and there's a part of me that wishes I could have been the one to see the light drain from Sherritt's eyes. Not only to spare Joe the memories. I hope the traitor knew his death was on me.

Joe had made the final decision about Aaron's end. He had spoken to Sherritt's mother only last month. Told her, face-to-face, that he'd kill her son with his own hands, if given the chance. That was Aaron's warning. Joe had insisted upon giving Aaron a chance to escape Kelly country; but he'd stayed. Perhaps Aaron didn't seriously imagine his childhood friend could murder him. That the boy who he'd spent almost every day with growing up, would watch him die on the ground at his feet. That was Aaron's arrogance and his downfall.

It's only a year ago that I stood in Aaron Sherritt's family home, surrounded by his sisters and their little ones. He hadn't been home that day when I'd called, nor his parents, but the girls had made me feel welcome and I'd spent an afternoon chatting with them. Their home was full of bodies, full of love. It was a warmth I was familiar with. I'd held the wriggling weight of Aaron's nephew, only months old, as the girls prepared bread for the evening. The smells of the kitchen and the softness of that young 'un had reminded me of home. I left their house that afternoon with the feeling of family. It reminded me that I was human, not the animal that I feel I'm becoming. Killing. Being hunted through the bush. The thought of the Sherritt girls, grieving the death of their brother, saddens me. I lament their feeling of loss and pain, in a way that I don't grieve for Aaron himself.

It turns easily, this right and wrong, good and evil. Which am I? I find it easy to judge others. Judging myself comes not so easily. Once Sherritt was as close to us as any man could be, one to be trusted and loved, now his blood runs on the ground. Rivers of blood will have pooled beneath him by now. But he was dead to me long before his heart stopped. This line that I'm walking, between what's bad and what's right and good, is narrowing with each passing week. It's not an internal compass that judges wrong and right for me anymore. Now the boys and I are open to judgment from every man and woman in the colony. Hell, maybe everyone in the country. People judge on what they see or hear—even if it's not the truth.

I feel in my pocket for the worn satin of the green sash that stays with me, never far from my grasp. The green and the gold are faded, the tassles frayed or missing, but I keep it close to me always: my talisman. A reminder that once, I was a cause to be celebrated, and that bravery and doing the right thing will be rewarded.

Joe and Dan will be thundering through the bush, racing to Glenrowan, knowing that they have to beat the train that will be sent for us. That's the beautiful part. Not only have we made a statement that informers will not be tolerated, we've created a diversion. A reason for the police to come steaming down the line to Glenrowan. They'll be receiving word of Sherritt's killing tonight. Then it will be Hare and his motley crew of coppers, armed and dangerous, barrelling towards us. Thinking they can take us. Armed they might be, but they're vulnerable, and don't yet know it. Racing towards Glenrowan, where they aren't expecting us to be, where the tracks will be ripped up and waiting. Hare's got no idea, but his head is next.

***

'Edward, bloody, Kelly.' James Reardon looks me up and down. 'Well, me missus is never gonna believe this.' He's not moving. He doesn't look scared, hand on his hip and chewing a blade of grass. Standing there in the darkness Reardon looks like a man weighing up options. I flick a glance at the shovel he leans on, with its thick wooden handle and the metal head. That would surely make a mess of my face if swung with enough force. Steve and a couple of the quarry workers were charged with cracking open the railway shed to borrow the tools which are now piled in front of the plate layer. His mate, Dennis Sullivan, stands off to the side of us, hands in his pockets and yawning widely. He looks placid enough. Like someone wanting to keep his head down so as not to get it shot off his shoulders. That's the kind of man I like. One who knows that I'm in charge.

It's just the three of us, waiting. I'm standing on the track just out of town, feet straddling the metal rails with a drop below us and a shallow gully to the left. The bush is thick on both sides and from where we stand, the lights of Glenrowan are hidden. If the train came now, we'd all be goners. Luckily, that train will be a while yet. I've chosen the place carefully. The perfect spot on a bend of track, with a gully that will send the trains smashing as they come from the tracks. I've sent Steve back to Glenrowan, Jane Jones in tow, like some starry-eyed pup trailing behind him. He's to retrieve Reardon's crowbar, which the plate layer conveniently forgot he needed to pull up tracks. He's stalling.

'Well, Mr Reardon, you'll have a grand story for yer missus. I'll wager there'll be a lot of people won't believe 'bout tonight's goin' ons.' I stand tall but try and relax my posture, laying my hand casually on the revolver which sticks from my waistband. I tap the handle meaningfully, but look skyward at the clearing night sky, leaving only silence between us. Reardon is by far the most forward of the two men. A surprise, considering we've got his wife and eight kids sitting in Glenrowan. Sullivan's said little since we left town, hauling metal shovels, an oversized spanner and hammer across our shoulders, to the place I've chosen. Now he stands separate to us. Clearly, he's leaving what's about to happen in the hands of his mate.

'Well, Ned. Can I call ya that?' I nod my agreement. He's a strong man. The muscles in his forearms are prominent, even in the dark. He's a good deal older than me, I'd guess a man in his 40s, if I had to gauge from the lines on his leathered face. He looks at me as he might one of his kids that's stepped out of line. 'Ned, seems like you've got big plans here, but I'm not sure that I'm ya man for the job.'

I nod at him, but I can feel the red flush of anger moving up my neck. This job, which should have taken us all of ten minutes, is dragging on. Joe and Dan are still not back and I've got this great loon standing here eyeing me up, thinking that he's got some choice in the matter. The only choice he has—pull up the track like I've bloody well told him to, or eat a bullet.

'You're right Mr. Reardon ... James.' I say with

drawling sarcasm. 'I'm expectin' a train from Benalla with a lot of police on it, and I plan on killin' 'em all if I can ... afore they get me. They're goin' to be pretty pissed about Joe and Dan puttin' some bullets in their mates in Beechworth las' night.' Of course, I don't know that. But I want to rattle him out of his hesitation. He needs to get on board, and quickly. 'If there are any left after the train's come flyin' from the tracks, I'll be takin' a couple wit' me. Some hostages might come in 'andy.'

His head snaps up. 'For God's sake, I've got a family to look after. You saw 'em. I can't be caught up in this. Killin' a train full of coppers. I'll hang for it!' His hand clenches the head of the shovel. My hand tightens on my revolver. If he wants a fight, he'll have one.

'Well, like it or not, you're helpin' me do it, Reardon. For yours and your family's sake. I don't threaten a man's family lightly, but I'll beat one of them senseless right in front of ye if ye don't get a move-on.' I'll be buggered if I'll be standing out here, looking at the railway, when the train comes roaring through Glenrowan, because of this finicky bastard. 'I wouldn't worry 'bout it though. Sullivan 'ere will swear that I held a gun to your head.' I pause and tap the gun again. 'If I have to.' The two men meet each other's eyes and a small nod passes between them. My body tenses, waiting for them to move.

Steve's timing is impeccable. I can hear his and Jane's voices as they approach through the darkness. The others hear them too. He's brought not only the crowbar, but welcome news as well.

'They're back, Ned. They're fine. They're havin' a drink at Ann's.'

Thank God. I breathe a little freer. Now things are ticking along, just as we've planned.

'That's grand news, Steve. You 'ear dat, Mr. Reardon? All's well. The boys are back, and we've got ye crowbar. Nothing's to stand in our way now, is it?'

Reardon takes the offered bar from Steve and nods at me. Without a word he looks at Sullivan and they move off towards the rails. Reardon hands his mate a spanner as they walk. Jane sits off the tracks waiting, while I fill Steve in on my words with Reardon.

My attention swings back to the two of them speaking quietly together. More time wasting.

'Ol' man, you're a long time breakin' up this road,' I call out. I'm past the point of friendly banter.

'I can't do it any quicker, Kelly. Even for a ball-breakin' bushranger, with a gun at hand.' Annoyance is written over his face, and in his body that turns to me. He lets the crowbar drop with a clatter against the rails and crosses his arms. If it's a challenge he wants, it's one he'll get.

'I can make ye do it quicker, Reardon. If ye don't hurry up, this gun's got your name on it. I want four lengths of track broken up. Get a damn move on.'

He scoffs at me. 'Four? One'll do as well as twenty!'

I look sharply at Steve. I don't know the truth of it, and I can see on Steve's face he's oblivious to it too. It's times like this that I need Joe at my side, not one of the young ones. Joe would know. Reardon can see he's caught my interest.

'Really?' I quiz him. He only nods. I don't know whether to take him at his word, or whether he's got himself notions of being a hero. Convincing me to take a small amount of track in the hope that the train might jump the gap and survive. But time is ticking by, and at this rate, I don't know if we've got time to take up four anyway. The coppers at Sherritt's place will have telegraphed Melbourne by now. The train could already be on its way.

'How's 'bout we make a compromise at two?' I pose it as a question, but my tone suggests otherwise. *Do it.*

The older men get to work with the spanner to loosen bolts and heft up the length of rails, sleepers still attached, throwing them down the embankment. It's a thrill watching the rails tumble down the hill. They hit the scrubby gums that grow by the side of the track and jar against each other as they fall.

Minutes later, the job is done. I clap Reardon on the shoulder as he passes, but he shrugs it off. He's no friend to me nor the boys. Despite the walk back up the line, the weight of the tools across my shoulders, I whistle a little ditty and exchange a smile with Steve. Things are moving along.

***

Sunday morning

THE watery sun rises through the heavy winter mist that hangs over the town. Back in Glenrowan, standing out the front of the Inn, drink in hand, Dan's the first one I see. He looks rough after the night's events, but it's Joe that worries me most. It was his bullet that split the skull of Aaron. It will haunt him.

Though he'd volunteered, I'm sure as Joe stood on the threshold looking at Aaron, the bigger piece of him had wanted to embrace the man rather than kill him. What Joe did tonight, he did for me—that's why he'll always be my brother, just as much as Jim and Dan are.

It had been Joe's own mother who'd eyeballed Aaron, those months ago, asleep on the dirt of the police camp. She was being dragged in for questioning; a routine for all of our families these days. As Mrs Byrne passed and they'd locked eyes, she'd nodded at him and he'd responded, 'I'm a dead man, now, ain't I?' He had known that he'd pay the price for turning against us. Just a matter of when.

'Ye orright, Dan?' I didn't embrace him, but laid a hand on his shoulder as I came alongside him standing outside the Inn.

He nods. 'We pushed the mares hard, but had no trouble on the way back.'

'And the coppers?'

'We left Aaron bleedin' on the ground. Dead. No sight o' the coppers, but we knew they were in there, hidin' behind the skirts of Aaron's missus and her Ma. Musta been curled up on the floor and pissin' 'emselves.'

They were gutless bastards to be sure, but even they must have crawled out from behind the women-folk and raised the alarm by now.

Joe wanders out and I throw an arm around his shoulders. 'It's done,' is all he says. I have no words for him. They look pleased when I tell them of our success at the tracks. Plans always seem better once they're set in motion. Now, holed up back at the Jones' Inn and all together, the real waiting begins.

Ann's establishment is one she's proud of, but it's not fancy. A small building of stringybark and weatherboard, lined with hessian and paper; but it's the more genteel establishment in town. There's irony in us choosing the Jones' place to be. Our numbers have steadily increased as Saturday night has rolled on into Sunday morning. We sit down to breakfast amongst the besieged townsfolk, all enjoying the hospitality of the landlady.

My night has been a busy one. After seeing Reardon and Sullivan safely back to the hotel, left in Steve's care, I made the strategic decision to avoid the single-manned police station and Constable Bracken— Glenrowan's excuse for a lawman. Word was that he'd gone down with gastric flu, barely able to move. It was a bit of luck that I'd not counted on and I guessed that he'd be fast asleep in his bed. Best to leave sleeping dogs lie, Red has always told us. Instead I'd dropped into the nearby postmaster's house, putting in a polite request that he keep an eye on the police barracks for us. In case the Constable made a miraculous recovery as morning came. Old Reynolds, the postmaster, is a well-known sympathiser to our cause. He seemed to think that playing lookout on the copper's station was a fair deal in lieu of me leaving him be at home. I clapped him on the shoulder as I left. All I'd heard was a hearty, 'Give 'em hell, Ned.'

Steve and I had gathered up other unwitting members of the public throughout the night and early morning. None had declined. Theirs were the faces that I stare at now, weighing up how many amongst their rank that we might call friend. When the time comes, the boys and I will be away. I'll need a few reliable friends left behind to keep troublemakers out of the fray.

As I look around, some faces are familiar, but most are staying put only under duress. We have to watch them closely. Any one is capable of ruining the plans that we've put into motion. Friends or not, it's evident that the night has taken its toll on everyone. Weary looks abound and some are laying their heads on tables to catch a few minutes of sleep. The adrenalin of being held up by bushrangers looks to have worn off and many are feeling the night they've spent away from their beds.

Right now, filling my belly with a warm breakfast of eggs and bread, my spirits are lifted. There will be little chance of sleep even if offered the finest bed in the colony. I wash my breakfast down with the mug of sweet tea that Ann brings out. The time approaches. Now we just need to be careful not to ruin our chances. Steve is the only one away, sent to the stationmaster's house to look after some of the womenfolk. Dan pushes his empty plate across the table and thanks Ann. His eyes are heavy with the adventures of the night before and a full belly. Rest will have to wait for him too.

I head out of the Inn, only a few steps from a view of the train line that links us to Melbourne. A great spine curving over the land of Victoria. A modern wonder laid only a few years before. I plan on using this great advancement against them. There's not a sound; it's as vacant as it has been for the last eight hours. Nothing to hear but the magpies' songs from the gums near the station. They sing a morning chorus and I find the familiar sound a comfort. The noise and chaos is coming. I embrace the stillness while I can.

Dan comes trailing out of the Inn and stops alongside me. He rolls his neck and shoulders as if loosening up before a fight. Trying to shrug off the night he's had.

'If 't all goes to plan, today could be the day dat we change history, young Daniel.' I grin at him and give him a good-natured thump on the shoulder. 'At the very least it'll change our fortunes and our destiny.'

Dan hangs his head. Something is dancing around in there. He's never been one to keep his emotions hidden. He carries his truth in every movement of his body. Hesitation. I know what he wants to say and I wonder whether he has the courage to say it to me.

'Are we doin' the right thing, Ned?' He surprises me. 'The heat's off us now. We can head up north and keep our heads down...' His words taper off, and his shoulders slump. He moves a little, uncomfortable in the silence that I let stretch between us. I won't give him what he wants. I can't, and there's no point him holding out hope that I'll change my mind.

'God, the quiet is unnervin' aint it?' He starts again, but I don't turn. His words are thick, no hint of our mother's Irish tongue. Not like me. I know that he wants to say more. I feel his doubt coming off him in waves. I shift my feet slightly, but keep eyes focused down the line, the endless steel that snakes in front of us.

'I know what you're sayin', Dan. The answer's no.' My words sit between us, heavy with unsaid meaning. I look at my brother, the boy that I've watched grow from a babe in Ma's arms, to this lad that stands before me. He looks so much a man now, much more than his age. Our time on the road—outlawed—has aged him. The things we've done don't sit as easily on him as they do on me. I'm built to carry the load.

'Aye Dan, I know you're worried, but we've been forced to it, haven't we? I gave them fair warnin' in Jerilderie to stay out o' Victoria if they've reason to fear us—but still they come. God knows, I don't want dis fight, but it's come for me anyway and I won't be backin' down.' The words come easily. They've run through my head a thousand times before today. 'That worm Fitzpatrick has done all he can to hurt our family. He's the reason we're in this bloody mess. The reason Ma is sittin' in that gaol, rottin' away.' Dan nods as I speak. He's turning from his own thoughts. Beginning to ignore his gut feeling, put his trust in me instead. It's what lets him follow me into any God-forsaken mess that we find ourselves in. Who knows if this will be his downfall. 'You know I've a fighter's heart, and tha' canna go unanswered.' My battle-scarred knuckles are evidence of this. I crack them in the morning cold.

I point towards the empty track, where we're expecting the special train from Melbourne to race up. 'The train'll come. There'll be no more runnin' for us. We're callin' the shots now. We'll take some of those coppers wit' us after the train goes. We'll use 'em to bargain Ma outta gaol and get that bastard Fitzpatrick kicked outta the force. They'll have to listen once we got some coppers sittin' alongside us.' We are shoulder to shoulder and I want to reassure him. 'I know we expected it to come steamin' through last night. Reardon took his time rippin' up those tracks and it didn't bloody matter! For sure it's a good thing though, that it isn't here yet. We've jus' gotta hope it's not about to arrive. It'll be in our favour if it's travellin' tonight, there'll be less chance of them seein' the track all torn up to hell. The darker the better.'

Dan just nods, the air between us full of his fear and regret. But he keeps his mouth closed.

'It's jus' taken the coppers longer than we thought. That's all. They'll be comin'. I feel it.'

He listens and follows my gaze down the track. Two Kelly brothers, side-by-side, looking for the train that hasn't yet come. He knows, as he's always known, my word is final.

***

Dan and Steve fell into this life—the thinker and the horseman. Whereas I was always bound for it. I can see reasons for all of the things that we've done. I feel each and every one of the injustices committed against us, from almost since the day we were born, as a cut to my soul. My heart bleeds when I think of the prigs on the Victorian Police Force throwing my mother into gaol and harassing my sisters. Fitzpatrick sniffing around the skirts of our beautiful Kate. Thinking he was worthy of her. She's tougher than that though. She told him where he stood but he didn't like it. Kate, Annie and Maggie are all tough Kelly girls.

Dan is different though: he's softer, perhaps kinder. He spends more time lurking around in his mind, second-guessing each step he takes, every word he says. My own actions and words are almost automatic, like they're pre-destined.

I was born in the shadows of the bloody Eureka battle between the Ballarat miners and the forces of her Majesty, Queen Victoria. They rebelled against the injustices and treatment they'd been served. My spirit of rebellion and distaste for the ruling class is mine by birth and blood. The blood of my father, who was given free passage to Australia, bound in chains for hard labour, flows through me. The injustices wrought on him, and all my people that came before, flood through my veins with each beat. But his is not the only blood that stirs me.

It's my mother that I resemble in all but looks. Since she landed on this soil at 9 years old, she's shunned restraint and expectation. She prefers her freedom and has a thirst for adventure. Always sharp-witted and sharp-tongued, if she lives to be 100, she'll continue to be so. She does not suffer a fool. She is as much my spirit, as I am her child.

All of us, as babes in her arms, heard her songs of Ireland. Her sweet, melodic voice singing of green hills and passionate hearts. Telling us to not forget where we've come from, even as we made this new life for ourselves in Australia. 'Ye got to remember where ye come from, Ned, if yer to get where ye be going.' She's a slight woman, but an exceptional horsewoman—a far sight better than Red ever was. It's from her that I get my seat on a horse, and the desperate desire to make my own path in the world. Red was a follower—always the weaker of the two.

He was a drunkard, pure and simple. Drank himself into a grave at 45, and I swore that I'd never let the drink take a hold of me like it did my father. I guess I loved him, but I didn't respect him. The older I get, the less I do. Never was there a soft, kind word between us. Having to report his death is a memory that haunts me. His weakness for the grog forced me to step up and become the man of the family. Too young and too much responsibility on my young shoulders. I don't resent him for it. I pity him. He was a man with strong ideals, but not the internal fortitude to realise them. It was his selfish choices and his weak death which dealt me my hand to play at 12 years old. It's a hand that's landed me where I am today. So all the cards fall into place.

When I look back, from where I stand listening to morning birdsong, I realise there has never been any other destiny for me. I was always going to be standing by this track, on the wrong side, ready to make my stand.

Dan is the opposite of my mother and me. He's a follower too. So, while I may blame Red for his part in landing me in this trouble, Dan has no-one to blame but me. Dan's made it clear that he's not keen to throw himself, and the rest of us, into the fight again. It's only his youth and naivety that let him think that we're out of the fight at the moment. Because he can't see the coppers on the corner or feel their breath up his arse, he thinks they've backed away. But I know that those bastards won't give up without me dead on the ground or swinging in front of a crowd. Him too.

We'd been under a cloudless, blue sky when Dan had first told me he was sick of the fight. A visit to the Moyhu Races earlier in the year. It's a small town not far from Wangaratta and in the thick of our country—Kelly country. The sun had been warm enough to prickle sweat on our backs under the light cotton shirts we wore. We'd all rested to the side of the track, amongst the thick cover of trees, hidden from unseeing eyes. My grey mare had felt the excitement of the day, ears pricked, wanting to race every time the horses came around. Our sisters had been there, and a few cousins, watching the races—always a favoured family gathering. Kate and Maggie had been keeping a lookout for anything out of the ordinary, but there was little interest in the familiar face on the big grey thoroughbred. The mood had been light. It had been a good day. A normal day; if we had the ability to know normal anymore.

Dan had thrown it back at me that night. 'Don't it show us that they're startin' to lose interest, Ned?' He'd enjoyed the hours when we hadn't been relegated to the half-life that we usually lived—a life hidden in the shadows. Dan must have spent the day in the sun thinking of a life without running. A future that might be normal. In a sense, I had too.

That had been my first day with Ettie, when I knew that I'd make her mine. We'd spent the day circling each other. Moving with an awareness of the other, which we hadn't known before. The sound of her voice was my compass and a brush of her arm sent electricity shooting through my own. She was beautiful, bubbling with life. And it was under that blue sky, hearing her laughter, that I swore I would have her in my life for as long as I had one. We'd both understood how far fetched our dreams were. Unlike Dan, Ettie and I know that normal will not be welcoming us into her fold anytime soon.

Dan's questioning of this life that we've made, leads me to wonder again that Jim was the more obvious choice of my two brothers to be in this mess with me. Jim, the brother that separates us, was always irritable and defiant. Even in looks, he is as tall and broad and just as stubborn as me. Except for the fact that he'd spent the last three years in Sydney's Darlinghurst Gaol, he might well be here too. His time away has been hard on him, in the shadow of bars, but it may be the blessing that's kept him out of this God-damned mess.

I was happy to have seen him only a couple of months ago but I'd found him much changed from the teenaged fighter who'd left us. He was nervous. His eyes darted around at every noise in the bush; the sounds that we've grown used to during our months living amongst the trees and undergrowth. The screech of a galah on a branch above us made him fly around expecting something at his back. He'd pleaded with me to break up the gang and give up our ideas of a North-Eastern Republic and of rescuing Ma.

'You'll only make it worse for Ma, Ned. They'll never let 'er out. It'll just be worse for all of ya.'

He knew what lay in store for Dan and me when things went wrong. Not if, but when. There had been tears in his eyes when he'd laid his hand on my arm.

Gaol was a place Jim never wanted to see again. Dan had spent barely a month behind bars in his years. Not enough to either harden or scare him. My time behind bars filled my veins with steel. Unfairly imprisoned, each day made me hate them more. But Jim was trapped by his experience and unable to escape the confinement and cruelty that he'd lived in. The fear of going back turned him. He wouldn't join us at Glenrowan, not directly, but he'd promised to be there to mobilise our supporters if it went to plan. I'd looked at him hard.

'When it goes to plan, Jimmy. Not if. I'll promise ye that.'

Three Kelly brothers, joined in our future, but so different in every other way.

The plan is a simple one. When the train falls, it

will announce that the Kellys will not go easily. We'll take our hostages and then we'll hit the bank at Benalla. From there we'll make them listen. Listen about Ma's innocence, Fitzpatrick's guilt. The money will keep our families and friends out of trouble. The takings from Euroa and Jerilderie are well gone. The Benalla bank will be left unprotected and at our mercy. Anyone working there won't know what's happening when four armoured bushrangers come wandering in to hold them up and clear out the money. Robbing the bank at Benalla will be the easiest part of this whole plan.

I make my way back under the verandah of the hotel. The dirt floor is smooth from the feet of hundreds of men. I have a perfect view to see Dan walking towards me, coming from the direction of the town.

'Where've ye been, Dan?' I realise I've not seen him for close to an hour. Since we parted at the railway tracks, I've passed the time in my own thoughts, pacing beside the line. Joe is playing cards with some of the others in the parlour and keeping a watch on those that are inside. He's never been much of a player, but it helps him pass the eternal cycle of waiting that we're stuck in.

'Been to see Steve. I wanted to tell him 'bout Aaron. 'Bout Joe.'

There is nothing else forthcoming, it seems he's avoiding my eyes. 'And?' I prompt him. His sigh is one of annoyance.

'And what, Ned? Our mate just blew his best friend's head off. How the hell do ya think he is?' He rolls his eyes at me. 'I had to let Steve know how it went down. He wanted to know how Joe was holdin' up.'

I nod my head slowly. 'Was it how ye thought?'

Dan shrugs. "T'was pretty bad, Ned. Aaron knew it were comin'.' Dan squats to pick up a stone, hurling it as far as he can from the verandah. It bounces off the steel of the tracks. He always did have a good arm for a scrawny kid. 'Joe won't admit it, but he'll feel it, Ned. I saw 'im hesitate - right at the end. Just a second he waited, 'afore he pulled the trigger. He knew he had to do it, but his heart sure as hell weren't in it. This'll eat 'im up.'

A silence grows between us as I take it in. I knew it. I could see it in his eyes when he'd returned. I push the thought away. The thought that when I signed Sherritt's death warrant, maybe I signed Joe's as well. It's too painful for me to think about. I won't linger on it. I couldn't live knowing that I'd caused such injury to a man that I love like another brother.

I change the subject away from my mate, to another matter that hangs over me. 'I need to see Steve too.' I'm careful not to let my hesitation show. 'To tell 'im that I'm goin' for Ettie.'

Dan's head jerks up, almost as if I've hit him. 'Goin' for Ettie? When?'

'After.' I hold down the urge to shrug my shoulders. I'm trying to look unconcerned but my heart beats wildly at the admission to Dan. 'After the crash. After Benalla. When dis thing is done, I'm goin' to go and get her. She's comin' wit' us. We've decided together—and we'll let 'er folks know.' The next I say quietly, not wanting to risk it by saying it too loudly. 'She's told me she'll be waitin'.'

Dan whistles low. 'Christ, ya better go and see Steve now.' I can tell he thinks it's a laugh. I hate this

feeling of vulnerability. The feeling of asking permission—
it's not me.

I shake my head. 'It's not the time. No' yet.' I can't
bring myself to go and see him. I know his reaction will be
explosive. Who'd want their sister caught up in this life?

Dan bobs his head, serious. 'Perhaps when we
know we've survived it all, eh? Then he'll be able to kill ya
without leavin' the rest of us in the lurch with a backyard
full of coppers and one man down.'

He grins at me and I punch his shoulder. In my
mind, I'm back at home. He and I up to some mischief or
another.

I can almost hear Ma calling to us.

***

Sunday evening

THE music is spirited and there's smoke and laughter
filling the air of Ann Jones' establishment. Despite most
being held at the Inn against their will, there's a sense of
joviality and friendship amongst those who are here
tonight. There are Delaneys and McCauliffes, even Paddy
McDonnell from the hotel across the railway line, rowdy
and raucous, along with his wife. There are sympathisers
amongst their ranks, which makes talk easy as the Sunday
hours crawl past.

The kitchen is separated from the main building
by a 6-foot breezeway, where a steady path has been worn
carrying food from the kitchen, keeping everyone full and
happy. It's as if Ann was prepared for a night like the one
ahead—with her 10-gallon keg of brandy on the bar, as

well as cases of brandy, gin and wine stacked in the corner. 'Nothin' aggravates a crowd like an empty guts or an empty glass, Ned,' she tells me, bringing more food into the Inn. I've promised her payment of course. I might be a thieving bastard in the eyes of some, but I don't expect Ann to be out of pocket on a night like this.

I watch her work her way around the room, expertly pouring and cleaning. A joke with those who look downcast. Handing out tea to those who have hit the booze too hard, too quick. She's old enough to be my mother, but there's a spark in Ann Jones that gives her youth and vibrancy. One of the younger lads grabs her up and whirls her around the floor in time to the ditty being played. She laughs with her head thrown back and her mouth wide, uncaring of who sees her or judgments they might make. Despite the children that she's lost, the homeland that she's left and the hardships that she's known, Ann Jones is a woman who loves life. She's a good one to have here today.

I've kept my words light and positive with the boys, as the hours have ticked by, but I can't believe that the day has passed with no sign of the police force arriving from Melbourne. I'm not a gambling man, but I would have laid money that they'd be here by now.

By early evening, we've more than sixty people scattered in and around the Inn. It's like every person in Glenrowan has decided to arrive for a drink. I'm sure word has got out to some of the locals, and a couple have dropped by wanting to have a sticky beak. Damn fools. I've even deputised Jane to some extent, given her a revolver, to help keep any peace inside the building. Much to her mother's disgust!

We'd all been nervous about whether Dan and Joe would get back to Glenrowan in time, before any police were dispatched here. We'd been sure that the fury of the police would be felt as soon as news of Sherritt's killing got to them. Joe thinks their late arrival can only mean those gutless pigs at Sherritt's hut didn't leave to alert Melbourne. It can be the only reason. Which means that eventually the police will come. But when?

We've taken off our armour, locked them away safely in one of the bedrooms of the main parlour. They're too heavy to wear the whole day. They're close by for when we hear the train coming, and for when we head to Benalla. The extra firearms and ammunition are under lock and key too; we don't want them falling into unfriendly hands. Ann had only nodded when I told her so. She understands that this is no place for gunfire. Outside, night falls early and as the sun sets, the mist descends over Glenrowan. A little hollow surrounded by the great granite hills and bush of the Warbys. Those hills have housed us many times, hiding places all over their rocky outcrops and giant grass trees. It gives me a feeling of home and I know tonight will be a success.

Inside, Joe looks across the bar at me, through the smoke. I smile at him but I know he sees the tension in my face. Not many others, if any, would notice the small signs—a furrow in my brow, a little quieter than normal. But Joe is a canny one. Despite all of my defiance and anger and plans, the risk I'm putting my boys under tonight weighs on my conscience, and Joe can read that. It would be less of a worry for me if Dan and Steve were not here. There are so many ways it could go wrong tonight, bloodshed is a strong possibility—most likely our own.

I've promised Ettie and my Ma that I'll look after the two younger boys, and keep them safe if I possibly can. Dan is her baby boy and a relative innocent in this mess. Only following me into this life out of loyalty. Across the bar I keep eye contact with Joe. He knows I may have sentenced us all to our deaths here tonight, and awful ones at that. He gives me a wink, and I think it should be me consoling and supporting him, not the other way.

Joe breaks my gaze to follow Ann, serving drinks along with her daughter. They wander through the men and women in the Inn, clearing and refilling. The seats were filled hours ago, so now many lean against walls or sprawl out on the floor. Joe's eyes move to Jane. They're a buxom lot, the Jones'. Jane will capture the eyes of many. A mass of dark brown curls and a ready smile. I can tell that she's caught Joe's attention over the night, as she had Steve's the previous one, and she's delighting in their admiration.

The faces around us are mostly friendly, if not a little in awe of being beside real-life bushrangers. We're lucky so many of the locals are sympathisers. It's what has kept us riding these bush tracks for as long as we have. Despite many local men having being thrown into the cells in the years that we've been wanted men, their loyalty remains. It hasn't hurt that the money from Euroa and Jerilderie has mostly gone to support their families when they've needed it. But still, the support we have is impressive. It infuriates the police. They don't understand how we can hide in plain sight for so many months without being turned in for the reward. It drives Hare to distraction – a superintendent with no power, and makes him hate us all the more. But that's because they don't understand loyalty, and how much the coppers and their corruption are hated around here.

After Euroa and Jerilderie, we kept our heads down. No more banks robbed or impassioned letters sent out. Despite what Joe thinks, I'm not naturally one to make the grand gestures, like I did with the letter at Jerilderie. But I was sick of reading the tripe in the newspapers all from the side of the coppers, calling us killers—killing innocents. I had to make my thoughts heard. We're not blameless, especially me, but I've never killed anyone that I didn't regret. I wish I hadn't had to take their lives, but I did. And I'm sorry for it. But, there you go.

Now the time is coming to implore the everyday man for resistance and support against those in power. Against the uniformed men, the bank men, the men who think they run things, and I need them to know my story before I ask for that support. After Jerilderie, the others told me to keep my head down. Pleaded, really. As well as the £2,000 that we had taken from the Jerilderie safe, I found and destroyed the mortgage papers of the selectors. Without them, the bank had no record of what was owed by the men of the land. It's gestures like this that keep us in the minds and hearts of the everyday people. They know that we fight for them as much as we fight for ourselves. They know where our loyalties lie and they give theirs in return.

Rumours have been circulating of an escape to Queensland for us. Some think getting out of the colony of Victoria is the only way we can stay away from the law. But it isn't Queensland that's beckoning. I'm reluctant to leave my family to the mercy of the Victorian Police Force.

Even after more than a year of no action from us, the Force is as intent as ever for us all to hang. Hare is determined to make us the next arrest on his record. He made his name nabbing old Harry Power. I know he'd love to finish his career with my head on a spike.

We know that we need to take the police head-on if we're ever going to have the freedom that we long for. There's no better place to hide than where you're least expected, so we find ourselves still in the bosom of our loyal supporters, in the North East of the colony. We know this country almost as well as the Pangerang people who've lived in these parts for a hundred generations. They've opened their arms to us too. Protected us at times. As if they know that our enemy is their enemy too.

But loyalty is a double-edged sword. Would these people be as friendly if they knew I'd ordered the death of Aaron? That Joe had the blood of his best mate on his hands? If they knew that Joe pulled the trigger without asking why Aaron had betrayed us all? Without demanding an answer or letting Aaron explain himself. Just shot him. Like I'd told him to. Because that's what loyalty is.

I see Reardon across the room, looking very merry with another large tot of Ann's brandy in hand. He's leaning in towards Thomas Curnow, the teacher from Glenrowan. I can tell even from this distance, that the plate layer is drunk and slurring. His body sways as he leans in, and Curnow screws his face up at the man. Distaste is written in every line of the teacher's body. Reardon reaches out and grabs the other man's pipe, helping himself to a deep inhalation before starting yapping again. This time, Curnow's face changes. He leans in towards the other man and I see his eyebrows raise.

Disgust turns to surprise. I can only imagine what Reardon is telling him. I'll need to watch the railway man as he could do us some harm tonight, if given a chance.

Joe interrupts my thoughts, calling to me across the haze of the Inn. A lopsided grin as he yells, 'Ned, do ya see that we're surrounded by friends!' There's a roar of approval and drunken laughter from many in the crowd. I cock an eyebrow at Joe in amusement. He's playing the clown; always one to be counted on to lift the spirits in a room, no matter the depth of his own suffering. He often hides behind his smile and his easy way with women. 'It's true, Ned, I read it in the paper.' With a flourish, Joe pulls from his trouser pocket a folded newspaper piece and holds it aloft.

I grin at Joe, seeing that he is working the crowd. I let him have his fun. 'Well, if it's in th' paper Joe, it must be true,' I reply slowly.

With this implicit approval to continue joking with the crowd, Joe stands up next to the bar and begins a dramatic reading of the piece. He straightens his body, holds out an arm and puts on a posh English voice. 'It tells me right here that, 'Ned Kelly is looked upon as a hero all over the North Eastern district, and Steve Hart is second only in popular esteem.' A drunken voice calls above Joe, 'If that's the case, the damn paper must'a been written by Steve's Ma'.

With Steve standing guard at the stationmaster's house, he makes an easy target for their humour. Another roar of laughter bursts from the crowd before a man right next to Joe pipes up, 'If Joe weren't number two, it ain't been written by no woman, that's for sure. Ain't that right, Joe?'

Joe throws back his own head, appreciating the ribbing. 'Well, I do love the ladies...' he leaves it hanging. 'Especially Steve's Ma!' The crowd erupts again. I can't help but wonder if they would be laughing so, if they knew of the bloodshed that is planned for tonight; the calculated derailment of a train full of people, hostages, killing. Will they all still be sympathetic to the Kelly cause once they know of Aaron? Once the train is destroyed? Tonight, their laughter is quick and light. Will their laughter and loyalty remain tomorrow?

***

After Joe's finished his recital, the music kicks off once again. Ann's young fella sings clear and sweet, keeping the faces entertained. The smoke from the fire gives the room a hazy quality and with so many bodies, the heat's getting uncomfortable. The door bangs behind me and with each step away from the hotel, the noise dims. It's a relief. After so long sleeping out, hidden away, it's a challenge being under a roof and surrounded by so many people. Being under an open sky again is a comfort. I turn at a noise and realise Joe is only a step behind me.

'Will ye come for a ride, Joe? Dan'll be fine in there for a while. I've sent Steve word to come back.'

I pull myself aboard the big bay, Joe alongside me on his own, and without another word we head into the night. The sounds behind us gradually meld into the night noises of the bush. Not silence, not even quiet—a different type of noise. One, that after all this time in the bush, is a balm to my ears and my mind. With every canter away from the Inn, a part of me wishes that we didn't have to go back. That I didn't have to finish what I've started.

I want to show Joe the track that Reardon and Sullivan ripped up the night before. To see for himself where our destiny is headed and how it's going to get there. With night having just fallen, it shouldn't be difficult to keep everyone in the Inn subdued. Annie's been instructed to keep the drinks coming. We won't be long.

I pull my mare up alongside the bend in the track and leave the reins loose over a hanging branch before scrambling down the bank to the line. I stand on the empty dirt, where only the indentation of tracks remain. The sleepers in front stretch out ahead of us in a seemingly endless line. It's light enough, even with a clouded moon above, which is just beginning to rise. Now that we're here, there's little to say in the face of what we've set in motion. The gap in the metal looks innocuous. That's the beauty of it. It may look harmless, but it'll be as deadly as the noose they have waiting for us. More so, as this will take dozens of people at a time. Whereas our walk to the gallows will be done one-by-one if they get a chance.

I take in the surrounds. Dense bush is close to the railway and seems to suck the light from the very sky into its dark canopy. There's no way that the train driver will notice the work of the plate layers, not in the dark. We've got to hope the train is on its way, right this minute, steaming towards us. The later tonight the better.

Joe is a dark figure in front of me, his outline softly lit by the light of the moon. He looks ghostly, staring into the darkness, just as I have been. The difference being Joe is focused on the view behind. He's watching our back, and waiting for what is coming. He's a spectre, looming, to tell me what is about to arrive.

'Is Aaron eatin' at ye, Joe?' My voice, though quiet, cuts through the night. He says nothing but nods, still gazing into the blackness. 'He had it comin', Joe. He would've expected it. He'd have known that the plottin' against us, workin' with Hare and th' coppers, 'twas a fuckin' dog act. The Aaron that we knew wouldn't have sold out like dat, Joe. He was a different man.' I'm rambling, trying to fill the void between us. Trying to find the right words to mend whatever hurt is ailing him. His mind, his heart—I don't know where his pain is sitting, only that it's there.

'He knew it, Ned. I seen it in his eyes. He looked sad and scared. He knew that I'd be the las' person he ever saw in this life.' He lets the silence settle. Emptiness. Then he nods, slowly. Resigned to his guilt and despair. 'I hear what you're saying, Ned. The problem is, I loved 'im. And I killed 'im.'

I watch Joe Byrne, wanted man and bushranger, wipe the tears from his face. I'm glad that he's had no time for sleep yet. I know that every time he closes his eyes, for a while at least, Aaron's shadow will dance in front of his eyes.

But Aaron is gone. The tracks are gone. Glenrowan beckons.

***

There's a man that I see; his face floats in front of my eyes, though I know that I have them closed. I can feel them—heavy. The man in front of me is thin. A learned man, with eyes that pierce into my soul. It's too late, he knows who I am.

His mouth opens and though I know he's talking to me, I

can't hear him. He limps towards me; just a step or two. C'mon, listen Ned. I need to hear what he's saying and I strain, trying to get a whisper of what he's telling me.

I fear that if I don't hear him, if I ignore him, it will be the death of me.

But his words are drowned out. Drowned by the drone that goes on in my head.

***

When we return to the noise and hustle of the Inn, the teacher draws my attention. Thomas Curnow is huddled in a corner with his little girl cradled asleep on his lap. His wife, who sits beside him, eyes barely open, looks fit to deliver another any day. Curnow has no smile and, other than to Reardon, I've not seen him speak to any others in the Inn. I can tell this isn't a place he frequents. He sits too straight and too still, trying to stay calm in this place which is so foreign to him. It makes him look awkward and out of place. Having his wife and child here must add to his worry.

Thomas Curnow is the teacher at Glenrowan. Someone mentioned it to me after we'd brought him and his family back to the hotel earlier in the day. He'd been on his way back from Greta Swamp, having enjoyed a family picnic that day. I called him to a stop just past the Inn, about to cross the railway tracks. Stepping into the road, pistol pointed, he pulled his horse to a quick stop. That had been just after 4.30.

Dan's dancing a jig in the middle of the room and swinging young Jane around, ending his dance in front of the teacher and his young wife, looking for someone to join him in his adrenaline-induced revelry on the dance floor.

'Come on, Mr Curnow. Come and join in the dancing, I'm sure ya wife'll look after the little one.' I can't tell if Dan is truly inviting Curnow to join in their fun or whether he is poking fun at the man, who gets around with a pronounced limp. It isn't like Dan to be cruel, so I think to myself that it must be youthful exuberance on his part. Curnow's eyes dart around, looking for an escape from having to speak with Dan, but my brother kneels down to look him in the eye.

'C'mon, Mr. Curnow. None of ya charges are about to see ya enjoyin' yaself. It's only right, what with you bein' such an *important* part of the community and all.' Curnow's eyes snap up at this exchange, a reaction to the sarcasm laden in Daniel's words. I am about to step in, but Dan is off, grabbing another lass around the bar as the music starts up again.

I grab at Dan's sleeve as he flies past me, which pulls him up quickly. 'What do ye mean, tauntin' the teacher like dat?' He shrugs, but looks over his shoulder towards the man in question.

'I don't like him, Ned. He's a squib and he'll throw us to the coppers as soon as look at us. See him over there, thinkin' he's better than the rest of us, with his learning and his hobblin' round.' I haven't taken much notice of the teacher since we picked him and his young family up. But now I want to talk to the man that's irritated Dan, normally the quiet, steady one of us.

Curnow notices me walking in his direction. His eyes focus on me. I stop beside him and nod to his woman, 'I'm hopin' your wife is well enough there. We won't be in here too much longer and then ye can all head back to your home.' I try to sound reassuring, but his eyes narrow and he throws my gift back in my face.

'You mean after the carnage, Mr Kelly? That's the talk of people. That you're going to blow up the train?' He poses it as a question; bravely, I suppose, or stupidly. He might look uncomfortable and out of place, but the man's no coward.

I look at him straight. 'Not blow it up, Mr Curnow, but you're right. There'll be some people brought to justice this night.'

He's quiet, nods a little and says nothing else. He doesn't look afraid, still awkward, but not scared, which makes me respect him a little more than if he was cowering in the corner. He looks up. 'I'd appreciate being able to take my wife and child home, sir, to sleep. They will be better out of what is happening tonight. They're innocents and need to be looked after.' His gaze has been roving around the Inn as he's spoken, but when he stops, he looks me dead in the eye. 'That's my job. You'll understand that.'

I nod at him. I've heard his request and it's not the first one I've heard from people tonight. He is the only one here with a pregnant wife and child though. He notices my pause.

'I could go by the Railway Department. Stanistreet tells me that there's a loaded revolver there. It might be used against you, Mr Kelly, or induce bloodshed near these civilians. I'd see it safely away if I was allowed to take my family home?' He leaves the question hanging, waiting for me to make a judgment.

I look hard at Curnow and try to judge the man. I

feel myself about to agree to the teacher's request. Neither his young wife, heavily pregnant and with another small child, nor the teacher himself, seem to be any threat. I don't know him personally but he's popular with his small charges and they always seem to be a reasonably good judge of character. I'll let the small family return home with the promise of checking in on them during the night, to ensure they stay tucked away.

I open my mouth to consent to his request.

As I do, the face of another teacher flashes in my mind. Daniel Kennedy. The teacher at the Greta school, not far down the road and very much in the thick of Kelly country. Rumour has it that he might be on the books as an informant. Annie's comments about my armour last night seem to support this assumption. I've no solid proof, otherwise I would have put a bullet through him as a warning to those who'd go against us. But if Kennedy was an informant, despite seeming innocent, could this teacher be working against me too?

I can't risk anything going wrong this night, with so many people relying on me. This young teacher, with his womenfolk and his limp, seems innocuous enough, but tonight is not the night to be testing unknown loyalties.

'I think not, Mr. Curnow,' I say quietly and turn to walk away. 'You and ye wife'll be home soon enough.'

***

I turn my attention to Ann. She's a deft hand with the men, a trick of the trade. She knows how to keep them drinking and jovial without it spilling into chaos and fights. It doesn't surprise me that the business has done well in its

short time, barely a couple of years, without even a
husband at her side. She takes stock of the scene around
her, shakes her head, ever so slightly, in disbelief I imagine.
She appears in front of me, barely level with my beard, but
still a force, and meets my eyes.

'Are ye finding ye'self in need of a drink, Ned? It's
too cold tonight, you'll need some warmin'.' She pours me
one, but I shake my head. I've not touched a drop all day
and night. I need all my senses in full working order.

'You'd better have it ye'self, Annie. Who knows
how long we'll be waitin' around here.' She doesn't need a
second invitation and downs the drink expertly.

'You're a likable lad, Ned, which is lucky for ye,
might I say, or otherwise you'd ha' been in her Majesty's
care a long while ago.' I can tell the drink she's taken hasn't
been her first tonight—makes her loose with her words.
Or perhaps it's the close proximity that we find ourselves
in. She'd not have expected to have a gang of wanted
bushrangers holed up and dancing in her hotel.

'You and the boys ha' been expectin' that copper
train for near on twenty-four hours now. Surely it would
ha' been here by now if t'was comin'?' She waves her hand
around the jumble of people gathered in the hotel. Adding
numbers every couple of hours. As the night wears on, the
drinkers continue, but there are a number passed out from
either drink or exhaustion, laying about the dirt floor of
the Inn. Curnow's wife appears to be asleep now, lent up
against him, while he cradles his small daughter. Rocking
her slightly with gentle movements. His mouth moves,
perhaps singing her a song or whispering her a story? She
looks fast asleep and I envy her comfort. A parent's arms
provide a bond of strength and comfort when you are a

little one. What I wouldn't give to sleep with such reassurance again, even for a night.

I watch the two of them. Content. Her face sleeps, without a care passing over it. *She doesn't know what happens. Not like I do.* It's as if she's not even here. Curnow's head snaps up and his gaze meets my own. If this goes wrong, his face will haunt me for years to come—him and his little girl. I look away.

Anne is still, and staring at my profile.

'You comparin' me to the posters, Annie?' I turn to face her and give her a grim smile.

'Per'aps. It's not a bad likeness, though I'd say ye nose is longer than in the flesh. I wonder who drew it? Had to ha' been a copper. Don't really know ye, do they? Your eyes in the papers are cold and distant, but they aren't like that, are they? They've life in 'em, yer eyes.' She continues to look at me, unmoving. 'I hope they stay like that, Ned Kelly. After tonight, I mean.'

'I hope so too, Annie. 'Cause, there's sure to be a train comin'. They're comin' for me as sure as I'm a Kelly. Full o' coppers and trackers, Hare too. He's desperate to capture the elusive Kelly Gang!' I raise my eyebrows and my tone is full of scorn as I face her. 'We're getting' in first is all. If the train goes, it'll send 'em a message. We're untouchable. That they can't bully us and th' men around here. They can't tread all over the men of dis colony with their corruption and greed and 'spect nothin' to be done about it.'

I watch her shrink away at my talk of fighting and killing.

I can see that my words unnerve her.

'You'll be crossin' a line, Ned. A very big, feckin'

line. This is cold-blooded murder tha' you're plannin', and there'll be a lot o' people dat don't want nothin' to do with it, and all the troubles it'll bring.' She looks around the bar at her family: young daughter and sons, friends and locals. 'What if they survive, Ned? The coppers. Won't they come lookin' for y'all here?'

I pat her arm, her red dress looks a little worse for wear after a night of drinks and dancing. I want to reassure her. 'Ah, don't worry, Annie, you'll all be grand. Yer kids'll be safe.' The two of us look up at the young boy on the other side of the Inn. He has a frailty in his body, but not his song. He's atop a chair and begins to sing the recently penned 'Kelly Song' to the cheers of those around him. John Jones is thirteen and clearly the apple of his mother's eye.

'Even the bastard Hare wouldn't open fire on a buildin' full o' innocents and children, Annie. We're not dat wanted!' I hope that my assertion is true. The last thing I want is for these people, the locals who I know, to be in the middle of a shoot-out. No matter what I say, I'm not convinced the police will draw a distinction between us—the locals and the criminals. Not if it means capturing the Kellys.

It won't come to that though. My plan is good. The train will go, and it will go hard. I look around the bar. 'You're witnessin' history, Annie, right 'afore ye eyes. Think of that!'

She smiles at me. It reaches her mouth but her eyes give her away. She's still watching John, her mother's worry written on her face. And a melancholy that I can't quite put my finger on.

As if she knows.

'Well, in that case, ye better carve ye name on 'ere, Ned,' she pats the red gum slab which we're both leaning on. 'People'll be comin' for miles to stand at the place where history was made. My little place'll be famous.'

She grins at that.

***

Ann's words spin around my mind. I'll have crossed a line. But didn't I cross that line so many years ago? When I think back, there haven't been too many times when I wasn't just a useless, bloody Kelly.

Dick Shelton had been a scrap of a lad at 7 and me so much stronger and four years older than him. I knew him well, both being local boys. That day, I was watching him from the bank of the Hughes River, swollen and rushing with the rains that we'd had. The current was always at its strongest just past the old stone bridge. All of us kids knew that. You knew to never get in down-stream of the old girl. But I watched Dick stand on top of a big gum, fallen years ago, which now stretched its giant arms across the river. Branches were ripped off by the wild water rushing around it. He was balancing, arms wide, and playing the fool. No fear on his face—until the moment his foot slipped. The old trunk was smooth with age and made slick by the muddy water running over and around it. He had nothing to grab onto when he slipped from it and went under the foaming rush.

I didn't know I was going in after him until I was running towards the riverbank. I'm a strong swimmer, always have been, and Dick was kicking and screaming, holding onto one of the thicker branches in the water. His head kept being washed over as the cold hands of the river grabbed at his body again and again. So many children have been stolen by the murky depths of the rivers and never returned. Dick would be next. I saw the terror in his eyes.

The current was fierce and grabbed at me as soon as I jumped in. Trying to throw me under, biting at my body, but my legs were strong and I was a fighter even back then. The water, though vicious, wasn't wide and I reached Dick in six strong strokes. Grabbing him with one arm, I was rough, shoving him along the tree trunk, both of us holding on for our lives. His face had deep scratches from the twigs and branches that we had scraped against along the way, but by the time I dragged him onto the bank, he was still breathing, and sobbing. Snot ran down his face, mixed with mud and tears.

By then several people gathered around us on the bank. They'd heard the screams and come running. Some carried Dick towards the Royal Mail. My own lungs were full of water and I gagged it up, where I sat. I looked as much of a mess as Dick. I remember hands pushing at me, smacking me on the back. Words being thrown over and around me.

'Well done, Ned.'

'Good work lad, ya saved young Dick.'

'Neddy, you're a hero, lad.'

By the time we reached the Hotel where Dick lived—half carried, half dragged through the street, news of the rescue had reached his parents. There were hugs and tears. It was then that his mother presented me with my sash; the finest thing I'd ever seen. With a kiss and more congratulations, the green and gold of my sash catching the light, I felt ten feet tall. The Hero, Ma had called me. Red had been proud too, boasting to his mates. He was more likely pleased about the constant supply of grog my rescue secured for him from Elizabeth and Esau Shelton, who ran the Hotel. Never one to give up an opportunity, was my old man. Ironic really, since it was the drink that probably killed him in the end. Maybe that's just another thing that I can be blamed for?

I keep the sash close, but I've never had that feeling again. That I've done something heroic and worthy. I guess Ann's words mean that now I never will.

***

Joe and Dan sidle up alongside Ann and me, which sees her move off to keep the customers happy. Beside me, Joe takes a fob from his pocket; a treasured gift from his father. It's a little tarnished but keeps time to the minute and I know what he's trying to tell me. His clock has ticked over midnight. We are officially into Monday morning, and it's reached almost thirty hours since he put a bullet into Aaron Sherritt's head. What the hell is keeping the train?

'You're a bloody dandy, Joe,' Dan laughs at him. 'Look at ya pullin' ya watch out, all fancy. The women are already swoonin' over ya. Don't have to go to any great lengths.'

'Get away, Dan. As if they have a choice, with you other smelly buggers about. I'm the best lookin' man in 'ere by a long shot. Let alone the best lookin' bushranger.' Dan slaps Joe's shoulder with a laugh and wanders off towards the locals who are kicking up their heels. Despite the late hour, they've gained a second wind. Even they must be feeling that the climax is coming.

As Dan leaves, Joe's face creases—the smile gone.

'By God, Dan looks young though, don't he, Ned?' Joe looks towards him. 'He and Steve are still boys. How the hell'd they get caught up in this mess? They should be home. Not in this shithole tonight.' He's talking but I know it's to himself as much as to me.

I step into his line of vision, 'That might be too much thinkin' for this time o' the night, Joe.' His gaze shifts to me and gains focus again.

Joe nods towards Dan and laughs, 'Christ, look at Dan's beard will ya. Me grandmother had a better one than what he's growin'!' I smile in acknowledgment. Laughing and joking across the room, Dan looks even younger than his 19 years. There's only six years between us, but it may as well be a hundred.

Joe lowers his voice and leans slightly in towards me. 'The thing is, Ned. What if it goes wrong tonight? I'm thinkin', are we doing the right thing stayin' 'round here as long as we have? We're sitting ducks. An' all these people waitin' here.' His gaze sweeps the room and he looks jittery. 'That damn train shoulda been 'ere hours ago. Even if the coppers at Sherritt's took their sweet time to come out. They shoulda been 'ere. What the fuck are we still doin' waitin'?'

My gaze follows Joe's. 'They must be comin' up by train, Joe. It has to be on its way. Hare won't let us get away with Aaron's killin'. They're sure to be comin'.' It sounded like the absolute truth, because I felt it in my guts. They are coming. 'They'll never shoot up the Inn. Not with all these people in 'ere. If the coppers slaughtered all these people, just to catch a few mangy outlaws, there'd be a bloody outcry.' Joe raises his eyebrows. He's not certain about any of it.

'I'm sick of runnin', Joe.' I sigh deeply. The resignation and regret in the words seep from my soul. Even I can hear it. It's only Joe that I can say this to. Not to the other boys, who I need to be strong for. Joe understands me as good as any soul in the world.

'I'm sick of bein' hunted like dogs. It's time for a stand. To show 'em that we can't be pushed over.' Joe sees that it's a futile argument against me. My decision is made.

Joe gives a slight grin, 'There won't be no runnin' from me, Ned, even if it does go badly. You might be able to get 'round in that bloody armour you've made, but I'm a goner! I can barely stand in it. Even without me fancy helmet!'

I shake my head at him. 'You won't need armour. Hare and his bastard police aren't comin' off that train in any condition for a fight. You keep ye fancy helmet for when we hold up the bank at Benalla. Then all you'll have to do is walk in. E'en a little saplin' like you can do that!'

Joe looks down at his watch. *Whatever the outcome will be, it will rapidly be upon us. The train has to come soon.* I move off to get suited up. I want to be ready.

***

Tick, tick, tick. Joe's fob moves around the hour.

Standing outside the hotel I lean against the bark slab wall to take some of the armour's weight. The leather strap cuts into my shoulders. From where the moon sits in the winter sky, becoming shrouded in cloud, I can tell that it's late–after 1 or 2am.

The noise from inside the inn sounds like a party. Energy bursts within the walls. If you didn't know the reason for the revelry, you might mistake it for a wedding, or perhaps a bloody good wake. Dan's in the middle of it all, dancing and laughing with the best of them. Trying to keep himself awake. Since we found ourselves on the wrong side of the law, he's come out of his shell. His confidence has grown. No longer is he the Kelly kid who everyone's grown up with. People are awestruck when they see him. Dan Kelly: bushranger. But along with that title comes others. Killer. Wanted. There's a certain admiration in people's eyes, even if the looks are mingled with fear.

The Kellys are a tough lot, and though she's a Quinn by birth, my Ma is as tough as any. Arrested when baby Alice was only a wee thing, thanks to that bastard Fitzpatrick, and I never even seen her cry a tear. Her mouth had formed a hard line and she just accepted it as her lot. That was what broke my heart. The woman we all loved expected no better from life. That was what being a Kelly had done to her. Rotting in Melbourne Gaol for something she didn't do.

The last time I saw her, a tongue lashing was handed to me for dragging Dan into this godforsaken mess, as she called it. She'd wanted us married, settled, earning an honest living and bringing her lots of grandbabies. We all know that's never going to happen now. Not for me anyway. Which gives her grief. She knows that I need Daniel at my side, but I'm still holding out hope that I might be able to get him out of this mess, relatively unscathed. Ma, and the kids of course, are the reason that I haven't been able to leave Victoria for good. How can I leave them here, at the scrutiny of the Victorian Police Force and the judgment of every man, woman and child in the colony? Locked away as she is, how could the girls fend for themselves? So here we are. The decision made and the wheels set in motion. Now, there is only waiting.

The clouds thicken across the inky sky and shroud the moon. That's good. The darker it is tonight, the better for us. Joe's worried the police train isn't coming but I can feel it in my bones, they're on their way. I tell myself their delay is a good sign, but not for those coppers.

My blood pumps harder and faster than I want it to. My heart is fair jumping out of my chest with anticipation. I thought our destiny would be already decided by this hour. Instead, here we are, along with half of Glenrowan, drinking and carousing. I was so sure that Hare would be frothing at the mouth at the thought of the Kelly Gang killing Sherritt. I had felt certain the train would come steaming through, as if we'd ordered the special train ourselves to come up the Wangaratta line.

But the longer we wait, I find myself with time to contemplate if this will all go our way. There is the problem. If this is the wrong move, I don't know what the right one is. If the police aren't heading to Beechworth, then where are they? Lying in wait for us? With what information? I've counted on Hare's insatiable thirst for the hunt. That his thirst to have me will drive him down these tracks, his mind mad with intent.

Perhaps I'm wrong.

I sense movement coming towards the inn— voices. I grab my pistol tighter as Steve walks around the corner, a bounce in his step. I hadn't realised he'd left the building. But here he is, a grin on his face and heading directly for me.

'It's the train, Ned. Blew her whistle. It's on its way, but she's moving slowly.' His body is rigid with nervous anticipation that the moment is here at long last. My tension melts away as he tells me the news. Now that the fight is here, I'll be fine. It's the waiting that I can't bear. The brawl, I'm ready for.

I burst through the doors with a clatter and turn my attention to Ann. I can't help but tell her, 'I'll show ye a sight now, Mrs. Jones. I'll kill all ye traps an' they'll be drinkin' here no more.'

Dan and Joe stand at the back of the room, silent and watching me. The dancing and music has stopped and the locals follow me too. The breathing is heavy, as if my own exhilaration is a fire that's lit the room. *As if they know history is upon us and they are part of it.* The younger ones amongst them look as if they'd like to join our adventure, but I know that once the bullets fly, most of them will shit their britches. It's never what you think it'll be like.

'Let's go, boys. The show's about to start and we don' want to miss the openin' act.'

I move deliberately, shifting my gaze around the inn. I know what has to happen now. 'As for the rest of ye, there'll be shootin' tonight and there'll be killin'. Best to stay here and keep your heads down. I won't be responsible for ye getting' shot if ye head out. Mrs. Jones'll keep the fires and the drinks goin' here for now.' Ann gives a single nod of agreement. We understand each other. A few other heads bob as well. We've enough friends here, and they'll not be letting anyone interfere. I stride from the hotel and grab my mare's reins, laying across the wooden rail just outside the doorway. I haul myself on top of her, and despite my size and the armour, I let down lightly onto her back. The success of my night will be entwined with hers and I need her steady. We're ready.

***

The noise of Stringybark, where my killing began; the cries of the wounded officer, the men pleading for their lives, has haunted my dreams since it happened. I know people see me as a blood-thirsty, murderous bastard, but even killers have a conscience. I've feared sleep since that night, as Lonigan's, Scanlon's and Kennedy's faces have haunted my hours of dreaming. Faceless wives and children calling for their husbands and fathers. But in an instant, I know their faces will be supplanted by the sounds and sights of this night.

The four of us gallop from the town, following the track, and our horses quickly approach the first bend out from Glenrowan. The first of the trains—it must be a guide train—moves along beside us for only a few beats as we pass through the bush to the East of Glenrowan town. I let out a full breath. They're passing through the town. They don't know we're here. I tighten my hold on the reins and squeeze my legs. I need the mare to fair fly if we want to see the trains hit the broken track. She pulls ahead of the others. We're lucky the railway line is cut into the hillside, almost as if the train is running on a step below us. I imagine for just a second that I could jump my mare atop the train. Now that would be a sight! I have a clear view of the train rolling beside us. This giant mechanic beast which breaks the night with its puffs and rattles. In contrast, no-one will have seen four horsemen galloping through the edge of the bush above them. The cloud is heavy and the bush is thick with silhouettes that weave themselves between trees and bushes beside the track. It's a night of shadows and ghosts.

The trains move slowly, full of caution, as if suspicious we have something up our sleeves. Despite their steady speed, they have no hope of seeing the missing pieces of track. The only chance they had was if they'd stopped at Glenrowan. *Or if someone had stopped them.* As soon as they drove through the town, at this time between night and morning, I knew the train must surely fall. The driver may see the yawning gap of line in front—but too late. He'll know it for only a few seconds before the train plummets from their step in the hillside to the floor below. He'll barely have a chance to cry out.

Riding hard along the line, we're almost there. I'm doing my best to dodge branches. I'm low on my mare's neck. She's moving expertly through the bush, missing wombat holes and leaping fallen branches. She responds to my urging, but still the first train pulls ahead. I hear, rather than see, when the first train leaves the track. A massive crunch of metal and wood. The train seems to fly off its guiding rail, and crashes from the track. I pull my mare to a halt above where the rails have been removed in time to see the carriages of the first come to a stop below. The noise is deafening. I'm not sure how I expected a train to look as it derailed, but I hadn't expected such force. I'm hypnotised by the scene. Then comes the screech of the brakes, animal-like, from the second train. The boys pull their horses up near my own. The driver's realised the first train has gone, with the glowing red lights ahead dropping from sight. But it's too late for him. In the time it takes the driver to register the carriage in front has gone and slam on his brakes, any chance of pulling up the train has disappeared as well.

This time we have the perfect vantage point to watch it leave the tracks. The bend in the line adds to the train's vulnerability. The brakes and the initial smash as it hits the carriage below is ear-splitting. I see Dan and Steve jolt and cover their ears. The horses start and shy away, dancing on their toes, eager to get away from the chaos. Debris flies into the air and bits of wood and metal land around us. We sit ten feet above where the tracks had been, overlooking the destruction we've created. A twisted mess of metal. They've fallen a further fifteen feet below where the track runs. Carriages on carriages twisted into strange, darkened shapes. Once the carriages settle, silence descends over the scene for just a second. We all catch our breath. The screech of metal is replaced by the screams of the people inside. And now I want to cover my own ears.

I feel like the young boys back at the hotel—full of bravado—until I see what chaos we've caused. I've an overwhelming urge to get away. But I don't have that choice. I've imagined the destruction of the train from the outset; it was my suggestion to tear up the tracks. What I couldn't imagine was the agony of the deaths that would come to those aboard.

The carriages are broken open, horses scattered around. Some beasts stand, shocked and trembling, but on their feet. Some writhe in agony on the ground; thrashing around broken limbs, while others remain trapped in carriages. Their noise is gut-wrenching. The shrieking is the sound of the banshee in my mother's stories, keening for her dead.

The cloud clears and moonbeams throw a spotlight on the carnage. The horses grab my attention first, despite the people scattered in the darkness: sitting, crying, wandering. Some are climbing from the ruined carriages. There is nothing but groans, cries, sobs, retching, screams escaping them. We're too far away to see the blood and torn clothing. But the noise will stay with me for a lifetime. From where I sit, they seem dazed, but in the moment, it's the pain and fear from the screaming horses that claws at my gut. I need to get down there. I have to settle them.

My eyes flick across the scene, taking in the mess. A woman. She's on the ground, her face searching. Her pale dress catches the moonlight and balloons around her on the cold earth. What the hell is a woman doing on the train? Some idiot bringing along his bride to see the action, no doubt. Fucking hell. My eyes flick to another lying awkwardly, half-strewn from the carriage. She looks dead. I feel sick to my stomach. Joe echoes my thoughts, 'Ah Christ! There's bloody women in it.' Dan and Steve swing their attention to where he's pointing.

It's too late for regret. The plan has been realised and the moaning, writhing bodies below us are evidence of its success. I straighten my shoulders, a show for the other boys more than anything.

'We've been pushed into dis situation, boys. It's not what we wanted. But we have to present ourselves as th' blood-thirsty gang they think we are. We'll make some noise and put some bullets down there. Keep ye wits about ye. They might be dazed or injured but get th' weapons.'

'Do we take the best of them as hostages, Ned?' Dan looks pale and I hope it's just the moonlight casting its glow over him.

I wheel my mare around. 'Lemme get down there and see how many coppers are about. If ye see Hare, ye put a bullet in 'im. But he's the only one, unless they give you cause.'

I kick my mare down the hillside, leaning back into the saddle as she scrambles downwards. She's sure-footed and it's not the first time that I've put my life in her hands. I hear the boys scrambling down behind. Young they might be, but they're as game as they come.

My mare drops level with the mess of metal and steam. The train hisses and burning embers spill from the firebox at the front of the first train into the leaf litter and brush. Thank Christ it's damp from the winter rains or I'd be dealing with a bushfire as well as a derailed train. I hold my pistol in the air and fire a warning shot. My voice is loud and clear, defiant. It's exactly how I want to sound in this situation. It's how I want people to remember me here tonight. Self-assured. Murderous. Not a retching, gagging fella, barely out of his teens, which is how I feel watching the maimed bodies struggling to move away from the wreck. Adrenaline surges through my body as I come face-to-face with our handiwork.

'I am Ned Kelly. Throw away ye weapons or I'll cut ye down.'

I whip the mare around in tight circles. She's tense and flighty underneath me, feeling my adrenaline and spooked by the unfamiliar noises and smells—the screaming of the horses. My voice is muffled by the cries and moans around me, so I raise my own to be heard.

'We'll no' shoot an unarmed man.'

Up close, the scene is worse. The broken bodies more angled, the horses writhe and thrash more intensely. For the few who are conscious and standing, I see pistols being thrown away and hands raised. Some are uniformed, some in plain clothes. Newspaper men, maybe. There are coppers and trackers. But there are none in any state to resist.

I yell over my shoulder, 'Steve, you and Dan round up anyone that can stand and put 'em into that carriage.' I point to the one that is most intact and standing upright. We've had to pick our way through the wreck from the back of the carriages. There is barely room for movement between the tangle of trains and bodies in the gully, rocky and steep at both sides. The boys yell instructions behind me and wave people in. I see Joe jump from his gelding, draw his gun and put a bullet in the head of one of the horses. It has been the one screaming, overtaken by agony and fear but unable to move. Perhaps a broken pelvis or back. Joe's bullet gives us some silence. There's no fight in these people before us. All that remains is the hissing of the busted boilers throwing steam into the night air.

'Hare, ye bastard,' I yell to the night, 'Come out and face me. You've wanted this meetin' for so long. Well 'ere it is.' I throw the challenge.

My mare whips around and I half expect a shot to ring out and the pain of a bullet to pierce my back. None comes. 'We've put a bullet in Sherritt. We know he was in yer pocket, but ye'll get no more from 'im.'

He doesn't appear. He doesn't call out.

Instead, it's the woman on the ground looking dazed, who calls out.

'He's dead, Kelly.' She sits beside another woman who is dead. She's stroking her hand gently, her own face smeared in dirt and blood.

It's a strangled sound as she points away towards a body. I'm hesitant in case it's an ambush being staged.

'Joe, keep an eye out will ye?' I dismount and move across the prostrate body. There's no movement. The body is in uniform, with a portly belly and bearded— he resembles what I know of Hare. But his head is badly crushed. Barely recognisable as human.

He's dead. Relief floods through my body. The surge of excitement rises again. He's not the only enemy I have. Truth be told I'd prefer if it was Fitzpatrick lifeless in front of me, or that bastard copper, Ward. But Hare will do.

'I warned ye. I warned ye all to leave this colony if you'd somethin' to fear from the Kellys. Let this be me final warnin' to the police. You cannot catch us. We're fightin' for the injustices against those innocents who are sufferin' at the hands of a corrupt police force. I told this in my letter from Jerilderie, of wholesale and retail slaughter and dat is what has come. I warn you again— leave this colony. Do not shame your ancestors and country by joinin' the Victorian Police Force, and you may live.' I grab my mare's reins and swing myself onto her back, the pistol still ready in my hand.

'We've been hounded by the police. Unjustly accused. My mother sits rotting in the cells because of you lying dogs. This is not unprovoked.'

I aim my words at the police I see scattered

around, but then I see one of the trackers. A man cradling another, keening, amongst the chaos. He looks shocked, as if he can't believe what has happened. They are more innocent victims in our war with the Victorian Police Force.

I count the local Pangerang people as my friends. They've helped us to evade the police at times, passed us information when we've needed it. They're brave. Underestimated by just about every white man I've spoken to. They know this land intimately. It runs in their blood. The Pangerang have been our brothers: marginalised and on the very edge of this life as well. Not by any damn choice of their own. After the kindness they've shown us, the deaths of those trackers feels like a betrayal. I'm sorry for it. Those Queensland men have just done what they've been bid to. Now their spirits will walk this country, instead of their own. I hope the Pangerang spirits are welcoming to these Northern brothers.

I have nothing more to say. Hare is dead and carnage surrounds us. I doubt that those who are living will remember much of what I've said, such is their state. But they'll remember it was the Kellys.

Joe is mounted up, pistol drawn, while the other two stand near the only upright carriage, now filled with the few who can stand.

'How many have ye in there, Dan?' He peers in, counting up quickly.

'Only six. Three coppers. Do we take 'em with us?' I shake my head. Thoughts are bounding around. What to do now? The plan had been to take hostages with us and use them to secure Ma's release. Give those in charge a reason to sit down and listen to the Kellys. But what we've done is past derailing a train. It's fucking carnage—a dozen dead at least. Premeditated murder. If we were wanted men before this, now our names will be spoken about in every corner of the country. The biggest bounty in history. Dead or alive. Jim had been right. Trying to get Ma out now will only make things worse for her. No-one will be sitting down with us, unless we had guns pointed at our heads. Hostages will only hinder our escape.

I look to the younger boys by the carriage, and get a start. A face peers from the darkness of the carriage and I can just make out the shape of his face. It's the bloody school teacher!

'Dan! Is that bastard Curnow in there?' I look straight down the pistol, aimed directly where I saw the face in the doorway. Dan and Steve exchange a glance, before Dan looks again into the darkness. His hand shoots out and grabs the shirt of the bloke lurking in the shadows, shoving him out and into the full moonlight.

'Curnow's not here, Ned. Just a copper.' The man cowers in front of Dan with his hands raised. It's not him. Bloody shadows playing tricks.

'Curnow'll be back at Annie's. He'll be no more trouble,' throws in Steve.

I'm frozen on the spot, shocked at my mistake.

'Put him back. Mount up. We're not takin' anyone—we're away boys!' I need to get out of Glenrowan. I face my mare towards town and call over my shoulder, 'Don't come lookin' for us. There are men crawlin' all over the town. They'll put a hole in ye as soon as look at ye.' Our work is done here and the Benalla Bank of New South Wales beckons. The confusion of seeing

Curnow's face is gone, replaced with elation. We've fulfilled our destiny. No matter what, we'll not be forgotten.

This was meant to be. *It was never going to be anything else.*

***

The signal is given. It's Jim or Tom Lloyd who sets off the fireworks—the signal for supporters in the area. Get ready to ride to Benalla. The lights and colours burst above the town in an explosion of light. They'll be heading to the hotel. The noise of the crash, followed by the silence of our guns, must have alerted them to the success of our plan. Tom is an integral part of the inner circle, as a cousin should be. I wouldn't be surprised if he'd snuck down to take a look at what happened.

We'll storm the bank at Benalla—kitted out in the armour we've fashioned. The people of Benalla will think us the devils themselves, walking in to rob them of every note within their walls. Blood rushes through me with the force of the river that pulled Dick Shelton away. We canter from the train wreckage, first along the gully, before driving the horses up along the line. There'll be no more trains.

The crowded inn has emptied and a hundred faces stare at the rainbow being painted across the night sky, turning to watch us gallop up from the railway track. A wave of euphoria goes through the onlookers. A few have gathered already, more keep coming. The minutes tick on, men and horses ready to leave with us at a moment's notice. The horses are toey, dancing around each other, responding to the tension and frenzy of the riders. A large group, including Stanistreet, Curnow and even Ann Jones, looks shocked. My eyes lock with Curnow, standing with his wife near the veranda of the inn. Of course he's here. The lack of sleep must be getting to me.

Constable Bracken, the lone Glenrowan copper, has been roused from his bed and hustled to the inn by someone—Jim is my guess. He stands beside the others, in his nightclothes with his hands clutching his stomach. There are stares of disbelief. Their eyes burn into me with disgust and even hatred. They've separated themselves from the others. They want to be in no way connected to this mess.

For Ann the risks are even greater. With us in this place that holds everything and everyone that she cares for in the world, she is uneasy. With a pull of my head I call her across to me. She comes across and puts a steadying hand on my mare's neck, who is still geed up after the noise at the wreckage.

'No' to worry, Annie, we'll be away soon. We'll just give the others time to arrive, then I'll be gone from ye place. Don't fret. The coppers won't be amongst us any time soon. There's none in fit state at the wreckage.'

She nods, relief plain on her face. 'Thank ye, Ned, but I think that you'd best call me Mrs. Jones. Won't do me no good, bein' on good terms with ye all, after this.'

I'm taken aback by her words. I look around at them all again. I've divided them. For many, we've crossed a line tonight. For the likes of Ann and Curnow, I've crossed into the heartless murderer that people have long assumed that I am. For others, those that have readied themselves to ride, I've crossed from a bushranger into a rebel. Tonight, today, tomorrow, I've lost track of the time, will mark the start of our freedom, just as we've planned. We start at Benalla.

But it will be bigger than a bank.

These past months, secreted away, Joe and I have written the Declaration of the Republic of North-Eastern Victoria. Now they're printed and awaiting distribution. We've armed supporters: men and women willing to fight for this freedom with us. Joe's kept records in the books of our meetings with those in the inner circle, as we've discussed our plans and how we'll achieve freedom in the north-east. Liberated, like my Irish cousins want to be— free from spiteful British rule. It's been nothing but a dream until now. But perhaps this night will prove to be the moment that we take the next step. I think of the clandestine midnight meetings, when a republic has been nothing but a far-fetched dream in our hearts. *It is a dream, isn't it? And yet here I stand, within touching distance of it.*

I leave Ann to join the others and whip my mare around; she's fresh and raring for a ride as much as I am. The run down the tracks has done nothing to dampen her enthusiasm. The other boys are astride as well, their own mounts jogging on the spot, or turning tight circles, much as mine is. Steve is closest to me, sitting in the saddle with ease. In the adrenaline-fueled success of the morning, I can hold in my news to him no longer.

'Steve, I'm away to get Ettie after Benalla. She's agreed to come wit' me. She'll be waitin'.' He looks at me, hard. But it's without surprise, and I wonder whether Dan has betrayed me to his friend. Or whether my feelings for Ettie are so obvious, that he knew this moment was coming.

'You're a dead man, Ned. My father'll shoot ya if ya try and take our Ettie. He won't 'ave it.'

'I'm as good as dead without her anyway, Steve.' He simply shrugs, unmoved by my declaration. With the horses the way they are, there is little more to be said.

'We're away to Benalla then,' I call to those on the ground and those in the saddle who surround me. It doesn't matter now who hears me. 'We're makin' history now.'

There are at least 25 on horseback, who roar at my words, sending another surge of fire through me. Some on the ground clap, caught up in the revelry.

Despite this, a thought niggles. I thought that there would be more. There's sure to be more joining us along the way. We'll take stock at Benalla. I urge my mare on. She understands the urgency and launches into a gallop. The clatter of hooves follows me in an instant.

***

Monday

IT takes us little more than an hour of fair hard riding to reach Benalla. The bush is dense only a stone's throw from the township. It astounds me that so close to the bustle of a town we can be protected in the native bush of this land. Invisible. It's been our ally in the life the boys and I have become a part of, cloaked in darkness and deception. There is a sense of nervous excitement amongst the trees and brush from the riders as we approach, though they're quiet. They're waiting and looking to me. What will we do next?

I know what we've planned to do, but things haven't gone to plan since I knocked on Ann's door. We have more than enough people to storm the bank at Benalla, plunder its safe and burn the mortgage papers of the people who struggle around here. We even have enough bodies, with big enough hearts, to raise a flag—to declare Benalla a free state, no longer under British rule. Given a little time, we could move on to the next town. But what then? In our meetings, where countless hours of talk have centred around this very moment, we knew what we'd do next. Take over Benalla, recruit the men, move onto Greta or Glenrowan, hold that and recruit again. But here lies the problem that I find myself facing. In our plans, we'd imagined men flooding to join our cause. Giving us numbers to withstand assault. And they might. But I saw the faces of those at Glenrowan, the ones that I'd alienated when the train crashed. What if the numbers don't come?

My mare breathes heavily still. She cares not for my contemplation. She wants action, as much as those around me. For many it's their first taste of blatant lawlessness and they're intoxicated by it. I look around at the faces I see in the dawning light, scattered amongst the trees and undergrowth. Most are still on horseback. A couple of the boys, I can't see which ones, have jumped off to take a piss behind trees and have a laugh. Bloody fools. It's a bit of a lark for them. They don't realise it's life and death, these choices that we're making. That I'm making for them. I see mostly faces that I know, but there are a few more surrounding me that I can't make out. I don't know who exactly or how many we've gathered on the ride. But I do see Jim, who has only come tonight in support of Daniel and me. There are Harts like Ettie's beloved brother, Dick. There are Quinns and Lloyds—cousins both. I see the faces of friends amongst the group, but mostly there is family. In the breaking light of the morning, I spot the feminine profile of Kate Lloyd, mounted up and chatting to the others quietly. I mutter under my breath and push my mare towards hers.

'What the bloody hell are ye doin' here, woman?' I scowl at her. I'm not mad at her, which is what I seem to be, but terrified that the beautiful 17 year old is prepared to join this gang of raggedy murderers. She's my cousin, but she's more than that. She's a confidante, a love of my life. Another of the precious Kate's that I hold close. I'm lucky my sister hasn't joined us here as well. I'm furious that my cousin has decided to throw away hers like this. *Her life will be just another one on my tally.*

'You put out the call, cousin, so I'm here.' Her seat is good on her gelding. Like all the Lloyds, she was practically born in the saddle. She'll hold her own in any ride, and we both know it. She wears pants, like any man, and rides astride. She's modern and fiery and far too good to be dragged into this mess.

'I put no call out for girls! Only for those who have nothin' to live for but the cause. You've everythin' to live for; ye whole life ahead of ye.'

She pushes her gelding up to be beside me, our legs nearly touch, and the horses stand companionably alongside each other, weary from their ride.

'There's nothin' for me if you aren't there too, Ned. If you're dead on the ground or hangin' within the walls of the Melbourne Gaol, then there's no point to all of this. I won't see you do it alone. The boys won't neither.

We're all here for you.' Her eyes hold mine. She's not one to look away.

And then it dawns on me. I feel it almost as if someone has hit me in the guts and taken the breath from my lungs as it dawns on me. These people are here—my family and my friends—because they believe in *me*. Not necessarily in the vision. They want to help me, maybe even save me and the other boys from the spectre of the noose that looms above us. They aren't here to liberate the North East from British rule at all. They are here because of loyalty, because of blood. The same reason Dan sits beside me.

The four of us: me, Dan, Joe and Steve—we're dead men already. We can't be helped. But for these others, it isn't too late. They don't have to be bound to death by their own actions. There is still time. Who knows, without this action, what they might become. Can we be liberated in the next generation, without guns and killing? I don't know. I doubt I'll live to see it. But if we go on to take the town now, for how long could we hold it? How many would they send to kill us? Their only purpose to kill my family. I know in my heart that freedom is what I yearn for. What we all yearn for. Freedom from the bastards who look down their noses at us, who lock us up, who close doors on us. But I'm not willing to swap freedom for the lives of the family that I love most. *Could I really have done it?*

And so I tell Kate, it's not the time.

***

The four of us can take the Benalla bank—we've done it before. There is little argument from the riders milling in the trees behind me when I tell them we won't be taking the town. My decision is made and with no Ned Kelly then there is no rebellion. No republic. I don't tell them why, only that the timing is off. I move my mare into the fold. My voice is firm but little more than a raised voice. We can't draw attention. I need to have them all away from here.

'You're loyal and I thank ye for it. I couldna ask for a better group of men behind me.' I look pointedly at Kate and grin. 'You're a gutsy lot and we'll need ye support. We're nothin' without ye all. The papers call us the Kelly Gang, but we're more than that. But today is no' the day for spillin' more blood. Head back to ye homes. To ye people. Wit' our blessin' and our thanks.'

Murmurs run through the ranks. Heads turn to and fro as they consult each other. But they don't question. Even the boys just look at me hard, and nod. Dan's eyes hold mine and then flit to Kate, mounted nearby. He understands.

Those gathered melt into the bush with barely a word. Heading for home and away from the life that beckoned them only hours before. Given permission to go, none wants to be caught in the wrong place now. Their quick agreement to leave reassures me that I've made the right move. They were here for us—not the republic, but still, the weight of my decision sits in my chest. Tightens as I think of what I've just done. The call for them to leave is the right decision, gifting them their lives. For my family, a reprieve. For the republic it's a death-knell.

Kate is the last to depart. A chestnut horse hovers

at the edge of the tree line waiting for her. A brother, no doubt. She pulls her horse next to mine and leans for my hand, which she brings to her lips.

'Be safe, cousin.' It's her final goodbye.

That leaves only four. The four that started this journey together and will finish it the same way. The bank is in view from where we stand. We fade into the trees and brush that surround us, our brown coats near indistinguishable from the earthy tones that encircle us. Taking the bank is vital. Now with no hope of having Ma released, I have to secure enough money for the girls to last them. Plus the other families. This money will be their lifeline.

I swing my leg from the mare and jangle as I hit the ground, but she doesn't flinch. The other boys rattle and clink as they too come from their horses. We stand in a line and focus our gaze upon the target, The Bank of New South Wales, no more than a hundred paces away. The wide front doors are closed and I see no movement from inside or out. Silence. The morning is too early yet, the manager most likely asleep out the back. I plan on being in and out before any are about. It is as if the bush itself is holding its breath and waiting for the word. Two magpies fly from an overhanging branch and the silence is so that I hear the beating of their wings as they move off in search of what's next. And so must we. I slip the steel helmet I've been holding over my face. Cutting off any view but that which is right in front. No distractions. With a shrug, I adjust the chest plate on my shoulders and draw my pistol. My heart beats steady and strong.

'Heads up, boys. Let's in and away quickly. The money is as good as ours.'

***

The four of us step as one. Suits rattle with each footfall. The building doesn't sit alone, there are shops and a hotel either side, but I see no movement from there either. It's barely six-thirty by Joe's fob and the first watery rays of light break through the Broken River mist, which sits not far away, and seeps across the town. News of the crash has not yet got out. Telegraphed news would have sent the townsfolk of Benalla scuttling around, but there is nothing. Luck is on our side. Unlike at Euroa, where our clothes raised no great interest, four of us clad in metal would cause a great uproar if we are noticed.

'Pistols out, lads. Be ready for any bolters. We can't have word out yet.' I carry one in each hand. 'We're takin' no prisoners. So give 'em a warning and if there's any movement, ye cut 'em down, ye hear me? We haven't got dis far to be taken out by some cocksure bank grub.' My steps lengthen as I get closer to the doors. I turn my head slowly. The helmet impedes my view, but the others don't wear theirs.

Two steps up to the door and I lean back to slam my foot into the locked double doors. There is no resistance. They break apart, wood splinters as they fly open. The pane of glass on the right-hand side crashes to the ground, showering the wooden boards in glinting glass.

'Dan, stay here at th' door. Joe, head round th' back. We need to grab the manager 'afore he gets away.'

'Righto.' Despite his protests about the weight of the suit, Joe jogs down the verandah and leaps onto the ground, heading around the back of the bank to the living quarters. Steve and I crunch over shards of glass and into the dark interior of the bank. The rich wood counters gleam with polish. I can smell the money in here.

'Still no-one, Ned.' Dan's call comes from the door, where he's sticking his head out to keep an eye down the street. The door at the back entrance of the bank swings open and I expect to see Joe. Instead, a man dressed in a suit, with a bowl in his hand, wanders in. He stops dead and looks from myself to Steve and then Dan, crouched by the door. His bowl trembles and he takes a step backwards.

'I, ah, oh dear. I heard a noise. I….' Joe comes up behind him, pistol arm extended into his back. The bowl drops to the floor, smashing and spilling oatmeal up the walls, splattering his pants. His fear turns to bluster, as he realises there is no way out.

'Who the blazes do you think you are? This is a bank. You are….are…committing a terrible…' He is a stuttering mess. There's no threat from this man. I lower my weapons and hook a thumb in my belt.

'I'm Ned Kelly. That there's Joe Byrne with his gun in yer back. This is Steve, and me brother, Dan.' I point my weapon around making the introductions. 'We'll be needin' yer help wit' yer safe there.' My voice echoes from the metal of the helmet still covering my face. The man blows air out in short, shallow breaths, his moustache bouncing around in protest.

'I'm not opening this safe for a bunch of criminal thugs! I'll have you know, that is protected property. You could be anyone under there!' Joe prods him in the back again, harder this time. His head whirls around. 'Just you mind, sir.' His voice is indignant. 'I am the manager of this bank!'

Joe shakes his head. 'Christ, man. Have ya lost ya marbles? I've got a gun in ya back and he's Ned Kelly and ya givin' me lip?' I pull the helmet off and let it clatter onto the floor. The thing was damn near suffocating me.

'I *am* Ned Kelly, sir, and I'll thank ye to shut yer mouth and listen. We're no' here to argue with ye. Ye either open that safe or I'll blow a hole in yer guts and find someone who will!' My threat is serious. He sees the truth of it in my eyes but still doesn't move. I cock the pistol and take aim.

'Is there anyone else in the buildin'? Yer wife perhaps?' He shakes his head and pulls at his shirt collar.

'No, my wife and daughter are in Melbourne.' His voice has lost its confidence, and he sways a little. I take a step towards him, but he leans over and vomits the rest of his breakfast onto the floor. Doubled over and breathing heavily, Joe lays a hand on his back.

'Up ya stand, mate. Open that safe and you'll be fit and strong when ya missus comes home.' Head still down, he nods. He sucks in some deep breaths and braces his hands on his knees before standing upright.

'Now then, what's yer name?'

'Dennis,' he croaks.

I wave my gun towards the counter. 'Well, Dennis, open it up.' There's no further argument as he and Joe step over the pile of mess on the floor.

'Is Benalla a sleepy town, Dennis?'

Concentrating on the combination for the safe, he shakes his head. 'Not normally. The local constable is around most mornings before opening around 9.' Without a word, Joe flips out his watch. 'Almost seven.'

I give a nod. Dan and I exchange glances and I dig

the fellow kneeling on the floor in the ribs. 'Hurry up, there. How much is in it?' The manager hesitates, his fingers fumble.

'I'm, not…not exactly sure.'

'Don't lie to me,' I growl at him and jab him harder this time. 'You'd ha' counted it last night.' The lock clicks and he swings the safe door open.

'Almost £4,000.' His voice is hollow. Steve's not said a word, but this grabs his interest.

'Shit! That's double what we got at Euroa.' He's excited, but I'm not. My gut churns. I'd expected it to be more. We needed more.

'Steve, put everything in th' bag.' He pushes the manager out the way and shoves notes, coins and gold bullion into the hessian sack he's carrying. The bank man shuffles back against the wall, his mouth set in a hard line. The wafting smell of fear and vomit is strong.

'Have ye been robbed before?' I ask him. He closes his eyes and shakes his head.

'No. I've always thought we were safe.'

Dan butts in. 'Well, now ya've been robbed by the best. The Kelly Gang.' I throw Dan a look and he turns back to the front door.

'Dennis, I'm wantin' the mortgage papers too— and any other papers ye have layin' around.' He's sat on his backside beside the safe, seemingly without the strength to stand.

'Mr Kelly, I can't give you those. I'll lose my position. That's bank property and I can't…'

In frustration I slam the metal of my pistol hard against the chest plate I wear. The noise pulls him up short. I would have unloaded a round to shake him out of his stupidity, but I'm hesitant to cause any more noise that would bring the constable running. I kneel down in front of him, his mouth still open, mid-sentence. My voice is barely above a whisper. 'I've had enough of yer bullshit, sir. Either find me the papers,' I poke the muzzle up under his chin and draw back the hammer, 'Or yer job'll be the least o' yer worries.'

Steve takes a step forward. 'Ned…'

I see Joe raise his hand at him, but I don't take my eyes off the man in front of me. He swallows and pulls a key on a chain from his breast pocket. His voice is weak and breathless.

'In there.' He points to a solid oak door to the right of us. 'In the top drawer of the desk.'

I leave the others watching over our solitary prisoner and move towards the desk.

'Dan?'

'Ya right. Not a soul.'

I fit the key into the lock and try to turn it but it doesn't give. My voice rings out from the office. 'Ye'd better not be fuckin' wit' me, Dennis!' I jiggle the key again and ram the desk with my hip. It gives and turns. I open it and find he's right, it's full of papers. I read the top one—L Baker £230. I rifle through them. S Lancombe £1,250. T Curnow £170. I hold it out and the paper shakes just a little. Curnow? That can't be the teacher. He wouldn't have a mortgage. I stuff it back on top of the paper pile and grab it all, tucking it into a leather satchel that sits on the desk.

The manager is still on the floor when I go back into the main room. His head leans against the safe, but he sits up as I walk back in. I nod to Joe. 'I have 'em.' My gaze falls back to the floor, 'Goodnight, Dennis.' Confusion crosses his face and he doesn't see Joe's pistol until it's too late. It hits the back of his skull and he slumps to the side before hitting the floor.

Steve's voice breaks the silence. 'We're done ain't we? We're bloody done!' No gunfire. No intrusion. *It's too easy.* There are grins all round. I rub my shoulder, which aches under the weight of the chest plate. Dan ducks his head around the corner.

'We're still clear, boys.' He can't mask the surprise and bursts out laughing. 'There's no-one, Ned! Can ya bloody believe no bastard's on the street?' *It is unbelievable.* I smile at him. He's just a boy.

'Well, what are we waitin' for?' We leave without even a backward glance.

My strides are faster on the way out—relief maybe? But also apprehension that this was too easy. All the way to the tree line I keep waiting for the screams to start. But it's only clanking of armour that we hear. Once in the trees, Dan makes a noise like a whoop. He and Steve embrace, jumping around like a pair of pups. I grab at the leather strap over my shoulder.

'Stop it, you two. Joe, give us a hand will ye? I need this bastard off.' I indicate the chest plate. I've left the helmet in the bank, and I plan on leaving the rest of the armour where I stand. I'll not need it now. Joe grabs the back plate, while I hold the front and together we lift it over without cracking my skull. It drops to the ground with a clatter which makes the horses jump. The others help each other out of their own chest pieces and drop them in relief.

'Whatever's about to come for us, we'll need to be

swift. We won't be needin' these.' I pull myself onto my mare's back and stare at the discarded armour. A calling card. That's when I hear it. A shout. Then another. Followed by two quick shots, which wipe the smiles from Dan and Steve.

'Shit, lads. Let's get outta here.' At a gallop, we leave the alarm to be raised without us. The two young ones give a cheer as we leave. Deep into the bush on the ride out from Benalla, I slow my mare a little, to pull the bundle of bank papers from the bag slung across my body. As she canters, I let them fall. The wind catches them and they blow across the bush. Let them rot where they land.

***

'Benalla is done. Ettie is waitin'.'

It's all I can yell over my shoulder as my mare and I take off at break-neck speed back towards Wangaratta, and the Harts. The others will be away to near Woolshed Falls, until we can sort out our next move. I hear a growing thunder of hooves behind me, but I don't slow. I know that it can only be Steve. No other man can ride like he can, and he must be fair flying. His voice barely carries over the rumble of the horses as he draws alongside. I slow my mare a little.

'I'd better come. Save Dad from bloody skinnin' ya alive.'

So it wasn't to stop me? Maybe it's even in support that he's come along. This is our plan—hers and mine. There's been no discussion with the others. Neither of us could have guessed the success at Glenrowan, so Ettie and I had agreed to keep the plan between only us.

No need to worry the others with what may not even happen. But here it is. Exactly what we'd spoken of. The time has come for me to declare my feelings for Ettie Hart. My decision to take the bank at Benalla, but no more, will be to our advantage. I'll reach her all the sooner.

News will be slowly filtering to our families and I know she'll be waiting. Ready to start a fresh life. A different and damned life. What else could it be, eloping with Ned Kelly, after one of the bloodiest acts against the Victorian Police Force to ever have occurred in the colony? But, already the sister of a bushranger, she's no girl with her head in the clouds. She's tough and determined. Despite her tiny frame and delicate features, looking as if I could break her with a firm hug, she fiercely knows her own mind and she's told me: she'll be waiting.

If nothing has reached her, our thunderous arrival will be the first news to them that we're not bleeding out, dead atop the Glenrowan dirt. I know that her heart will be in her mouth for both Steve and I.

It's more than 20 miles from Benalla to the Hart place. It's not far from Wangaratta and we have to be alert past Glenrowan. We can't go too hard. The horses have had a big night and have to return to the boys outside of Beechworth as soon as we're able to.

Ettie and I have had our plan for months. We've known that our futures will be together—if fate gave us the chance. It is now or never. There won't be another chance to take Ettie with me. I won't give her up—not for any of them. None will be pleased about it, but it's not up for discussion. Faced with the anger and disapproval of her parents, I hope she doesn't relent.

Steve and I throw caution to the wind as we

approach the Hart home. We round back through the bush, but I don't hesitate to jump from my mare. She's happy to wander in the green pick around the homestead. If there are coppers around, we're goners, but I've no time for watching and waiting. My long strides head to the door, Steve now a step or two behind. Off the horses, I'm at a distinct advantage over the smaller man who falls behind.

I haven't reached the door when it flies open. I flinch. Shit—the traps! I'm at eye level to a barrel aiming straight. I freeze. I realise that the face at the other end of the rifle that's aiming at my head is familiar. One without a uniform.

'Best be gettin' on, Ned. There's nothin' here for ya.' Dick Hart has the same build as his son, fine-boned and lanky, but he's as ballsy as any I've known. He's been a friend for years. One I've respected and who's opened his home to me. To see him down the barrel of a gun sends my heart plummeting. It's not going to be easy. 'It's good to see ye, Dick. I'm guessin' dat she's told ye then.'

Steve reaches us at the door, stepping between me and his father. 'Dad, this ain't the way to deal with it. Sit down and talk it through.' He tries peering over his father's shoulder into the darkness that obscures any vision of inside. 'Where the hell's Ettie? She's a part of this.'

Dick Hart seems to heed reason when the suggestion comes from his son, and nods at him, lowering the rifle without a word. 'You'd better come in, then.'

I hesitate. It's been unnerving to see him looking at me with distrust and a gun aimed at my head. I can't see him, but Dick's voice carries from inside. 'You'd better 'urry up. Christ alive, ya s'posed to be a bushranger, out there cowerin' at the door!' A smile breaks across Steve's face and like that, the tension breaks. This is the man who's known me for years, grown up alongside his own children. He's cross, but he's still in my corner.

A figure sits at the table—wooden railings bound together, worn smooth from the meals of this family of ten. Inside the house is dark but for the hearth with a heavy cast-iron kettle hanging over it. Ever on the boil in the Hart house. I'd kill for a cup of tea. A small sense of home in a day which has been surreal. My eyes adjust to the dark and I see that the figure is Ettie. She looks up, a smirk creeping across her face, a newspaper in her hands.

'I'm glad he came to his senses then, and didn't blow ya brains out.' She stands and folds the paper before placing it atop the table. Then turns her face directly to me. 'Ya late.'

My mind races. Yes. I'm late. She's waited. An overwhelming relief floods through me and warms me from within. The ink from the newspaper has blackened her hands and spread to everything she's touched. How long has she been sitting there leafing through the pages, pretending to read them? I notice a small smudge across her cheek and another near her chin as she comes towards me. I reach out a hand and wipe the one from her cheek. I try and put everything into that small touch—my joy at seeing her and my relief to be standing here touching her. I turn my attention to her father, who's watching our every move, his mouth set in a grim line.

'Dick, I don't want to upset yerself or Bridget. Ye've both been second parents to me. But, I've come for Ettie.' I leave some hesitation in my voice. In my mind she's mine, but I need her family's blessing for this to ever work. Without it, she'll come to resent me for the love in her life that she's had to sacrifice. 'I love 'er, Dick. And I think she feels the same.' I don't want to speak for her, so I leave space for her own voice, but she doesn't get the chance before her father speaks.

'Gah, love is it? That's a laugh. Neither of ya's more than kids.' I go to object, but he silences me with a hand. 'I don't care what ya posters say, Ned, ya not old enough, or wise enough, to take on me girl. She deserves better than the life you can offer 'er. Which may not be any life at all. After what's happened at Glenrowan, I'd say the coppers won't stop at nothin' to get you lot.' The news has reached them.

Ettie stands herself to full height, but she still only reaches my shoulders. 'It ain't your choice, Dad. I love 'im. Either I go with 'im now, or I'll follow on me own. We've decided.' She isn't going to fight; her father can only accept what is happening. Movement catches my eye through the back door and Bridget walks in. There are no kids with her so she must have shooed them out the back, though I bet none of them are too far from the raised voices and visitors. She's clearly heard the exchange between us.

'Esther Hart, I didn't raise ya jus' so you can run off with any old crim that comes knockin' on ya door. Bad enough that ya brother's gone off like he 'as.' Steve hangs his head at his mother's words. 'And now it's ugly.' Her voice breaks off, and she catches herself. 'It's too late for the boys now. They knew it'd turn out like this. They all knew.' *I know it.* 'They chose to send those people to their deaths, Ettie. I can't abide with that. People won't neither. Ned won't make it out of the North East alive.' She sniffs and looks between Steve and me. 'I'm sorry, boys. But it's a bad business yer in now.' Steve walks across to her and takes a hand, which she grabs onto tightly with both of hers. For all her callous words, I sense the thought of losing her son is a stone, heavy in her guts.

'So you'll throw your own son to the wolves then? You've got no conscience.' Ettie shoots back at her mother, venom in her words. Her body is so close to mine, we stand as one. Bridget has a temper as fiery as that of her daughter and she doesn't stand for the accusation.

'What do ya know 'bout a mother's love, Ettie? Steve'll always be me son, no matter how this ends. And it will end, my girl. As sure as he stands there next to you, they're gonna swing for what they've done. I just don't want you caught up in its endin' as well. No more than we're all caught up already.' Her face is drawn, with dark smudges under her eyes, as if she's slept little in the days and weeks before. 'There's no future with Ned, and I don't say it 'cause I don't like him.' She looks at me. 'I do, very much. An' in any other situation I'd give you me blessin' with a full 'eart. But it's gone too far now, there's no future for 'im.' Her voice is strangled, 'No future for any of 'em.' Steve wraps her in his arms and she cries a mother's broken tears against his shoulder, her body heaving with choked sobs. Everyone else stands still and I can't look away.

Ettie places a hand on my arm and we look at each other, trying to read each other's minds. I need to know what she wants of me. I know her mother is right— I shouldn't be here. I've nothing to offer but dreams and hopes. And we should know by now that nothing much comes from the dreams of a Kelly. She doesn't need me to speak for her.

'I love 'im, Ma. I won't wait 'round here, to be laughed at and ridiculed, and married off to the only no-hoper that'll 'ave me. The Hart name is buggered thanks to Steve and the rest of 'em. I know that. But what I won't do, is stand here pretendin' that life'll be any better if I stay 'ere, safe. I know that I'm riskin' everythin' to be with him. And I'm happy to do it.' She turns to her father. 'I'd rather do this with your blessin', but I'll do it without if I have to.'

In the end, hers were the final words on the matter.

***

Esther Hart is known as Esther to only the police and strangers. To anyone who truly knows the vivacious, quick-witted girl I love, she is Ettie. To me, she's always been Ettie. At first she had been Steve's Ettie, his little sister. But she has slowly become my Ettie, and I've become hers. *Oh how I want to be hers.*

She has delicate features, quite like Steve, though they fit her better, and an inquiring mind that could put many to shame. A catch for any young man, she was always destined to land someone above her station in life with her beauty and charm. Not now though. Now her family are tainted with the stigma which infamy brings. Steve's as good as branded her. There is likely no man in the colony, let alone the district, who would marry her, bar a sympathiser, and there are few of those with any prospects. But that's not why she's agreed to be mine.

Ettie was never going to grieve over lost marriage prospects, though her mother might. The subject of cross words between them a number of times.

'I'll not be stuck with some lug-headed local boy with nothing to do but pump out children for him and mend his clothes,' she had told her mother. Not a popular opinion in the Hart household.

The fact that I am now the most wanted man in the Colony of Victoria is inconsequential to her. Neither a deterrent, nor enticement. To her I am simply Ned. The last time I saw her, she had found a moment when it was just the two of us.

'Did ya know I've loved you afore there was a beard on ya chin or ya face was plastered on posters all over the colony? I've loved ya when you were just Ned. Friend of me brother, Richard, and then of me brother, Steve.' Then she kissed me and my heart had soared.

At first I had thought of her as another sister. But as she grew older right in front of my eyes, and more outspoken with each passing month when I spent time with the Hart family, I'd begun to truly see her. I found myself trying to catch moments alone with her. That was it. I fell hard.

And now she's here, riding alongside me, skirt flaring out behind her. With a seat almost as good as her brother's, she flies through the bush tracks heading back towards Beechworth. She barely moves as her gelding props and jumps over a small log in front of him, before taking off again at a gallop. She's ghostlike, white skirts fanned out, in the dawn light. Almost an apparition which has appeared in front of me—*is she even here?*

But then her face turns to see mine, and we lock eyes. Of course she's here. We're both here—together. Just how we planned it.

PART 2

THE PLAN

IT'S been five days since the crash and the dense bush surrounding Beechworth is our camouflage. We know every inch of this inhospitable countryside, Joe especially, having lived here his whole life. To the police who have flooded Benalla, Glenrowan and Wangaratta in the days after the train derailed and the bank was taken, we hope the bush that surrounds us will seem menacing and impenetrable. We're counting on the threat of coming face-to-face with the bloodthirsty Kelly Gang in amongst this rugged bushland holding no appeal to them. For Ettie, the boys and me it's cold and unglamorous, but it's a haven nonetheless. For now.

The carnage that surrounded us at Glenrowan was more than I'd expected. It sounds naive, even in my own head to say that, considering I'd demanded the tracks be torn up with the sole purpose of crashing the train. But the reality of the smash and the consequences of it, came as a shock. There is frustration about Hare—at not taking the man out myself. He'd made it his mission to hang us— each and every one, he'd promised. I would have liked the chance to tell him that he'd lost. That the Kellys couldn't be taken down.

I've spared Ettie of the most gruesome details of the train crash. She knows what happened, knows the casualties, knows the police are crawling across the bush after us, but I refuse to open her world to the horrendous physical violence that I saw that night. I tell myself I'm doing it to spare her the dreams that I have—the ones I know must creep through the brains of the others during their deepest sleep. But, if I'm honest, I want to hold back the worst of it so that she can't see the worst of me. I'm afraid that I'll be mirrored in the horrendous violence that has occurred at my hand. That she'll see me as worse than the killer bushranger I already am.

It's not only the deaths on the train, but the sheer audacity of the crime that's seen us become the most wanted men in history, or so the newspaper reported yesterday. The rewards have been increased and our faces are plastered on every available space in the Colony of Victoria. £10,000 for Joe, Dan and Steve and £15,000 for me. Dead or alive. It's a fortune, and no small incentive. Joe tells us of stories he'd heard as a boy, about rich rewards on the heads of wanted men. His ma would tell him of grand adventures as they lay in their bed.

'I hadn't thought Ma's stories would be the life I'd end up with.' We all agreed that it sounded more romantic in the stories.

Tonight, the five of us are huddled together, cramped beneath an overhanging rock, shrouded by thick scrub. The smell of the Eucalypts surrounding us is sweet and familiar in its intensity. Despite the success at Glenrowan and Benalla, every move we make sees us further cornered. We know that the troops are rallying and that the bush, unwelcoming to them, will only keep the police at bay for so long. If they get wind that we're here, not even the bush will hold them back. We've reached a stalemate; with no agreement on our next move. The younger boys look for leadership, but both Joe and I are undecided on the best move for us all—one that won't end with any of us swinging from the hangman's noose. Ettie is caught in the middle, trying not to look overwhelmed by the situation surrounding us. Her face is defiant, but a shadow of doubt flits across it at times as we argue back and forth. She's surely weighing up the stage on which we find ourselves.

Joe clears his throat and directs his words to me. To him the next move is simple. 'We need to get out o' here Ned. Out o' the north-east.' He draws a steadying breath. He's been forcefully campaigning to us for the past day and he's agitated at our reluctance.

'I don't jus' think it, Ned. I know it. We've got s'porters here, I know that, but informants are bloody everywhere. You think Aaron was the only one in their pocket? And there'll be more linin' up after Glenrowan. 'Twas a bloody affair.' He runs his hands through his hair and lays his head in them. 'They know we planned it—we wanted it to happen. We can't keep playin' the boys who are caught in a mess. We need to get away, somewhere unexpected. It's the only way we'll dodge the noose.' He's said his piece before and come up against my steely, silent resistance. The fact of the matter is that I'm just not sure. Joe watches me, waiting and thinking, before I speak.

When I do, the message has changed. My mind has cleared from the fog that's clouded me since the train came screaming from its tracks. I can see our futures as clearly as if they're laid out on a map before me. Maybe it's having Ettie beside me. I know I've got something to live for.

'You're right, Joe. I see it too. We need to get out o' here, that's true, but we need to get our families out too. The kids are gonna need to move, even afore Ma's out o' gaol. North into New South Wales. They'll have enough to set up a small plot. They can tell everyone there's too much pressure down 'ere.'

'Ain't that the truth though, Ned,' chimes in Dan.

It sits heavy, the thought of moving my family from the land that they know. It's not a move that they're going to want, and not a decision that I take lightly. Ma can join them up there in time. I look at Joe before I keep on, my eyes steady. 'Your family should go too, Joe. And yours, Steve.' I look to Ettie. 'We need to make sure that our families are safe out o' this mess we've made.'

Dan's agreement is important. He nods, so I go on. 'We're mad to stay in dis colony. We'll send the family away, maybe Wagga? People'll say it's the end of the Kellys in Victoria.'

Joe looks at me, not quite understanding where I'm going with my plan. 'So we'll be heading to Wagga

with 'em, Ned? Won't it look a bit obvious all of us trailin'
off up there? I don't know if we'll even make it cross the
border.'

I interrupt him. 'We won't be crossin' the border
with 'em, Joe. No lads, we canna go with 'em. That's not
even an option.'

***

The three boys look at me as if I've gone stark-
raving mad when I announce the plan that has slowly but
surely lodged its place into my mind.

'Ettie and I've decided, boys. We're away to
Ireland. We 'ave to leave these shores forever if we're to
have a chance of livin' a life.'

Ettie nods next to me. 'We'll never be safe here.
Someone'll always know 'im. One day his past'll catch up
with 'im. You too.' She pointed in the direction of Steve.
Though her future is entwined with mine, her heart rests
firmly with Steve's future as well. She wants him along
with us.

I keep on. 'So we'll head to Adelaide. We can get a
ship from there. We figure it'll be a damn sight easier t'
leave from there without bein' noticed. They're all
expectin' us to go north, Sydney maybe, or Queensland.'

'Adelaide? How, for Christ's sake, are ya gonna
make it all the way to Adelaide?' Joe's voice is full of scorn
at our plan to cross the colony, but more, I think, at feeling
left out of our plans. Until now, he and I have always
agreed on the next move for us all. But it has to be
different now with Ettie amongst us—shifting dynamics.
'Don't worry 'bout the rest of us either now, will ya? What

the hell are we to do? Hardly any money left after settin'
up our families. Coppers after us, crawlin' all over the
colony.' He looks somewhat disdainfully at Ettie. 'And no-
one to warm *my* bed.'

Her face flames, in anger more than
embarrassment, if I judge right from her clenched teeth
and balled fists. 'Damn you, Joe Byrne, ya bastard. You're
just jealous that he's thinkin' of someone other than you.
You've had him for years and look what it's come to. He's
thinking straight for the first time in a long while. You and
ya bloody liberated north-east. You all need to give up
anythin' 'cept getting' away alive.' An uncomfortable
silence hangs between us, which I try and break into.

'It's a plan for all of us, Joe. We can all head to
Adelaide. Catch a ship to Ireland. We can make our own
fortunes over there, without our troubles hangin' round
our necks and holdin' us back.'

'Don't it put ya off that ya own parents wanted rid
of the damn place so badly that they jumped on a ship and
sailed half way round the world?' Joe throws his hands in
the air and Steve sniggers. Ettie elbows him in the side.

'Well, I'm sure Da' would've chosen to stay, if he'd
a choice in th' matter,' I tell him with a gruff laugh. 'This is
th' way, Joe.' I stop then, to let it sink in. 'If not for all of
ye, it's the right way for Ettie and me. I canna stay in this
place. If I do, it's certain death for us both. I won't risk
her—not now.'

'And what about money to get us all there?' He
interrupts again. 'Are you plannin' to hold up the ship's
captain and demandin' our passage, afore loading on the
entire Kelly Gang for a nice little sail 'cross the world?'

I'm exasperated by his hostility. 'Ah fuck, Joe. I

know it's not ideal, but it's a start ain't it? A plan? Imagine ourselves livin' free together. We'll have to do a final job 'long the way. I dunno what yet, but it'll show itself.' My mind races, trying to think and plan as I speak. But I can't get my thoughts straight: Ireland, Joe, Aaron, Glenrowan, what next? We sit, each in our own thoughts, thinking of a different life. Ettie's voice breaks through.

'What about Ballarat?' Ettie's been silent since Joe's barb. 'It lies between 'ere and Adelaide. Probably big enough for ya not to stand out straight away, rich enough that it could be worth ya while.' She stops. 'Our while,' she corrects herself.

I look around at the boys—these faces that I've grown to know as well as my own. I think it's a good idea. I haven't considered Ballarat, but it could work. It's a beautiful city I'm told, and where there's beauty, there's money. I don't want to be the one to give my opinion first. Ettie has to earn her spot here with the boys. It has to come from them.

The seconds of silence stretch. Stretch to breaking. Not a single word fractures the sounds of the bush that surrounds us. I realise I'm holding my breath.

'It could work.' Joe finally relents. Maybe this is his peace offering to Ettie. She meets my eyes and smiles. Joe continues, 'I know a bloke near Ballarat. Not well, mind. But probably well enough.'

I exhale.

***

Ballarat. I look at the girl beside me in absolute wonder. It makes perfect sense. A definite risk but with the possibility of a reward great enough to grant us all the freedom we long for.

I've never been to Ballarat. Da' had been to the goldfields of Bendigo in 1853, recounted the hard life of the miners to us. It'd proven too hard for Red to make a living there. With his drinking and him sending money home to his family in Ireland, there'd been little left for his wife and family. He'd told vivid stories though, on the odd night when he wasn't too full of the grog to remember. Spinning tales of a harsh life on the diggings. His stories are all I know of a mining town. None of us have been that far west. We won't be mining our fortune in Ballarat. I'm not sure how our money will be made just yet, but it sure as hell won't be mining. I'm sure there'll be enough coin in the richness of Ballarat for some to come our way.

Our most pressing problem is how to get there. With the police swarming around Glenrowan and Benalla at this very moment, finding a way out of here and half way across the colony is going to be damn near impossible. Saying it out loud sounds treacherous. Getting our families out is key. Moving them to New South Wales will be the perfect distraction. Everyone knows that the Kelly loyalty to family is steadfast—most often the cause of our troubles with the law. No-one will believe we're moving in the opposite direction to them. We'll head them out as soon as possible using the money from Benalla to set them up.

Ballarat will be unknown territory for us. No sympathisers. No family. A town of prosperity and hope, but where the police are heavy in the streets and always on the lookout for troublemakers. We know the story of the Eureka Massacre in Ballarat, decades before. Men refusing to be bent to the crooked hand of the law. It feels right for me and the boys to be heading to the place where they spilled their blood. Joe would call me an idealistic fool for the thought. But I've always made decisions using my gut. *Isn't that what got me into this trouble?* And this feels right.

We'd made the biggest of stands at Glenrowan, taking the fight to the law and then thumbed our noses at them by robbing the bank at Benalla. Heading to Ballarat to do the same, gives me a thrill. Another way for us to show they can't keep the Kellys down. My dreams of liberation are dead but maybe freedom is enough. Our freedom will be the ultimate act of revenge.

I yearn to be bigger; if we can't have the republic that we've dreamed of, then we need infamy. Ettie will call me a damn idiot.

I want my name spoken of for years. Only by being unforgettable, will the injustices we've suffered come to light. No more cover-ups and lies from the police. But I'm no fool. I know that this run, this rampage, can only continue for a short time longer. If we push too hard or too stupidly we'll all swing or be on the end of a bullet from someone keen to collect that reward. We all know it. Then we have to melt into this wide country, well away from anyone that we know, or more to the point, anyone who knows us.

In quiet times, I catch myself imagining my life as it could be, if this all ends how I hope it will. *You've let it run away with you.* I see myself surrounded by the lush, rolling hills of Ireland; imagined from my father's stories and my ma's songs, with Ettie by my side and her belly big with our child. Our life is simple and free. But I know in my heart that this ending will be near impossible. Not just because of where we've found ourselves in this moment, but because I know Kelly dreams seldom work out.

***

Faces swim in front of my eyes. They look distorted, as if underwater. Hard to focus on. I see eyes, lips. Only outlines of chin and cheek. I know each and every one of them. I love them. But why won't they talk to me? Why won't they stay? I'm sure that's my mother—maybe. And faces from my childhood. I can't put my finger on who they are. But I know them.

They know me better than anyone. They all love me.

They might be the reason I'm here.

***

Life is laughing at me.

His bearded face looks familiar, staring out at me from the small gap at the door of his hut, gun pointed at my heart. Maybe I'm only finding similarities in his face because his name is Harry. But I swear, he looks so much like the other Harry that I knew in my younger days that it takes me by surprise and I take a step back. That one was an Irishman too, and a slippery one at that. Life is just one big coincidence.

We've made the decision to come unarmed to his door in an attempt to look non-threatening. If that's even possible for four wanted bushrangers.

On the other hand, Harry Price looks every inch the hardened, life-long criminal that he is. He pokes his head out a little more when he sees our raised hands. The resemblance is less then. This Harry wears past exploits in every line of his face. His eyes hold suspicion and mistrust as he runs them over us. He's dirty, bushy-bearded and gruff; not the kind of man that I'd invite to join me for a casual drink. He greets us at his door, at dusk, with a revolver in each hand and a growl. You never know who might turn up from a man's past, and he looks as if he's not one to abide strangers popping in for a visit at nightfall.

His stare moves from one to the next and stops on Joe. A spark lights in those suspicious eyes.

'Joe Byrne. I remember ye. A little older than when I last saw ye.' Then his eyes flick to Ettie, hanging onto Steve's hand for dear life. 'Got no weapons on ye?'

Joe is our spokesman. 'Good to see ya again, Harry. We've left the guns with the horses. Didn't wanna startle ya.' He spreads his hands open.

Harry gives a snort and once he accepts that we're unarmed, grunts at us to come in. We cram into his sparse bark hut and his rattled breathing is the only noise other than the wind whistling through the bark slats around us. Now we're in, grateful that none of us has ended up with a bullet to the gut, I am at a loss of what to say.

Getting in has been the first step. What do I do from here?

***

How the hell we've made it here, all five of us and all alive, I'll never know.

As our plan had formed, the fear was palpable. How were we going to get from the bush around Beechworth, all the way to Ballarat?

But arrive we have. And alive we are. It's taken us more than two weeks to get here; the utmost caution taken at every step. Every town, every day, every night. The constant watching and waiting, often in the harsh light of day, has worn down all of us. We're all dirtier, skinnier and smellier than we've been in a long time. I could feel my arse bones pushing uncomfortably against the saddle as we rode for hours at a time, day and night. Throughout our journey, Ettie was quieter than I'd ever known her to be, and I wondered whether the consequences of her decision are sitting heavily with her. The further that we rode from her home and family the more I worried for her. We'd left without their blessing—a sadness she carries with her. I'm fully aware that I have to be her family now.

The lack of food over the past fortnight has taken its toll. Ettie's had a greater share than the rest of us, but even she's gone hungry for many nights. Joe and Dan travelled ahead of Steve, Ettie and I. We'd thought it safer to travel in smaller numbers. The horses did it equally tough, managing without good food for most of the ride, except when we could snaffle some from local properties we chanced upon. We didn't dare risk it much. We could leave no chance of discovery. We'd travelled as close to the heavy bush areas as we could. Past King Valley to Violet Town, bypassing Bendigo to head through Castlemaine. Staying off the main roads and away from people all we could.

Against the tide, Joe's family refused to be herded out of Victoria. His mam wouldn't follow Steve's and the rest of the Kellys. The Harts were angry over Ettie's decision to come away with me, but it didn't stop them from accepting a way out of Victoria, to their idea of a better life. They packed up their belongings, collected my sisters and Jim along the way with the little they owned. Joe's mother though had steadfastly refused. Even with many in the area blaming the Byrnes for the death of Aaron, she refused to leave her home.

The Benalla money was delivered to our families through the sympathisers. Trusted men and women who would do right by us. News filtered back to Joe that his own mother had refused it.

'Those boys ha' crossed a line. I don't want nothin' to do with that money,' she'd spat on the ground and closed the door in their faces.

I fear this has played on Joe's mind every day since he heard it. If she'd refused the money, would she also refuse him? Does she disown him, her own son? I fear the guilt of Aaron's shooting, coupled with his mother's disapproval and anger, has sent his mind to a black place.

The mass movement of the families has caused untold speculation in the papers about what this means for the gang. No-one knows the truth, not even our families, but that doesn't stop every man and his mangy dog from having an opinion. Both families wanted to travel freely, with little hassle from the police. There was never a chance of that. Word is the coppers tailed them the whole way. It had been the perfect distraction, leaving only the day before we did.

It was Joe who suggested Harry Price. Once the decision was made, Joe was with us. There would be no split yet.

Harry was an acquaintance Joe had met only once before. He'd only been a teenager, but he'd a strong recollection of the man's story telling and easy laugh, which boded well. Apparently he was a man familiar with the law, another benefit for all of us. Harry Price was one of the many names that he was known by and he'd served his time on a number of occasions. Living not far from Ballarat we'd hoped he'd see us fed and perhaps given some information for a small token of our appreciation. We knew that we'd need somewhere to hole-up for a while. We would see if it would be with Harry.

These are the reasons that we knock on the door of a man we don't know, just as the sun sets. These are the reasons we are in Smeaton.

***

Now that we sit in his hut, with introductions made, Harry warms to the idea of us arriving on his doorstep. He's more hospitable than I could have hoped. He's moved a billy over his small hearth and set a few cups on a table against the wall. The hut is sparsely furnished, with only a single chair and a small cot at the back.

'Ye ain't the first wanted men I've met boys, you don't 'ave to look like you're 'bout to mess ye trousers. Si' down will ye? Ye makin' me nervous.' He indicates the floor to us, but pulls the chair out for Ettie. I like him already.

Despite the decades that he's lived in the new country, his Irish accent is still heavy, and its familiarity reassures me. We might not know him, or he us, but I can tell that he's one of us.

'I must say though boys, yer the most valuable men I've met. Fancy th' Kelly Gang standin' in front of me verra own eyes. What I could do wit' the £45,000 on your heads! I'd be a rich man, not livin' in this shitty bark hut, that's for sure.' He's joking, but the mention of the reward puts my nerves on edge. I watch the boys' shifting feet out of the corner of my eye. Ettie's eyes dart to me as he says it.

Harry seats himself in front of his small fire and runs a hand over the matted beard that hangs well below his chin. His face breaks into a wry smile, and even this does not improve his appearance. He looks many years older than the 50 or so that he is. He's not put off by our lack of reaction.

'Well now, I canna imagine that ye came all the way over here, to stop at me door to catch up about me own good ol' convict days. So,' his words hang in the air and his eyes hold fast on me, 'why are ye here lads, and miss?' His gaze moves to Ettie. A question, jovially asked but serious nonetheless.

I rub my hands together, enjoying the warmth of the fire after a day of cold riding. 'We're no lads, Mr. Price, but ye right we've come wit' a purpose.' He nods.

'Call me Harry,' he tells me. He doesn't look unfriendly but his tone keeps us at a distance. 'Well, if it's th' banks at Smeaton that yer after Mr. Kelly, you'll be sorely disappointed. There are two of 'em, the National is th' biggest. Right across the road from the Hotel, which is th' busiest place in town. It'll be a hard one to knock off and not much reward.' He gives a small grin again which creases his face and lends it a more friendly countenance.

I shake my head. 'We're not after th' Smeaton banks, Harry. We're not after any banks. And my name is Ned.' He stands to pour the tea into tin mugs and drops an open bag of sugar on the table, spoon sticking from it.

'No banks, hey? Well, after th' mess ye boys caused in Glenrowan, I'd imagine that nothin' is beyond ye. You're a well-known lot of buggers, I'll give ye that.' A silence stretches amongst us. The truth is, I don't know what the plan is yet. But I know that it has to be something smarter than robbing another bank—less predictable. Right now, every bank in the colony is on high alert, keeping only the bare minimum of cash on the premises. Managers, no doubt, armed to the teeth.

Harry breaks the yawning silence and into my thoughts, 'I told ye, ye ain't the first bushrangers I've met. But p'raps the first to have a lass in their ranks.' He nods in Ettie's direction. 'I'm not in a mind to shoot ye or turn ye in, so you can all si' down and breathe.' He takes a drink from the mug still in his hand. We follow his lead. 'I knew one bushrangin' fella from these parts; Gowrie was 'is name. He'd hold up fellas along the way.' His hand waves vaguely. 'Held up some big sheep station, just out of Ballarat—Ercildoune I'm sure 'twas. 1872 I reckon. Didn't end up well for him though, did it now?' He's rambling, though its purpose is to make us feel at ease. 'Highway robbery was 'is only game though. Nothing quite so fancy as you young fellas.' His story of Gowrie has grabbed the attention of the younger boys.

'The Joker?' asks Dan with interest.

I've heard of The Joker, the nickname that most bushies know him by, though never crossed his path. We're feeling each other out with the light banter of criminal connections. Neither of us is yet sure if the other can be trusted entirely. Or at all, for that matter. 'I didn't know the Joker was from around here. What happened to him?'

'Have ye heard of Ercildoune?' He waits for an answer and I shake my head, so he goes on. 'Big place, out near Lake Burrumbeet, no' far west of Ballarat. Grand lookin' house built on it they say, not that th' likes of me has seen it! Samuel Wilson owns it now, Sir Samuel it is actually, can't forget the toff's title now, can I?' A glob of spit hits the fire with a hiss, a full stop to what he thinks of Sir Samuel Wilson.

'Breeds bloody good merinos though. I'll give him that. Took over th' place not long after Gowrie raided the property back in '72. Gowrie'd holed himself up in a cave on the hillside and made raids around the area for a time.'

For us boys, who've spent a good part of our short lives in similar dwellings, the Gowrie existence doesn't hold any appeal.

''Twas big news at th' time. Took all the gold from Ercildoune and then headed for the Robertson's on Mt Mitchell Station. One of the Learmonth brothers, who owned Ercildoune at that stage, got there first though. He must've ridden that countryside bloody well to have beaten him there, gotta give him that. He might have been a snobby, rich bastard, but he was a horseman orright. Learmonth got the Robertson's to hide their 1500 gold sovereigns in a sack of flour apparently, and much to the Joker's disgust, he couldna find it.'

'I didn't know he'd been around th' area,' I tell him, trying to keep my voice neutral. I don't want to acknowledge that my interest is piqued.

'Oh, aye. Didn't last too long though. Ended up wit' a bullet through his skull not long after. I'm guessin' that don't suit you all that well?'

I shake my head. I decide that Harry Price is

someone we may be able to trust, if only for a short time, to be in our corner. 'Harry, I hope we might trouble ye for a meal or two, and your silence. Both of which we'll compensate ye for.' I pause, giving him time to think. 'We're men in need of friends, but ye'll find that we're loyal to 'em.' Harry stills at my request, mulling over the situation in which he finds himself. In his shoes, I may not have been willing to take on four wanted men and a slip of a girl as house guests.

'I'm no innocent, Ned. I've killed, I've robbed and I've served time—a lot of it. I'll no' judge you boys on what ye may've done in the past. I take a man how I find 'im. You'll have me silence, and I'll take yer word of loyalty as reward enough, but I'm tellin' ye to keep yer heads low. Ballarat's not friendly for men like me. It'll be deadly for the likes of you lot.'

Our mood lifts at his words and there's a change in the feeling of the small room—a lightening of spirits at the thought of an ally in this unfamiliar place. We'll be safe tonight, with full bellies and a good night's sleep. The first in many weeks. The thought feels luxurious.

But better for me is the quiet, creeping thought stirring around my mind. Perhaps our future lay not in gold, but in sheep?

***

Harry lives hidden away from the small town of Smeaton. His place is heavily scrubbed, making it easy enough to stay away from curious eyes. Harry's clearly not a welcoming fellow to those in town and with his well-known past, he isn't one to have neighbours dropping by, which suits us perfectly.

That first night of safety and sleep has been a relief to all of us, though I know that Steve feels wary of our new ally. He slept with one eye open for most of the night. Every time I woke, he was restless or sitting up, staring into the darkness around us. Perhaps his dreams are haunted by mangled men and screaming horses too?

That first night turns into days, which turns into weeks, laying low at Harry Price's. Each day brings a bigger feeling of comfort and safety. It's given us time to heal, to eat and regain our strength. For the younger lads, it's given them time for what we've done at Glenrowan and Benalla to sink in, and to understand what it means for us now. Dan and Steve are sleeping better and not jumping at every small noise that happens around Harry's place. I watched them those first few days that we were here, when they were jumpy and unsettled. Their fear at staying put and getting caught was written in their every move, though they tried to laugh it off. For Ettie and me, it's given us a chance to reacquaint ourselves with each other and think about the future we might have.

After the initial days at Harry's, I found a quiet moment with Joe as we checked the horses in the yard. 'Jesus, Joe. Ye never told me that Harry was a dead ringer for ol' Harry Power. Fancy him comin' back into my life, all these years later.' The resemblance sat strangely with me for the first few days after meeting Harry, not to mention the coincidence of the same name. *Old ghosts of my past making their faces shown.* Faces arriving when everything in my life is balancing precariously. Freedom. Survival.

'Christ, I hope this one's a bit more on th' straight

and narrow than that old bugger, or else we'll have the coppers landing here any day. I reckon he'll outlive us all. He's still goin' strong—given up the game though, after his last stint.' Joe shakes his head, clearly not believing that Harry Power, bushranger, would ever be able to walk the straight and narrow line of the law, despite what he may declare.

'Thanks to Hare,' I chip in. Joe looks over the horses, back at me.

'You fixed Hare. For Harry and for us.' I nod and move onto the hooves of my own mare. Lifting them to cut the length from them. They need some care after the trek they've had these past weeks.

'Argh, old Harry's not a bad fella. He used t' call me his apprentice. Showed me th' ropes with nickin' the horses.'

Joe raises his eyebrows at that. 'So ya could say he's one of the reasons that you're here in the shit right now. Thanks to 'is trainin'. Let's hope this Harry doesn't land us in the same mess.'

I'd always thought of Harry Power as an ally who looked out for me, a friend in my corner. But listening to Joe speak, I begin to think that I had less to thank him for than I'd ever thought about. Would I have managed to get myself into the trouble without that start in life?

I've spent the last weeks at Harry's reading any papers that I can get my hands on, dissecting bits of news that Harry picks up on his infrequent trips into Smeaton. The papers are insatiable for news of the Kelly Gang. They've interviewed the manager who recovered after his knock on the head, not to mention a number of locals who weren't even there. The stories get bigger and more full of tripe by the day. I'm trying to read through the stories, the lies and fancy words, deciphering if there've been any sightings of us out of the north-east. As far as I can tell, the police are still in two minds. They think we're either following our families North or we're still playing bush-rats around Beechworth and Glenrowan. No-one knows we're here.

The safety of Harry's hut has been unexpected and welcomed by each of us. But now, in the middle of August, the time has arrived that we should start thinking about our move away from the safety of Smeaton. The question is, to do what?

I gather our group together, all happy with full bellies and hands warmed by the fire. I speak honestly of the situation in which we find ourselves. 'We've overstayed our welcome, Harry. I hadn't thought ye hospitality or your cookin' would be so good.' I've warmed to Harry with each day that's come and gone. It's become increasingly obvious that the older man will not expose us to the law, or others, despite the enormous rewards on our heads. In fact, Harry's gruff demeanour has faded and he's turned out to be a man with a flair for storytelling and an insatiable willingness to speak about most things—great entertainment for all of us. Ettie has taken to looking after him as she would her father; cooking and cleaning. In exchange, Harry's taken to calling her 'my girl' which always gives her a smile. I haven't thought to find a friend again in this life that I didn't already have. With the money reward for us, and our notoriety, I imagine that finding a true friend will be as rare as hen's teeth. He's a find that's almost too good to be true. *And yet I believe it.*

'I've enjoyed havin' ye 'bout lads. It makes me

remember what it's like to have company, when I'm no' being a miserable ol' bastard.' His grin fades. 'I have to say though, that I reckon ya might be right. It's time for ya to make some plans. You can't stay 'ere forever. It's no' safe for any of us. If the newspapers are right, yer story is no' dyin' down. They're out to get ya, come hell or high water.' His words remind all of us the risk Harry's taking on himself—harbouring wanted men will not bode well for him in the eyes of the law. Given his history, he'd undoubtedly be branded as one of us and punished the same way.

I nod to Harry and open the conversation to all of them. 'Now that we've had time to gather our thoughts boys, what do ye think about th' future? The papers have slowed down on us a little, but if we give 'em the slightest sniff, the bastards'll be droolin' like mangy dogs again. They seem to be puttin' their money on the fact that we've headed to New South Wales. That could work for us, if we keep our heads down.' The other four sit silent. Steve shuffles in his seat. He's not one to speak up, generally going along with whatever we plan. But he's had things rolling through his mind, and I've seen his fitful sleeps of a night time. Like Dan, he's barely a man, at only twenty-one. He's not on his own now that Ettie is with us. Like Dan and me have each other, having his sister here is a comfort. But it also brings responsibility and maybe guilt.

He clears his throat and looks embarrassed to be speaking his mind in front of us all. 'I've been thinkin' I wanna go to Queensland. Far North as I can… with the canes. A man can disappear up there. I'll work hard and keep me head down. I know you'll look after Ettie. I need to look out for meself now.' No-one else speaks. Steve's words hang in the air and dance around each of us. I wonder how long he's dreamt of Queensland and canes? We contemplate the freedom that our friend barely dares to speak of. The threat of the noose weighs heavily upon Steve, perhaps more than the rest of us. It's what haunts him at night and causes him to call out in the dark and sit up, sweat dripping into his eyes. In his dreams, the taste and smell of the hessian bag over his head becomes suffocating and he grasps at it frantically before waking with a start. I've watched the fear etched in his face as he wakes.

I give a slow, measured nod, wanting him to think I'm mulling over what he's said. I don't want him to see that I've dismissed it outright. 'It's a good plan, Steve. The time for us to melt away is nearly 'ere. I see th' green hills of Ireland in me own dreams. Freedom calls to me, and to Ettie as well, so I know how you're feelin', man. The need to get away… The problem is, we've no money.' I give it a few seconds, letting this thought settle upon them. 'We 'ave to pay for these new lives and the freedom we're longin' for. The money from Benalla is all but gone.' The room is heavy with disappointment as the others realise that even though we're close to escape, we can't go yet. 'I'm beginnin' to see a way through our money troubles. Since we've been 'ere it's gettin' clearer.' I look around me. 'We're gonna have to be smarter than just stickin' up th' next bank we see. They're not the way for us anymore. Benalla was a lark, but they'll not be like that no more. They'll be waitin' for us. But boys, the call is yours. Ye can leave now and head for where ye heart is tellin' ye.' I nod towards Steve. 'Queensland, or anywhere else yer yearnin' for. Or else, we stay together until th' money is made, and den say our goodbyes—as men ready for new lives. For Ettie and me, there's no choice. We need that fare to Ireland.'

Harry is still, listening with the others. He shakes his head, his eyes heavy on me. 'It's a cryin' shame, lad, that ya been caught up in a crim's life. Ye've the presence, the wit and the tongue to have gone far. There's honesty in the way ye speak. Ye believe in every word ye sayin'. It's a powerful thing.'

Ettie smiles and nods. She's told me the same before, but at Harry's words Joe gives a loud 'Ha!' and then swings around to me. 'But that's just it, Harry. Maybe they sound honest and passionate to you. But I don't believe our *heroic* leader.' Joe's sarcasm is clear and cutting. I know he's hurting. Still aching for what passed at Woolshed Falls and Glenrowan, and he's sending that guilt and anger in my direction. It's been simmering for weeks, since he pulled the trigger. *I knew it would break him, but I still made him do it.* 'Our Ned's not gonna be satisfied with makin' some money and slinkin' away into the bush or the canes or even the far-off Irish bloody hills. If he'd wanted that, he woulda done it already.' Joe is up and pacing the hut like an animal, caged and waiting to be cornered. He's always been the one to openly challenge me and he's warming up to it.

'Our great Ned Kelly here, he sees hi'self as a leader, but not just o' the Kelly Gang, his lowly gang of ruffians. No. He sees hi'self the leader of a grand rebellion, where the men of the colony rise up against those in charge. Where the corruption is exposed and everyone realises the justice system only gives justice to the rich. Do ya disagree, Ned? Will a few coins in ya pocket be enough for ya to slink off into ya dreams with Ettie? 'Cause I don't think so, my friend.' He takes a moment to look at Ettie with such directness that she holds his gaze for only a few seconds. His eyes beg someone to challenge him. Daring us to tell him he's wrong.

I stand up from the dirt floor to meet him eye-to-eye. The hut is cramped with the two of us standing and moving. Our size fills the empty space in the room but it's the feelings that cloud the air around us. 'Leaving dat chance of rebellion at Benalla, was one of the hardest fuckin' things I've ever done, Joe. You know it as well as me. That coulda been our one chance to send the message of rebellion. The one chance for us to be bigger than just rippin' off the local bank and dyin' like dogs at the hands of a copper. But that chance is gone. I knew it, standin' there. You saw who was there. Not enough. I wouldn't risk me family and friends. I wasn't gonna sign their death warrants for a bloody dream.' My finger points at him, an accusation. 'And they weren't jus' my dreams, were they?' I wave my hand in the direction of the others. 'I still got dreams that dis colony can be a better one. Fairer for our brothers and sisters and their children. That one day a man won't be caught in this life because of who his father is. I 'ad no choice. We was pulled into dis life afore we knew what it even was. By the time ye know, it's too bloody late. I hold hope a time'll come when the rabble coppers aren't persecutin' a man's family 'cause of what he's *s'posed* to have done. But I don't know how to get there from where we are now. We thought we did, didn't we? But it's no closer than it was afore Glenrowan.' I stop my pacing behind Ettie and place my hands on top of her shoulders. Her bones feel small and fragile. 'But I'm done wit' that,

Joe. I wanna life and I want freedom—like you. I've sworn it to Ettie. I canna have rebellion and a life. I choose life.'

No-one moves, nor speaks. There's neither support for me, nor Joe. We each have our own dreams of escape, the types of lives we want to live away from the persecution of our youth and the mess that's followed us. This is the moment of decision for us. Is it time to move on now and let fate show us what she has lurking in shadows for each of us? Or does our future lay in the Kelly Gang for a little while longer?

Steve's the first to speak, breaking the standoff between Joe and me, as we continue to watch each other. How have Joe and I got here? Challenging each other? Discord amongst us? Steve nods slowly, and his words come out as if he's thinking about each one. He avoids Joe's eyes.

'I'm with ya, Ned. All the way. You're all me brothers and we should finish this together. One more job. Then it's Queensland for me.' He stands and grabs my hand, leaning in to embrace me. This show of emotion and loyalty electrifies the others and breaks the tension. Dan joins in the show with slaps on the back and a confirmation that we will indeed be in this together. It's broken Joe's icy freeze. He nods and takes Dan's hand. It's unspoken, but I know that none of us feel ready to leave the safety of the group. To go our separate ways will be to part for life. This gang of friends and family is all that we know in this mess of a life that we've created. To let that go, at this stage, is unthinkable. *My heart can't bear to lose these brothers of mine.*

I look to our host. 'In that case, Harry, we'll be off in the mornin', but I wonder if Ettie might stay on for a while? We'll be back within a week and stay for another short time?' Harry nods agreement, but I can see that he's nervous about the idea of us returning. Ettie will be safe here though, which puts my mind at ease.

'I can't tell ye the plan just yet boys,' I tell them. 'But it's formin' and I need ye to trust me. Steve, we'll leave you and Dan near Lake Burrumbeet. Just for a few days or so. Keep ye heads down, but see if ye can find out anythin' about that station, Ercildoune. If ye can get a look at her, even better. We want the lay of the land around there.'

***

Burrumbeet's not a peculiar name for someone who's grown up near the town of Wangaratta. Town names in the Aboriginal tongue are common in the northeast. The name Burrumbeet means 'muddy waters' in the local language. Dan muses about his new-found knowledge. 'No wonder it's called muddy-bloody-waters,' he mutters as we water our horses at the banks of the lake. 'Who'd swim in that?' The water is cloudy with mud that spreads just below its surface, but the ducks seem not to mind and delight in the muddy shallows along the water's edge.

Eighteen miles around, the lake is the focal point for the township of Burrumbeet, which lies on the north bank of the lake. The town is substantial; a coach, post office and a number of hotels. A few hundred dwellings are situated quite closely. The size of the town, so close to us, makes me jumpy after many weeks spent hiding out at Harry's. I'm glad that Joe and I have ridden to Burrumbeet with the younger two to see them settled.

Our hair is longer—after the short crops we'd all worn at Glenrowan—and Dan and Steve have grown as much of beards as are possible for them. I hope it means we're less recognisable. Dressed in the same clothes that miners around Ballarat wear, we should pass as prospectors trying to make our fortune and future in the goldfields of Ballarat and surrounds. It's not an uncommon story. Despite the steady decline of interest in the goldfields in the past years, there are still many of the hopeless and hapless trying their hand at digging in the area.

Joe and I plan to leave the other two here in the morning. Give them time to scour the district for information about Ercildoune. We pull our horses up at the southern bank of the lake to water them and set up camp for the night. We'll lay low in the scrub tonight, and Joe and I will head off tomorrow morning, once we know that Dan and Steve are alright.

The lake is a pretty place. Gums loom overhead, gnarly arms stretching over me in a large, welcoming canopy. They seem almost protective of those who stand below them. There's a peace to the place. Grassy meadows are scattered with the odd kangaroo picking at the new shoots, and small sandy beaches lead to the edge of the water in many places. There's a strong breeze today and it causes small waves to lap along the shore edge. Birds surround us and the ducks are plentiful and will make good eating for the boys over the week. My mouth waters at the thought of it, after the diet of mutton stew at Harry's in the past weeks. Strange how what seems so wonderful at first, becomes the normal and the mundane so very quickly. *Isn't it so with life itself?*

If everything goes as planned it will be a pleasant few days spent on its banks for Dan and Steve. They'll enjoy spending the time together away from us; crisp, clear days spent riding out as two mates. They've already been yahooing their way through the bush this morning from Harry's. As always, Steve's skills on a horse amaze me. He jumps fallen trees without a thought and barely moves in his saddle.

Steve was born at 3 Mile Creek in Wangaratta, ironically close to the racecourse. He could have been a jockey. He has the build for it. In a way, he is in a constant race—one of out-running and survival. No cup for winning that though. Steve's own brother, Nicholas, was a race jockey, but it ended badly for him, killed in Wagga only a year ago. Horses were in Steve's blood but weren't lucky for him. His first run in with the coppers in Wangaratta had been for horse stealing and using them illegally. That was where Dan and Steve had first met, behind the bars of Beechworth Gaol—sent for his exploits with the horse. And now here they are, likely headed behind bars again, if they are lucky. If they're caught, gaol will only be a short stop-off on the way to the gallows.

I'm sure the boys will be able to ask some passers-by about Ercildoune and get the answers that we need, which is why I've given them the job. In the meantime, Dan and Steve can just be boys. Enjoy the winter sunshine and pretend that a life of adventure on the goldfields is what lies ahead for them. It will be a nice change: an escape. If only for a few days.

***

Despite the lateness of the morning, the mist hangs low over Burrumbeet, swallowing the lake and all the land that edges it. People say that mists like this blanket the land, but that's wrong. Blanketing implies warmth, comfort and cover. As I stand here waiting for the boys to emerge from their misty embrace, there is no warmth and comfort. My heart beats hard and heavy, racing at the thought that I'm the only soul here. *The others all ghosts.* It's dreamlike, except that the hairs along the back of my arms stand on end and tell me that this wouldn't be a dream—more a nightmare.

Then my eyes catch a flicker of movement and they focus on what's in front as Joe's silhouette becomes clearer with each step towards me. Spectre-like he emerges, until he is so close I can reach out and touch him.

'There ya are, Ned. Christ I thought I'd lost ya in this fog. I can't see three foot in front of me.'

I'm uneasy. His voice is light but even this can't stir me from the eerie foreboding that ripples through my body.

'Ned? Are ya right man?' My eyes snap up to meet his. He smiles and it flicks a switch. I breathe. The boys are right here.

Joe continues. 'There's a hawker nearby, apparently heading back to Ballarat. I talked to him. Said he's got some finery on board. Might be what we're needin', without headin' closer to town.'

'That's grand, Joe. We need the clothes, but stayin' out the way o' anyone else'll be perfect.' Away from our Smeaton hideaway I'm edgier. More aware of every person I come across. This seems a good option.

We seek out the trader, his cart resting under a

large canopy of gum branches, not far along the western side of the lake. He's on his own and sits whistling and boiling up a cuppa. We agree; he seems to pose little threat. It turns out he's a trader of all manner of clothing and more than happy to show us his wares. Some seem to be cut very finely, not that I have much experience in such matters.

'Oh yes! Only the finest quality,' he tells us. 'I have a reputation to uphold.'

'What are ya doin' out here with such things? Not much call for it in Burrumbeet.' Joe asks, holding up an embroidered women's petticoat. The hawker is dressed himself in a most handsome and somewhat outlandish fashion, bright against the dulled greens and browns of the bush. He seems slightly odd, but amusing, out here amongst the bush tracks.

'I've found you, haven't I?' he gives a laugh. 'I'm from Adelaide, but I'm heading to Ballarat,' he tells us. His voice is English and educated, which makes him stand out as much as his clothes. 'I'm hoping to find some who have struck their wealth and need my expert assistance to part from it.' He erupts into a fit of giggles. Joe and I raise eyebrows at each other. In the few minutes since we've introduced ourselves, the hawker's done nothing but confirm our suspicions that he's a man who's not quite right. He's a lucky find for us. Should he recognise us, most likely no-one would believe him if he said so, given his eccentricities.

I introduce us with false names and he shakes our hands feverishly.

'I'm needin' a set of clothes meself, sir.' I tell him. 'A little more subdued than yours though, if ye please. I'm impressin' the in-laws ye see.' His face is grave as he nods. He does indeed see. 'And I'll be needin' two fine dresses as well. I can't outshine my wife now can I?' I pat the small bag of coins hanging from my belt. About the last of the money from Benalla.

Despite his quirks, and being easily over fifty years old, the hawker is adept at his work. He quickly measures and then moves to do minor alterations to the outfits we pick. He works from stock he carries, letting out and taking up.

We spend more than three hours in the man's company. He's a talkative fellow and passes the time amiably chattering about his dearly departed mother-in-law and reciting his favourite ballads to us. He stitches and talks, stitches and talks. I find the whole situation amusing and am quite enjoying his company, but I can see that every minute that's passing makes Joe more anxious.

'We're makin' ourselves stand out to this fella, chattin' and such in the middle o' the bush,' he hisses to me as the old man moves away to take his billy from the fire. I admit that it feels comical to be standing out here in the dirt in top-hat and tails, but the man must be used to it. He hasn't blinked an eye at us since we approached him. Joe's happy demeanour of the morning has vanished. He's quiet and sullen.

'Ah Joe, he don't know either o' us from Thursday! Don't worry 'bout it.' I am certain this man has no inkling of who we are.

With a few more stitches, the old hawker finishes and hands over the final products to me, wrapped together neatly in brown paper packaging and tied with twine.

'Good luck, young man. You'll be sure to shine in

these to even the crotchetiest of mothers-in-law.'

I shake his hand. 'It's been a pleasure, sir. Travel safely, now.'

He continues to hold my hand in both his own. Dragging me in close to him, he looks around furtively, before leaning in to whisper. 'Now you travel safely too, boys. There are all manner of rogues roaming this bush. You make sure that you're bedded down before nightfall. Murderous men like the Kellys are wandering around somewhere. Though I dare say they are baking in the Queensland sun by now, if the papers are anything to go by.' He grins widely and looks at the sky, shrouded in cloud, so we can barely glimpse the watery sun. 'It'd be a fine thing, some sun to warm my old bones!' He sighs.

I nod politely and gesture to Joe. 'I'm a big man, but I certainly wouldn't mess with th' Kelly Gang, dat's for sure. Thanks for ye concern.' I clap him on the shoulder and he releases my hand. His warning as we part company has amused me all the more, but has the opposite effect upon Joe.

It's mid-afternoon and we should head back to Harry's. I turn my mare east, heading towards Smeaton, but realise Joe isn't following.

'Ned, you've given the boys a few days to look around and see what they can find about ya fancy place. I need some time away as well.' My friend is jumpy and his face has lost all colour.

'Where are ye wantin' to head to?' It's a simple question, which I don't ask lightly, because I'm sure that I already know the answer.

'Ararat.' A one word answer, loaded with unsaid meaning. He will be drawn on it no more, but is anxious to go. We both know that Joe's trip to Ararat is for only one thing: poppy.

It's something he hasn't done in months, though the pipe's been his friend throughout his life. It's easy enough to find a place to cater for his needs. That he can speak to the Chinese in their own lingo helps him, as it's often them running the hazy dens. Smart on their part, as it's all the other buggers who frequent it, overwhelmed by cravings. Joe grew up around the Chinese. They'd taught him as a lad, running in and about their dirt heaps. He spent years getting to know them and would often visit the Chinese village in Beechworth to eat and drink with his friends. But language wasn't the only thing he was introduced to.

Only once I've followed Joe into one of the dingy houses, filled with dark rooms and a cloying smell, not completely unpleasant to my nose. Those around us, clearly used to the place, had lain mostly silent, each in their own world. A few others talked in low, monotonous voices; the drone of voices a gentle hum through the rooms. I couldn't tell if they were talking to themselves, or to someone only they could see. Most of the men appeared to be miners and a few settlers. One young man was well-dressed with the appearance of money, except for the angular, un-natural way that he lay. The shape of his body sticks in my memory. Poppy dens don't discriminate. Anyone can get their drug-induced happiness for a coin.

A pretty girl, one of several standing along the edges of the hovel, came to us that day. Her dress was bright blue, in the oriental style, and the only burst of colour in that soulless place. She sat beside Joe, stroking his arm and body. She was young and attractive, but her eyes were dull and glazed over, sunken into her face; whether from the over-use of the drug or the misery of her situation, I couldn't tell. In a flurry of Cantonese Joe gave her some money and told her to leave him. He hadn't needed her company that night, the pipe would be his mistress enough. I left him to it. I couldn't stay to watch him be taken away. His eyes had turned as cold as the girl's.

After, he had whispered, 'I wish me end could come by the burning ember of an opium pipe. It seems a peaceful death.' His eyes had been hard as he'd watched me. 'It lets me escape.'

Since his bullet had cut Aaron down, I imagine the poppy has called to him insistently. Aaron and Joe had been side-by-side from the time they could both walk. Their families lived closely. Days, weeks, months spent on boyhood adventures around the Woolshed bush. Time spent at each other's houses when they were kicked out of their own. But for a few key decisions, Aaron may well have been the fifth member of the gang. Instead, he'd married a lass of sixteen and promised to be our friend.

In the weeks following the siege at Glenrowan, headlines had been about the train derailment and robbery and also Sherritt's murder. We'd read the reports. Aaron's informing to the police had been for more than a coin. It had been in lieu of Joe's safety, when we are inevitably captured. I'd read the words aloud and watched Joe's face crumple in front of me. Steve had put a hand on his shoulder, but he'd shrugged it off.

'Don't. I'm damned either way. I 'ad to give up one brother to save me other ones. Now I 'ave to live with it.' He had spent many hours that night quiet, looking into the flames in Harry's hut.

I know that the pipe will be no good for him, but it's what he needs, so I say nothing as we part ways just outside of Burrumbeet. Joe will be gone for several days, I hope staying low in Ararat. The pull is too great, and there is nothing I can say that will stop him. I can only hope this won't be the last I see of my friend. I have to trust that the poppy hit will be enough and that he'll return to us at Harry's.

'Be safe, Joe. I'll see you at Harry's in a week or so.'

He pulls his hat low, nods and whips his horse around. Ararat is west.

***

I'm endlessly amazed at the elasticity of time. The speed and slowness with which it moves. Upon leaving Burrumbeet, the days that I spend back at Harry's, alone with him and Ettie, awaiting the return of the others, are fruitful. Each day I feel more strongly the direction that we should be moving—where our futures lay. When Dan and Steve return with their news, for me the decision is sealed. Joe's arrival only a couple of days after the younger two, brings relief and joy.

It starts, as most ideas do, as a tiny fleeting possibility running through my mind. At first I dismiss it as ridiculous. But, with each day that passes, it's stuck, and grown. I've been cautious about announcing it to the others, only growing it from a fledgling idea to a fully-blown plan of attack in my own mind.

In the weeks after the rush of Glenrowan and

holding up the bank at Benalla, it's become clear to me that our time as bank robbers is limited if we fancy keeping our necks intact. The guessing game is headlining the newspapers, with every person in the colony voicing an opinion about where we'll turn up next. Every bank on the eastern side of Australia is waiting for the Kelly Gang to burst through their doors, iron clad and guns aloft. They are wrong.

The conundrum is, in order to outrun the law and fade into obscurity, we need a significant windfall. The question that hangs in the air is, how do we do it?

When Harry had spoken of Ercildoune and its history with Gowrie, the seed of a plan lodged itself into my brain. Slowly this seed has branched into my dreams and now sits growing in most of my waking moments as well.

Steve and Dan's return from Burrumbeet with information about Ercildoune tells us that the station is at the forefront of the country's merino movement, with high quality stock and wool. The most interesting point that they return with, is that Ercildoune will hold its third annual Ram Sale on the property in the coming month. This piece of information is the key to our future wealth, freedom and happiness.

I decide to use Ettie as my sounding board. I want to see her reaction to it, before throwing my idea out to the boys. I start to explain the idea rattling around my head, but she interrupts.

'So, you're plannin' to rob this fancy ram sale? Is that ya game?' There is no confidence in her voice and her hesitation sends doubt spinning through my own mind.

'Well, yes. Dat was th' plan. Less obvious than a bank. They'll not be expectin' it.'

'You'll just walk on up, hold 'em up and take the money?'

'Mmmhmm.' I'm lost for words. Hers are cutting, and I'm not sure what else to tell her.

She scoffs. 'There must be a smarter way! A way you can be a part of the sale—see who's got the money?' She thinks out loud, bouncing her thoughts between us. My eyes follow every movement as she speaks. It's as if I can see the ideas playing across her face, her hands moving with her words.

'What if ya could pass for a gentleman, Ned.' She looks at me closely, a faint smile playing on her lips. 'Well, if not a gentleman, maybe an owner, lookin' for a prize ram maybe? Imagine workin' from the inside. You'd know who 'as the money and who to take it off!' The more she talks, the more it makes sense to me. She's right. If we can manage to get on the inside, we'll be able to gain so much more. Take so much more.

I kiss her, square on the lips. I look down at her, holding her body tight against my own. 'You're a smart one, my girl, aren't ye? I'll ignore th' crack about me not bein' a gentleman!' This time, she's the one on tip-toes kissing me. Her reserve is fading more with every day that we spend together. She's giving herself to me, as I've dreamed she would. She winds her hands around the back of my neck and moulds her body into my own. Pulling my mouth down onto hers. I'm hungry with wanting her, but I can hear the others outside. I break away from her mouth, giving us some space, which is the last thing that I want. I kiss her nose.

'Now then me beautiful girl, any bright ideas about how to get us on th' inside?'

***

The final piece of the puzzle all but throws itself in my lap, only a week after my conversation with Ettie. Scanning the headlines of the Ballarat Courier for any news of us—supposed sightings and fanciful ideas of where we were headed. I chance upon an article about the upcoming Ballarat Agricultural Show. It grabs my attention and I stop to read it through more carefully. The paper is most enthusiastic that the show will be attended by a number of notable dignitaries. Most importantly the Duke of Manchester will be at a celebratory dinner later that night.

Could that be the path forward? The last place the public or the police will expect to find the murderous Ned Kelly will be rubbing shoulders with a Duke. To infiltrate the sale and be accepted by those who go, those with money, I'll need to be part of the scene. My face must be known to Samuel Wilson and the local elite. Without being known to those around me, I won't be able to attend the ram sale without suspicion. Clear though the plan is, it's risky.

Becoming known is crucial to the success of robbing the ram sale, but it also goes against the past weeks, months and years that we've been living, attempting to be almost invisible. The Ballarat Show will be my way in. Playing the role of gentleman and running the risk of being captured. The others must be kept at a distance until absolutely necessary. It's clear in my mind.

It's time they know.

***

Five pairs of expectant eyes watch me as we huddle in the warmth of the hut. It feels like a second home to us now after the many weeks spent here. Harry listens as intently as the others—he will be a part of it if he's keen. Our way out might be his own escape into a different life.

I launch in, my voice full of belief about how we will set ourselves up to rob the ram sale at Ercildoune. Ettie sits further back, perched on the edge of the only bed in the hut, removing herself from the discussion. Watching the others.

The more I speak, the more I focus on Joe shaking his head in disagreement beside me. Back from Ararat, his mind seems no more settled, nor his countenance any more agreeable.

'Spit it out, Joe. Don't jus' sit there shakin' your head like a bloody puppet!' I growl at him, stopping mid-sentence.

'Ya not goin' on yer own, Ned.' I'd thought it was the plan he disliked, not the idea of me going on my own.

'One man on his own'll be less obvious. I want ye there, I do, but I'll no' risk ye all if dis madness goes wrong.' I don't want Ettie or the boys anywhere near it when I first head to Ballarat. Those first moments will be crucial if I'm to be recognised.

Dan nods. 'It's a daft bloody plan, Ned.'

'It is.' I look around at them. 'It's completely mad.

But they won't be expectin' it. If it comes off, we'll 'ave the money we need to start our new lives.' My eyes flick to Ettie and she smiles. 'You'll 'ave to be at the sales—all of ye, if we're to pull it off. But dis first bit, I can take th' risk for us. I owe it to all of ye.' It'd eat through my guts if the boys were captured or killed. I couldn't live with that. 'I know ye don't like it, Joe. But it 'as to be dis way.'

If this goes badly, I will go down alone.

***

It's because of this discussion and weeks of planning that I find myself walking from the railway station, without my brothers for the first time in a long time. *I'd best get used to it.*

People swarm like ants on the Ballarat streets. Busily moving about their business, each following an invisible path to get to where they're headed. There are people everywhere and I feel conspicuous in this bustling city, rich with its new money from the goldfields and grand buildings lining the streets. Their stone and brick tower over me. Beauties demanding the attention of all who walk her streets. I've never been to Melbourne, but I cannot imagine a place that is grander than Ballarat. This town, birthed from the haunches of the gold rush, surpasses its rough and rugged beginnings. It's a city splendored. And I wonder how the hell I got here. My great, hulking body walking unnoticed amongst the crowd.

I step from the train, avoiding the chasm at the platform. I see the sleepers. Memories of other tracks flood back. My feet safe on the platform, I watch steam billow into the chill air of the morning and the imposing, white walls of the Ballarat Railway Station dwarf me. It looks far more striking than a train station ought to. I can't help but stop to take in the grandeur. Ballarat is surely set to be one of the finest cities in the world with its youth and vibrancy and wealth.

I've travelled from Burrumbeet into the city; new clothes fitted and looking the part. My face is clean-shaven and I'm dressed in suit and hat. A far cry from the rugged bushranger who stormed Glenrowan. Ettie had run her hands across the smoothness of my chin, bringing a smile to her face and my own. I know that I look like a different man, but I fight the instinct to hide my face. The train has unloaded its passengers, but it will travel on to Melbourne. People mill about, waiting to board, chatting amongst themselves.

My eyes roam across the waiting faces. I spot a familiar one in the crowd. My heart changes rhythm, then gallops so that I'm almost breathless. The man staggers towards me. Carried forward by the crush of bodies moving towards the train. Then I realise that he is not staggering—he is limping. It's the teacher, Curnow. His face has been everywhere since that night at Glenrowan. Is he an apparition? My gut churns. Why would it be him on this platform? On this very morning and at this exact time? *Why is it always him?*

Despite the chill of the spring morning, sweat prickles my brow at the hairline and along the edge of my hat. Curnow is with a woman, not his wife though. Is it his sister? She seems vaguely familiar to me. They get closer by the second and a decision has to be made. Do I continue ahead, steadfast? Or do I attempt to duck away, out of sight? I have but a second before the decision has to be made.

A gentleman would stride ahead, resolute in his direction. No indecision. Money and standing give an air of confidence. But none of this has been in my experience. From an early age, I've known that I am not enough. Every person except my mother: teachers, the police, people in town, even my own father, have looked at me as if I am tainted. None had ever doubted that the Kelly kids would follow in the footsteps of their father. One good-for-nothing Kelly after another.

For a moment after I'd saved Dickie Shelton, I'd been called brave, a hero, and given a sash of brilliant green. For a short time, I'd thought maybe I was better than I'd always been told. But as in every children's tale, the fantasy wore off and in the eyes of those around me I soon transformed back into the ruffian I was destined to become. People judged and looked and whispered all over again. I was no-one. The no-one that everyone expected.

'Too much of his father in him that lad. I always knew it,' they whispered amongst themselves.

These thoughts rattle around in my head. Now, in this minute, as I stride towards the limping Curnow, a thousand disapproving eyes from my childhood and youth set upon me at each step. I fight every urge to duck my head and lower my eyes. Instead, I channel the arrogance of all those who have ever judged me, who have judged my very name. I stride across the platform, wearing my air of superiority along with my new clothes. The sea of people parts in unspoken deference. People lower their eyes and instinctively move aside. Airs and graces are all it took.

Curnow himself walks by, oblivious, brow in a furrow and engaged in an intense conversation with the woman. My brow prickles, but this time it's relief. Have I escaped the hangman's noose once again? *Is it escape or prolonging the inevitable?* I stop in the crowd and turn, briefly. I know that I shouldn't. I should stride ahead, ignoring all those in my wake, but I can't help myself. I want to assure myself that he is real. That I'm not jumping at shadows. I search the heads for only a second before I spot Curnow heading onto the train, which blows its whistle impatiently. It's nearing the end of its idling before starting its trip to Melbourne. His face is in the window, bending to seat himself. He's really there. Flesh and blood. As he sits, for a mere second, our gazes lock as if we are drawn to each other. I'm unable to move for what feels like an eternity but is merely a heartbeat of time. He moves on first, eyes divert from me. He continues to speak to his companion. He has missed me.

I swallow and walk on through the train station, though a tightening of my throat reminds me that the noose is closer than I dare think about.

***

The sun of early spring is on my face. It's bright and while it doesn't take the chill from the air, I relish the slight warmth on my skin as I leave the grand white building. I feel relief in every step. I move away from the train, from the sight of Curnow and into the glaring light of day.

The clothes from the eccentric hawker do their job. No-one looks twice. But they are tighter than I'm used to. I resist the urge to fiddle and pull at the collar. I need to act as if I've worn these clothes since the day I was born, when all I want to do is to tear them from me. It's not just the itch and constriction of the clothes themselves which annoys me, but what they represent. I'm not this. I detest everything these clothes represent.

I move toward a hansom cab parked beside the station. I've never taken one. The black cab glistens in the sunshine, both horse and man wait patiently for their next fare.

'To the showgrounds, man,' I tell him. I don't wait for an answer before hoisting myself into the carriage and closing the door behind me. I can't help but break into a grin, nervous though I am, as the horse moves off carrying me through the streets of Ballarat.

Only ten minutes from the station, the cab leaves me near the entrance to the grounds and I hand the man his coin before watching him flick the reins gently so his horse moves off, headed back into town. Head up and shoulders back, I walk through the gates towards the main arena. It's a bigger version of the shows I went to as a boy in Wangaratta. All manner of people buzz about the showgrounds. I dodge a large cow with her udder bursting, being pulled along, horses with gleaming coats ridden through the crowds. A general air of fun and excitement.

There's a crowd of people here to watch the animals, or to admire the collection of craft and cooking in the home-crafts shed. Happy children run around in between people and animals. Squeals of excitement escape as they roll down the hillside near the grassed oval. It lends a lightness and carefree nature to the day. Their happy laughs and the sunshine are enough to bring a smile to my face.

***

I have to be seen. I have to ingratiate myself into this Ballarat society—and quickly. It goes against every instinct. I must meet other gentlemen, introduce myself and share my story. Carefully crafted over nights of talk in Harry's dimly lit hut. It must sound real. Not cause speculation from those I meet. I thought the story itself would probably hold up, but then there was the other problem: I have to be able to pull it off.

Our eyes are set firmly on Ercildoune and its prize ram sale. My story today has to find me a place at that sale, amongst the buyers of the district and the colony. Men who know their sheep and know each other. I'm confident I can bluff my way through about the stock. I've dealt with livestock all my life, albeit not always legally. It's carrying off being a gentleman that'll be the test. But there's no other option if our plan is to work.

I will be Jack Callaghan, a son of Irish immigrants, from the colony of South Australia. Money made in cattle, this sheep caper will be new to me. We want aspects of truth to the story, so it will flow more naturally for me, but are counting on the majority of buyers to come from the colonies of Victoria and New South Wales. I'm from a small holding near Burra, with my wife and two young children. Joe said talking about a wife and children will endear me to the women I come into contact with. Give me a sense of reliability. I can't argue with that. I know children, with all the Kellys that have come after me, and

I'm sure I'll be able to talk about them convincingly enough.

Once the story was set, attention was turned to my appearance. Harry has done himself proud, trimming my wayward hair and removing my beard. Cut throat in hand, out the front of his hut.

'Ye've missed ye callin' in the barber trade, Harry,' I'd told him. He'd held the blade in front of my face.

'Ye keep that up, lad and ye'll be lookin' for yer ear in the dirt.'

Once dressed, all had agreed that I looked the part.

'Yer a bloody dandy, Ned,' laughed Dan. 'Ya could give Joe a run for his money now.' Ettie had swatted at him and called me dashing, which sent blood rushing to my face. The weight of the suit I wore was heavier than the armour at Benalla. More was riding on it.

Heading to the show today I have a clear purpose. Dinner. There's to be a dinner held tonight in honour of the Duke of Manchester. All of Ballarat society will be there—and so must I. Though I don't know it, I'd bet money on the fact that a fancy dinner will have Sir Samuel Wilson in attendance. I need to establish myself here at the show today, if I'm to pass relatively unscathed tonight.

I have no bloody idea how to do it.

I head towards the grandstand. A small crowd of people gather to watch the show-jumping, mostly ladies, though one or two finer-dressed men are in discussion nearby. As I approach, the women acknowledge me with a small smile. The men nod their heads in my direction. One man even touches his hat to me. It seems so simple. I've done nothing more than acquire a nice set of clothes and cut my hair and beard. I haven't even opened my mouth and here I am, not just tolerated, but accepted as one of the gentry.

I head for the wooden railing around the arena. Families mill about and I don't look out of place. Just a man on his own, trying to get a closer look at the fine display of horsemanship on show over the jumps. I take a few deep breaths and try to settle into my surrounds. It sounded so simple during our talks in the hut, but now that I'm here, my heart beats heavily—as uncomfortable and anxious as when I was waiting for Hare to arrive at Glenrowan. Again, it's the waiting.

I lose a sense of place as I watch the daring and expertise of the men flying over the jumps. Brave fellas— and horses just as gutsy. The jumps are solid. Horse and rider will fall hard if they don't judge them right. The men jumping aren't from money. They wear old boots and the horses carry saddles that are work-worn. Men of the land, showing off skills they've honed during years of riding.

Their acrobatics give me pause to plan out my next step. It's one thing to attend a public place and nod and smile at passers-by, but how do I breech the inner sanctum of the upper class? It has to be subtle and natural. These thoughts chase each other, the enormity and stupidity of the task at hand descends upon me. Why the hell would I have suggested this? Frustration over my lack of direction floods through me and I kick my toe into the dirt along the fence. I feel an approaching body, authoritative, boots striding towards me. My heart thumps harder and my foot stills.

The shadow reaches me first, then the man, but I don't turn. My eyes stay fixed on the horse moving around the arena. If this is to be my final moment of freedom, I'll not run. The voice comes from my right.

'Damn fine riders aren't they? Quite astounding.' The voice is clearly Scottish, though the edges of it have softened. Dulled, I assume, by years of living away from his native country. I turn towards the voice, slowly. Rigidly. I've always said that the gentry walk with a stick shoved up their arse and I keep that image in mind today as I try to move amongst them. I consciously move with restraint and stiffness. A world away from how I normally move through my world.

I let my Celtic lilt hang on my words but keep them more formal than I'm used to.

'Yes, they put my ridin' to shame, I'm afraid to say.' I meet the man's eyes and extend my hand in introduction. 'Jack Callaghan.' He's shorter than me, barely taller than my shoulders but has a firm shake, which I admire in a man. I'm not sure that extending a hand is the right thing to do for a gentleman, but I have to forge a relationship somehow and it feels the natural thing to do.

'Angus McCulloch. A pleasure to meet you, Mr. Callaghan.'

'Please, it's Jack.' I tell him, hoping my informality is accepted. Angus McCulloch doesn't blink.

Formalities out of the way, he steps closer towards me and takes up a position beside me, leaning heavily on the top wooden rail. His face is rapt watching the jumpers and he hangs over, looking desperate to be out there himself.

'Much of a rider yourself, Angus?' I nod towards the man guiding his horse over a low rail that looks simple but is deceptively wide. It almost catches the man and beast.

Angus shakes his head. 'Ah, no, Jack. I wish I were though. I can stay in a saddle but I'm not one for the jumps. Never have been. Looks grand though.' His gaze doesn't leave the field. 'Are ye a local?'

I shake my head and give a small sigh. 'No. I'm from South Australia. A long way from home in fact, and missin' my wife and little ones quite badly, I must say.' I weave my story. 'I'm a cattle man by trade, Angus, but I'm lookin' to branch into sheep and I hear this region is one of the best around, if I'm looking to pick up some quality merinos. Which I am.' I shrug simply and look away. The seed is planted.

'Aye it is. I'm a sheep-man myself. We pride ourselves on the quality of wool that we're producing here. Ballarat is the up and coming place for quality sheep in Victoria.' A small smile creases his face. 'Despite the appearances,' he indicates his own suit and hat, 'I run my own property: a smaller affair than a lot of the men who own stations around here. I hope that you don't mind me saying; you seem the type who might work his own land as well?'

It's politely posed, but alluding to what I lack in carriage, speech and name. I silently thank God for sending Angus McCulloch my way. If I'd approached a steadfast gentleman, I might have been called out immediately. Instead I'm presented with a hard-working, self-made man who appears to be straddling the classes. Almost a comrade.

I laugh and run my hand self-consciously over my bare chin. 'It's rather obvious isn't it?' I pull at my necktie slightly. 'I'm more at home in the paddocks and amongst the cattle yards. But my wife, Elsie, has insisted that if I'm intendin' to make the acquaintance of Sir Samuel Wilson and company and purchase some of the finest stock in the country then I should look the part!'

Angus nods and smiles at my apparent discomfort. 'I ken a strong-willed wife, Jack. Yours sounds like my own.' He half turns to indicate the taller of the women I've passed on my way to the fence.

There's a small silence, though not uncomfortable, when we turn our attention to the next competitor entering the ring to begin his flight around the course. It feels as if Angus is taking stock of me.

I draw in a sharp breath as I focus on the next competitor called in. I'm too far away to hear the name announced, but I am damn sure that the attendant hasn't called 'Steven Hart'. Yet there he is—larrikin bushranger and wanted man, jumping the logs as if they are made of pillows. I set my mouth in a hard line. That bloody fool. I'll wring his neck when I see him next. He might well be welcoming the coppers by the time I get through with him. I last saw him at Harry's with the others. He and Ettie had come to cross words not long before I'd left.

Despite my anger at his stupidity, Steve's riding is first class. A natural. He easily clears the final jump and the Scot beside me launches into applause. Begrudgingly, I join the clapping.

'He damn-near flew over those last few,' Angus exclaims, his voice breathy. He slams his hand against the top rail in delight.

'A bit showy for my likin'. But he's ahead of the pack for sure.' If he wins the competition he better not have the hide to collect the trophy, I think.

Angus' voice rips me away from my violent thoughts about Steve. 'Are you attending the dinner tonight, Jack?' I weigh up how to approach the answer. This moment is crucial. I can't be worrying about Steve. My palms prickle with sweat.

'I've not heard of a dinner. I only arrived in Ballarat recently, ye see, and I'm on my own really.' I leave the statement hanging, too nervous to add anything further. These gut-churning nerves are enough to make me lose my bowels, not a feeling I'm used to. Sparks shoot through to the ends of my fingertips and a light-headed feeling comes upon me. I'm not a man to wait—normally one of action.

Angus seems oblivious to the torrent of emotion flooding through me, but his response is enthusiastic. 'Well, you've arrived with great timing then. There's a dinner on tonight to celebrate the arrival of the Duke of Manchester. I believe it will be all very grand. Katherine and I are attending.' At that moment, the woman herself arrives at the fence. The cut of her dress is modern and sophisticated; the shade of green matches her colouring, which makes her even prettier up close. Angus makes the introductions.

She faces her husband as he speaks and I make a short study of her. She carries herself in a graceful, effortless manner. It looks as if Angus has married above his station. Perhaps that's the reason that he's able to span the classes—she's given him a pass into the upper class. Katherine is animated and vibrant as Angus explains he's extended an invitation to the night's festivities.

'Oh absolutely! Mr Callaghan, you must come

along. It's set to be the dinner of the year!' Her gaze switches between the two of us. 'It will be a wonderful opportunity to meet many of the local breeders and owners. We have a ticket available, which you would be welcome to. It will allow you to put faces to the names before you attend the big sale.'

Angus interrupts her. 'And the not so local ones as well. Men from all over Victoria and New South Wales are here. Daresay there'll be a couple from around your way as well.' He means it to be reassuring, but the thought of it fills me with dread and is almost enough for me to give my excuses there and then. Angus gives his wife a small nod and continues, 'Well, Jack, if Kate has invited you, I'm sorry to say, that's all there is to it.' They both give a small laugh and kindness rings through them. I join in and it feels good to release the tension rising in my chest. She's a woman of considerable force. He's done well to win her over.

I warm to the two of them and it is her nickname, affectionately called, that confirms the great luck of my acquaintance with the couple. She's another beautiful and formidable Kate within my life now. I think of my sister, who has always had my back. *These people, so familiar and yet so strange, circling in my life.* Surely if I rely on a Kate, I am in good hands.

I give her a small half bow and a grin. 'In that case, Mrs. McCulloch, I gratefully accept.'

It is that easy. A contact made. An invitation accepted. One step closer to our goal: freedom.

***

With Angus and Kate as self-appointed chaperones to the dinner, I walk in confidently and receive nothing but smiles and nods of fellowship from those I pass. A crowd of people gather in the foyer, waiting to be admitted to the ballroom, set up as a huge dining room. The chatter and laughter in the room is intoxicating. It seems all of Ballarat is here. What I think will be the hardest part of the night is no difficulty at all.

My thoughts stray to Ettie and the boys, holed up in Harry's hut, waiting. They don't know how the day has panned out for me. What it means for all of us. It makes me feel somewhat pleased to have seen Steve flying around the course today. Though I was wild at the time over his foolishness, I hope he will have seen I was in no distress and this piece of news will give Ettie a little comfort through her evening of uncertainty.

The night passes quickly. Angus introduces me to anyone and everyone he knows, ensuring I'm accepted as a member of whatever invisible club it is that these people belong to. I'm incredulous. Is this how easy it really is? When you're a Kelly, stuck at the bottom of the human pile, living like this seems so out of reach. Yet here I am, no longer wasted space in the eyes of those who have been born, fought or bought their way to the top. The fortune of birth, or lack of it, has a bloody lot to answer for. It's what's driven me. At Jerilderie. At Benalla. A man's station at birth shouldn't define him. But it does. Be damned for it.

While speaking with Angus has been pleasant, the formality of the evening is confusing. I've not considered this element of fitting in. None of us had. Which no doubt speaks to our lack of experience. We are seated and I am across the table from both Angus and Kate. Confusion swells as I look at the array of cutlery in front of me. I counter my lack of knowledge by keeping a glass of wine in my hand, beginning to eat only after those around me start, which allows me to watch their every move. I assume an air of interest, but am vigilant of every action and listen to the exchanges around me. I parrot their words, expressions and intonations, and talk a hell of a lot less than normal. Though I feel conspicuous and phony, no-one around me gives even the slightest pause or question. Pretention is the art of the aristocracy. There are no uncomfortable silences or slightly raised eyebrows. No surreptitious glances from those around me, or whispered words aimed in my direction. No doubt the good food and liberal servings of wine help their lack of notice. Everyone is here for a good time.

Course after course is served once we take our seats. The menu has words that I've never even heard of, let alone pronounced. All I know is, tonight I have eaten food that I've never seen before and will likely never experience again. There are dishes of succulent duckling and green peas. When it arrives in front of me, I can't help but think of the squat little ducks kicking around in the mud of Burrumbeet. The meat is tender and delicious. Next, a sirloin of scotch beef, unmatched by anything I've ever tasted, served with finely grown vegetables, tiny carrots and sprouts. The meat melts in my mouth as I eat it. I labour over every mouthful, savouring it, while a steady flow of chatter surrounds me. When I think I can swallow not another bite, a pastry covered pie is brought, followed by a pudding, which leaves sweetness lingering on my tongue. I sit here, stomach bloated but satisfied. If the constabulary breaks through these doors here and now, I will go with them willingly, unable to move and knowing that I have eaten the finest meal to have ever been served. I cannot think how to describe it to the others when I return to Harry's. Words cannot do it justice.

The crowd appear adequately stuffed as the last of the dishes are taken away. Waiters make sure to fill every glass before the toasts and formalities begin. I find it mind-numbingly boring, particularly after the liveliness of the meal and the conversation that's surrounded me throughout the evening. It's conceited, but I've become accustomed to being the centre of attention. So now being relegated to the background, an unknown, is unusual and awkward.

It's clear who is in charge. The men at the front of the room, who arrive in top hats and dance around the Duke, lead the formalities. Eventually the Duke stands, though he seems distracted. He looks to be enjoying the flowing wine and the company of the finest young ladies Ballarat has to offer. His official duties look to be getting in the way of his social inclinations. His voice is light and slightly slurred as he gushes about the town, which makes all the top-hatted gentlemen tug at their moustaches and straighten their coat jackets.

'I had heard tale of this town's progress. A modern city striving forwards. But I needed a rather personal inspection to realise the truth of it!'

Those around me hang on his every word. He raises a hand. 'I'll be sure to take these observations of your city's greatness back to England, to the very highest realms.' He laughs, 'As I will the memory that I have never tasted a better piece of beef in all the world.' There is a roar of approval from the people on my table. I join in the applause.

At this point, I pay less attention to the words he spouts and more to the men around me. There are easily 200 people and I wonder how many of these dandies will be at Ercildoune's ram sale. They seem tightly knit, so I presume there will be many even if it is just to 'be seen'. The Duke stops, to be toasted by one of the faceless men, before going on. His voice rings out, clear and arrogant across the dining room, despite the many people present.

'This show of Merino sheep is not to be surpassed in any other part of the world.' There is a callout of 'hear, hear' from the floor, to which Angus beside me joins in with gusto. I give a laugh. I'm counting on this quality of which the Duke speaks to attract the many around me with their full purses.

I hope the Duke knows what he's talking about.

***

It's damned relief that I feel most of all as I ride towards Harry's hut. Not excitement, nor fear, but all-encompassing relief. We've a way forward. It's not long before dawn when I pull the borrowed mare to a walk approaching the now familiar thicket of trees.

At the conclusion of the dinner, I'd said my goodbyes to the McCullochs and promised to see them at Ercildoune. The contrast is stark between the brightness of the ballroom and the dark of the night. I thought of staying in Ballarat, as I told Angus I would do, but the adrenaline of the night sent me hurtling towards Harry's at a tremendous speed. Harry's place has a thick coverage of brush and trees in front, which makes it difficult to see unless you know it's there. A welcome sign of safety. The kookaburras overhead greet the newly arriving day and for the first time in a long time, it feels almost like I'm coming home.

Despite the early hour, Ettie's waiting to welcome me when I open the door to the cramped hut. I can see that she's barely slept. The floor is filled with familiar bodies; all are awake. Awaiting my return. Ettie moves to a seat near the fire to warm her hands. The open door has let the morning chill in. My own hands are icy, though the rush of success today kept me warm through the ride back. Steve moves beside her without a word. He sits in the shadows, the firelight flicking over him. I don't know if he moves next to Ettie in support of her, or to avoid my wrath.

'Steven.' I say it as if I'm greeting him, but a tension sparks immediately and crackles around the room. 'It's good to see ye again—and in one piece. I've been worried ye might ha' come off ye horse.' I feel my accent slip back into it's normal beat. A release as sweet as unbuttoning my collar had been as I rode from Ballarat. My words bring a snort from Dan. Maybe this is why they'd stayed awake. He's enjoying someone else being in my firing line.

'I'm not gonna apologise to ya, Ned. Others might reckon you're the leader of this gang, but I never signed up for that. Neither did any of the other boys. I'll go where I want, when I want. I was keepin' an eye out tis all.' Joe and Harry have been chatting, but stop as the tension in the room rises.

I feel, rather than see, the others move away from us, clearing themselves from the confrontation they think isn't theirs to deal with. My eyes are locked on Steve. Ettie stays where she is, but the other three leave the hut with barely a sound.

Steve hasn't moved. His best moments are when he's laughing in his easy style and making a joke, but now he's quiet. He clears his throat but won't look either of us in the eye. 'You know I don't like ya being here, Ettie. In this with us. With him.' Short and sharp. A stinging rebuke to both of us. It was what they must have been arguing about before I'd headed to Ballarat.

'So, ye thought ye'd show it by directly goin' against my orders?' I growl at him.

Steve's voice doesn't rise in its volume but it's cold as he speaks. He's not intimidated by my own gravelly tones. This time, it's directed straight to Ettie. 'Yeah, I did. I'm disgusted in the whole bloody situation. For me little sister to be caught up in the same mess as the rest of us, is a fuckin' crime. Goin' against our parents. What would Ma think of ya riskin' ya neck like this? Bein' here like this with 'im every night? His common whore, with ya not even married.' The words send a red flush galloping up her neck and into her cheeks, anger coursing through her. She holds herself taut.

I see she's fighting hard to control herself, refusing to give in to his insults. When she speaks, it's measured. 'I'm sorry to hear that, Steve. But there's nothin' ya can do about it. Quite frankly, it's got nothin' to do with ya. Ma and Dad know 'xactly where I am and why. This is between me and Ned.'

Steve seems itching for an argument, which she's

refusing to give him. He rubs his hand up and down his thighs, fists clenching. I stand ready to jump between them—if he's going to hit someone, it better be me. Ettie looks at him, straight on. No fear. There's no mistaking she's serious. I watch her face in profile, with her hair falling across it in the firelight. She's beautiful.

'I've loved this man for years. And seems that he feels the same way 'bout me. And don't pretend ya don't love him just as much. You'd give your life for 'im. For each other. It's why ya still here. But ya still don't think he's good enough for me?' Her arms are crossed, but her eyes plead to him.

'Ya makin' a mistake, Ettie. Ya beautiful and smart. The best of the Hart girls. To waste all of that, pinin' after a man whose future is buggered, is a bloody waste. Ma's always thought you'd be the one to better yerself. But there's no bloody chance of that if ya Ned Kelly's lover!'

I go to interrupt in our defense, but she's no need of me, this woman that I've tied myself to. She doesn't need a man to fight her battles and I love her for it.

'Better meself?' She spits at him. She takes a big breath and exhales slowly. 'Ya think ya didn't already seal my fate for me, Steven Hart? Is anyone with any prospects gonna want to marry any of us Hart girls? Or the Kelly girls for that matter? Course not. Me, Kate, Grace. We're as tainted as you are. We'll be good enough to bed, but that's about it. I love Ned. I always have. And I'm bloody lucky that he loves me back, or else I'd be resignin' myself to life as a spinster or someone's whore.' Her eyes haven't left his. 'You dragged us all into this life, Steve, and I don't judge ya for it. It coulda been circumstance or fate or damn bad luck. But ya sure as hell don't get to judge me for my choices, either.' That's all she is going to say. It's enough.

Steve gets up from the fire and paces next to it. He looks shaken by her words, which sting with truth. I'm taken aback as well, thinking about my own sisters. I've sentenced them to a life of trouble.

Steve looks at me properly for the first time tonight. 'You can get fucked with your escapin' to Ireland. I won't be going anywhere near a ship to carry me off to the other side of the world. When we're away, I'm headin' north to Queensland. And I won't be the only one.'

Steve storms out of Harry's hut, into the darkness, leaving Ettie and me contemplating our families and our futures.

***

The dawn breaks and the tension between us settles. Everyone has said their piece for now. We've got bigger things to think about. As Ettie cooks breakfast, I tell them what passed in the day I was away. There's firm agreement all round of our luck to stumble across the McCullochs. Their friendship has dropped into our laps and we can be nothing but grateful. The morning hours pass as I regale them with talk of dinner and the Duke. Ettie sighs as I tell them of the dancing and flowing champagne.

'I wish I'd been there. What a night! To have spent it dancin' with a Duke!' The boys chuckle, but I scoff at her words.

'I'd 'ave not let ya within ten feet of the letch.

Christ! Ya shoulda seen 'im wit' those girls.' There are laughs all round. It feels like a day of celebration now we are one step closer.

The stories come to a stop as the day passes into evening. Tiredness has caught up with us from the night before and even the elation of success has subsided. Dan stands and the others follow him to make their way out back to sleep. I'm staring at the fire and think of my own bed on the floor beside the hearth.

But tonight Harry doesn't lie out on his mattress ready to bed down as he has every night since we've been here. Instead he mutters, 'I'd better see to the boys. I, ah, might be talkin' for a while.' He's not needed to check on anything outside any other night. His reason for leaving is flimsy at best but Ettie and I accept his gift of privacy and take advantage of a room to ourselves, for even the smallest time. Steve, Dan and Joe have been sleeping rough outside under a lean-to woodshed, which is where I imagine Harry to be sitting right now. Sharing a yarn with them and keeping them from sleep for a little longer.

Alone, the emptiness of the hut encompasses us and I'm wholly aware of this woman near me. For someone who has spent a large part of my life avoiding others at all costs, I want nothing more than to be next to Ettie. With her. Together in every way. *It's what I've dreamed of.* I'm in my breeches, shirt thrown on the floor next to where she lays, under her blanket already, head resting on her makeshift pillow. I crawl under the rough woollen blanket next to her. We are close to the glowing embers of the fireplace, which send a little warmth into the sparse surrounds. Despite the chill, as I slide under I'm hard against her as soon as I lay my body alongside her own. I angle away slightly, removing the pressure from her leg. She's never been with a man, and I don't want her intimidated by my closeness. Every sense is heightened. The coarseness of the blanket against my skin sets me alight and I can feel her heart beating. I almost hear the thoughts running across her mind, I'm that attuned to her every movement, and every word.

She's only in her shift. It's thin and I can see the shape of her body through it. The skin at her neck is smooth, her back to me, and I find my eyes travelling down her neck to the swell of her breasts, draped in linen. They are mounds of beauty, so close that I throb with the thought of cupping them with my hand. Instead, I place my hand lightly on the rise of her hip. She's warm to the touch, which means my hands must have the chill of outside on them still. But she doesn't flinch, in fact she moves towards me, nestling her round arse into the crook of my groin, clear in the knowledge of exactly what she's doing to me. It's as if our argument with Steve has spurred her on. Where we've refused before to give in to the wants of our own bodies, it's almost as if we've agreed that tonight she'll be mine.

I lean my head to her ear and groan quietly. This is the moment that I have thought of, dreamed of and rehearsed in my mind since that day at the racecourse, where she caught my eye and my heart.

There was a time when I'd been sure my decisions, my destiny, would never bring us here. That this moment would only come to life in the creases of my mind, where love and hope would fold onto each other to create a moment of perfect, like this one. And yet, despite everything I know, here she is. I cup the roundness of her arse in the palm of my hand and the blood pumps harder in every inch of me. *She's so real.*

'Ettie, girl, ye know that my heart is yours? Yer the woman I love. The only woman. Ye know I'd never have ye like this, if ye weren't mine for life?' It's a question to her, but she takes it as a statement of fact and smiles up at me—she knows. I see the love that I feel for her, reflected in her eyes. She turns her body to face mine and lifts her mouth to meet my own, without having spoken a word, without having needed reassurance. I'm the one who is taken aback. Her hand runs along my face and her tongue across my lips. God, she even tastes like I imagined she would, like sweet tea and the smokiness from the fire where we've been talking and eating through the night.

As her tongue touches my own, her lips meeting mine, I'm overcome with my need for her and any thoughts that I have about taking things slowly and carefully are forgotten. I press against her. 'Can ye feel what you're doin' to me? I've never wanted anythin' so badly in all me life.'

She grins, matching me with equal force, a small rhythm to her movements doing nothing to decrease my desire. I don't know whether it's the smoky haze in the room or the intoxicating feel of being alone with Ettie, but her movements are dreamlike. She moves slowly, purposefully and I savour each moment, to replay in my mind. Who knows when we'll have this opportunity again?

I tug at her shift and bring it up over her head, causing her hair to spill out over her shoulders and breasts which gleam white and perfect. I reach out a hand and cup the fullness and run a thumb gently over her nipple, which is already stiffened with desire or the cold breeze that whips through the cracks in the wooden slabs of the hut. Her body is soft and supple next to the muscled strength of my own and I think again, that we are the exact complement to each other. How did I know that she would look like this, feel like this? There's no explanation, other than this was always in my destiny, this moment together.

Her hand runs down the length of my body. She drags her fingers across muscle and skin and I strain against the tenderness of her touch. She leans into me and I breathe in the smell of her; a mixture of woman, and sweat, and smoke.

'I can't believe that we're here, Ned. Together like this. Feelin' ya body next to mine. This was never gonna be. It can't be real, can it?'

I kiss her, hard and deep, before I roll over the top of her. My arms holding my weight from her small frame below and I growl to her, 'It's real if I say it's real.'

Then I lose myself in her, and there's never been a moment that I wanted so badly in my life.

***

Ettie's snores are even louder than Harry's have been over the weeks that we've been guests, though God knows that I'd never tell her that. Everyone else is sleeping. Harry still with the boys I'm guessing, but sleep will not come for me.

The adrenaline of my success in Ballarat, mixed with the apprehension of the coming events is too much for me to relax and I'm unable to let slumber wash over me, despite my physical release with Ettie. She sleeps contentedly across my body, her face relaxed and her hair loose down her back.

I have a growing anxiety that by sleeping I am wasting what may be the last hours and minutes of my existence. Of course, the lack of sleep makes this worry worse, and so the cycle continues. I wasn't like this, even at Glenrowan, but having Ettie here makes the toll heavier, the gamble even greater. Even the gentle patter of rain that has started, which would normally soothe me as it always did as a we'an, does nothing tonight to settle my mind or body.

Ettie shifts beside me. The noise of her deep sleep stops and her breathing changes, signalling that she is awake. No doubt disturbed by my own sleeplessness. As if one soul can sense the restlessness and unease in the other.

She reaches for my face and lifts herself to kiss my mouth. 'I feel quite scandalous bein' here with you like this. With Steve and his whingin' right outside. Do ya reckon he's drunk himself silly out there? He was so angry. Bloody fool.' She's whispering to me, close into my ear. We're both under no illusion of Steve's feelings. We also know that were she with any man other than myself, Steve wouldn't tolerate it. But tolerate it he must.

'He knows I mean to do right by ye. No matter our endin', your life is just beginnin', my girl. Steve knows that too.' I look into her eyes and see the slight doubt that lingers there. She's thinking it too, as much as I am. This may be one of the final nights that we will ever have together—the only night. The memory of this night may have to last her a lifetime. She snuggles in closer and I wrap my arm around her shoulders protectively and kiss the top of her head.

'It's all settled, Ettie,' my voice barely carries to her ear over the wind that surrounds the hut and pushes its way through the cavities in the timber. 'I want ye to come to the sales with us. Ye can play my wife well, I think.' I wink at her and she smacks my arm gently. 'Ye won't be dancin' wit' the Duke, but ye'll make a fine lady.'

'We'll be makin' our escape from the sales. It's the only way to get us all away safely. We'll need to go our separate ways and say our goodbyes at haste. The minute we leave Ercildoune, there'll be no more Kelly Gang.' It has to be that way. I feel the gravity of those words, but the fire lights behind her eyes and she sits up onto one elbow, looking at me seriously.

'You needn't get all wistful and romantic about it, Ned Kelly. If we can all manage to get away and breathin' it'll be a bloody miracle. So don't lay there as if the end of the Kelly Gang is the worst thing that could 'appen. We're all puttin' our lives on the line for ya plan.' She stresses the *all* and again the weight and guilt floods back. She moves in closer to me, laying a hand on the bare skin of my chest, as if feeling the rhythmic breath coming and going from it. She places a kiss where the skin is smooth.

'I'm not sayin' it to make ya feel guilty, but it's all I can think about. This,' she signals her resting hand, 'ya breath, it's a sign of yer life. And it can be taken away so easily. Ya strength and laughter. Taken away from me.' Her eyes well with tears as she looks at me. The honesty in her words is raw. 'A life lived without ya, will be only a half-life. I don't want it. But neither do I want to see you as a grisly, danglin' puppet from the end of a rope. Just the thought of it makes me feel as if I can't breathe at all.' She puts her head to my chest, but I can feel the wetness of her face against me. She is as strong as they come, this woman I love, but I am pushing her to the brink.

'The Ballarat plan is our chance. Our only chance to make enough money to start a new life. So I'm willin' to risk it all for us. But we're gonna need a hell of a lot of luck. Still, we're here now, so ya must have some luck of the Irish about ya.' She wipes the tears from her cheeks and I smile at her. I'll not let the Victorian Police Force, or a bunch of rich graziers, stand in the way of making a life with her. A life for the both of us.

'You say ya love me. Well, I need a promise from ya.' She sits up straight, the blanket covering her. She's serious. I don't even ask what it is, but nod my head, eyes intent. 'Ya can't be a saviour.' She goes on. 'Ya can't sacrifice yerself to be the hero for the others.' I open my mouth to respond. She must know I'm about to launch into denial. She cuts off my words. 'Don't. I know ya fancy yourself as savin' the little man—on a one man crusade to burn their mortgage papers and show a man is not his father and can better hi'self. I've always admired that about ya. Despite the killin' you've done, and bein' a wanted man. I love that you're a romantic. But you're also a pig-headed bastard. A selfish one even.' I stiffen at her accusation, but I don't move. I need to hear what else she has to say. I need to if we're going to make this life together. I know I've a streak of selfishness; too much like my father in that regard.

'Ya need to promise me you'll put me first. You first. Us first. You 'ave to promise me that we're gonna leave if this plan goes our way. If ya can't promise me now, that ya can walk away from your big ideas, then I'm not comin' with ya.' Her gaze is steady, as it was when she spoke to Steve. 'I've gone against me family, and I can live with that. But I 'ave to know that this… isn't all for nothin'.'

I push myself onto an elbow, close enough for me to feel the heat of her breath on my face. I move away slightly, trying to create a small distance between us. The chill of the night air sweeps between our bodies.

'What? Walk away from all dis glamour?' I throw a hand around. My tone is jeering, but she bites back at my words.

'Don't bullshit me, Edward Kelly. You know damn well what I mean. Can ya leave ya name behind? No longer being THE Ned Kelly: wanted, hunted. Can ya live without it? Yer not one to fade into shadows—we all know that about ya by now. But that's exactly what we need to do. Ya can't be the leader, or the hero, anymore.' She holds her breath, her expression unwavering. ''Cept to me,' she adds.

She leaves her question hanging. Her eyes not moving from my own. The seconds tick by. There is no doubt on my part. This is where I should have always been—with her. I nod. As I do, the face of Thomas Curnow flashes into my mind, gently cradling his sleeping daughter. I don't know why I see him now, at this moment with Ettie. But I do. Then the distance between us evaporates and she and I move as one, and he's gone. If we're together, we will be enough.

***

Scenes from the Ballarat dinner fill my head. Snippets of conversation pop in and stop any chance of sleep. Sir Samuel Wilson, the pompous arse, barely looked at me when Angus introduced us. However, once he knew I was there to attend his sale, buy his stock and fill his pockets, he became most obliging. His great bearded cheeks puffed out as he'd slapped me on the shoulder. He took the time to remind me of it being a, 'Cash sale, my boy.' Even the memory made me grit my teeth. It had been a long time since I had wanted to hit a man so badly, but refrained. Maybe even this is a sign I can turn the cheek and walk away. A sign of maturity—I doubt it. I'm focused on getting this done for Ettie. I wouldn't risk it just to smack the man, much as I might like to.

Wilson's jokes had continued. 'I would hate you to miss out on the finest stock in the colony because of any *misunderstanding.*' He emphasised the final word and it told me all I needed to know about him. He was rich and arrogant, a man who always got what he wanted. He gave a little cough and pulled himself up to full height, which still put him well shy of my own eyes.

'Yes, I always think that cash stops any funny business going on.' The veneer of polite behaviour was thin. 'It does prevent any awkward misunderstandings.' I let the reply hang in the air and caught his slight falter. He was trying to decide if I was mocking him. I chastised myself for my pettiness in the face of such an important meeting, so I smiled. 'I'll make sure to bring along plenty, Sir. I'm very interested and my wife is most keen to come along and see the fine stock for herself.' I'd attempted my best deferential smile, which had been a struggle. Long ago I gave up bowing and scraping to the gentry. But this was for the greater good.

The glint of greed had flashed in his eye as I said

it. A man with such wealth and the greedy bastard still relished the thought of more. He smiled, nodded and moved on, making pleasantries with the next potential buyer. The exchange made me feel happier about what was to come. Wilson had it coming, a sure need to be taken down a peg or two. And I would be glad to do the honours. It is this thought, of the success that possibly lay ahead, that finally brings sleep to me.

***

Days pass quietly. Time moves as it will. But each day has done so with an undercurrent of worry that the police could storm Harry's door at any moment, pistols drawn and calling for our surrender. But not today. Today we have a purpose. Sale day. Though we all know this day will be the finish of the Kelly Gang, everyone seems pleased it has finally arrived and will bring an end to the mind numbing waiting of the past weeks. Spring weather can be inclement, but today has brought nothing but sunshine and a cloudless sky, which bode well for us today. I stand at Harry's door and look out. My heart is light.

The day ahead will decide whether we disband in glory and adventure, or if we go down amid blasting gunfire and violence. No matter what's gone before it, this will be our final act. It seems to me that Joe cares least which of these outcomes it will be. He simply wants it to be over quickly, one way or another.

He's quieter than normal and I can tell he's yearning for another hit of the pipe. As the weeks have passed since his return from Ararat, so too has his irritation grown. He's said nothing, but is distracted and melancholy. Folding in on himself, like the accordion that he used to play in the times before we were always on the run. *Oh to hear him play a tune again.*

In our discussions over the past few days, we've agreed if things go badly today, none of us plans on being caught. Between the five of us, Harry included, we've spent our fair share of time in Her Majesty's accommodations and all agree we won't be going back to those hellholes again.

Ettie is taking the biggest risk, innocent as she is, but we've agreed on the course of action she will take. If things go awry at Ercildoune today, she's to scream her anger at us. Not a hard task I'd imagine. She's to scream her innocence to those around her and align herself with the respectable ladies and gentlemen nearby. She's to say that she had no idea what was going to happen. It's a risk. She may well be jailed still. But I hope, if things go to hell, that the protestations and our own inevitable deaths will be enough to keep her from the noose herself. Steve agrees with me, and Ettie of course, does not. But I refuse to have it any other way. Her heart is so tightly entwined with mine, that if I were to be at fault for her demise, I'd only be half a man. Such is my need for her.

Harry is perhaps the greatest surprise for me. The older man has become a father figure to our rabble band in the time we've spent with him. I've looked to him as a voice of reason and experience in these weeks. He's made the decision, with the agreement of everyone, that he will take part in this day, for better or worse.

'The past weeks have made me remember the life I once led, lads. To go back t' livin' like a ghost like I was 'fore ye arrived… 'twas no life at all.' I'd embraced him.

He and Joe will attend the sale as well, though a distance from Ettie and me. Walk the edges, be there, but be seen as little as possible. Joe will partner Harry, dressed as a woman for the occasion. It was a difficult call, with both Joe and Steve sporting equally chiselled features. In the end though, I'd needed Joe, with his experience, to be close to the action today.

'It'll mean dressin' ye as a lass, Joey. Ye'll be on Harry's arm at th' outset.' He groaned but he'd also smiled for the first time in a week.

'Christ, what a way to be remembered. Frolickin' round in me finery.' He did a little two-step and dipped a curtsy on the spot, which had us doubled over.

He's happy with the decision to play a big part today. He's always happier in the thick of the action; gives him less time to think, a good thing when your mind plays awful tricks. Their distance from others is integral to the success of the plan. Joe might be feminine in appearance, but up close it's clear to anyone that he's no woman. Hopefully some distance from the crowds and a carefully placed veil will be enough to keep up the charade. It won't be until later in the night that he'll be in the middle of it.

Even with an unsettled mind, Joe's a sure shot and as brave as any man I've ever known. I want him beside me on a day like today. Ettie had a hand in the decision too. Steve's ended up with the least dangerous of the jobs, well away from possible fighting. If things go badly, it's most likely Steve will be the one to make it clear.

The mundane weeks of waiting have been filled with plans and discussions and dreams about what will happen if our freedom is won. The chances of us all surviving today are slim. Probably damn near impossible.

But we've not dwelled on it. Instead, we've made our plans.

For Ettie and me, we'll head west to South Australia, catch a ship to the Ireland I've only heard about. Dan is still with us, though Steve has decided that his future will be north. It is the hardest of decisions, to plan on leaving the shores of Australia forever. My family is my reason for living and breathing, so to make the choice to leave them with the mess that will land on them after this final heist causes me pain.

Joe suspects it will be much harder to make our way to South Australia and away, after the Ercildoune holdup. The police will be baying for our blood, but mine in particular, and he thinks I'll be more conspicuous with Ettie at my side.

He'd told me honestly and with resignation, only yesterday. 'I'll wish ya luck—yer the closest friend that I have in the world—but you'll not get away. It weighs down me heart to say it.' His melancholy fills me with dread. For Ettie, as much as myself, he has to be wrong.

For Joe himself, there have been no plans as yet, though he's packed his clothes up as the rest of us have. He's told the others he will head north with Steve; but I know he's not convinced his destiny lays in that direction. His plans are vague.

'There's no point makin' plans I won't be alive to do.' It's not lack of belief in the plan for today; it's superstition. He thinks our luck has to run out. It's as simple as that.

Dan will arrive with Ettie and me today—our driver in the horse and buggy from Ballarat. We assume these will be housed well away from the main homestead, so an extra pair of hands will be required. We know the parts we'll play. We've planned for what is possible but the rest is now up to good fortune and some bollocks of steel once we all arrive at Ercildoune, as none of us know how today will really turn out.

It might be the courage and confidence of youth, or an inability to prophesise my own demise, but I've spent little time pondering what will happen if the situation turns bad. What will be, will be. After our life on the run, how could we believe in anything else? Another part of this self-belief, which I dare not say out loud after the events of the past years, is that I'm beginning to think we're untouchable. It would feel like I am tempting fate to voice the thought. But I feel it: exhilaration. As if this is meant to be the Kelly legacy. The legend.

Joe feels dread. He'd confided last night, 'I've got the same feelin' in me guts as I did the night I went to Aaron.' He'd looked towards the window, eyes distant. 'And you know how that turned out.'

***

The carriage wheels drive a steady rhythm. It runs a rhythmic rocking motion through my body. The wheels are a constant stream of noise, but I don't mind, because she is here with me. And God, she is a beauty. If only I could hold her in my arms as I have before. I did hold her, didn't I? I can all but feel her body pressed against my own.

She smiles at me, and holds out her hand. I try and reach hers. I stretch, but can't quite grasp it, only brushing her fingers with my own. That's all there is, just a brush of her hand.

***

The day is bright and crisp. The sun's energy bounces through me and I'm ready to face what comes. Dan looks calm, driving the horse towards Ercildoune. My heartbeat keeps a careful rhythm with the trot-trot of its hooves along the dirt. The trip from Ballarat is a pleasant one, through gentle hills overlooking green paddocks. Collectively there's a sense of relaxed optimism, given what lays before us today. Dan seems focused on the events ahead, rather than the possible outcomes. Ettie also seems calm, despite the importance of her work in what's about to transpire. It's the first time that she'll be in the thick of any action, actively taking part with a gang of bushrangers. There's no way of preparing her for this. I wasn't prepared. I'm mindful she may become overwhelmed or nervous at any moment. For now, though, she looks thoughtful and relaxed, enjoying our outing as the 'happily married couple'.

I'm in two minds about having her so close to the action. It seems wrong to have her here beside me, but her presence makes our work all the easier and gives us the greatest chance of success. Whether I like it or not, this woman who I'll marry has a mind of her own. When I'd offered her the chance to stay away with Steve, that I could come to her after our business at the ram sale, she was livid.

'I won't be kept away, Ned. Not again. This is the life I've chosen. I won't risk bein' away from you and the boys through this, when ya safety, ya chance of coming out of this alive, is better with me at ya side. I'm no coward. And I'm no bloody wallflower.' I'd pulled her close and kissed her. As we'd pulled apart she'd whispered to me, 'Glenrowan nearly killed me. I'll not sit by waitin' again.'

To Steve's disgust and my own chagrin, Ettie is with us.

Dan agrees we are barely recognisable in our newly bought, well-fitted clothes. Ettie's shape is enhanced with a bustle, which she's never worn before. Accentuating her curves and tiny waist that I've held against me. It's unnerving to be looking so unlike myself. Ettie carries herself well in her new clothes, whereas I feel restrained. Caged. We look like the men and women who have browbeaten and oppressed us all. The kind that I've promised to break down if I can.

The property of Ercildoune sits west of Ballarat and is an easy drive in the buggy from the town. People are coming from far and wide for the sale, and to enjoy the genial hospitality of Sir Samuel Wilson. This is important.

Those attending the sale are invited to dine and dance at its conclusion. The business of money changing hands will happen at the dinner's completion. A fact which sounds bloody ridiculous to me, but is apparently the way things are done. We'll interrupt the dinner after the curtain of night has fallen and before too much wine is drunk. Timing is crucial. We want to catch them before they are full of booze and bravado. I don't want anyone playing the hero or reaching for his pistol. The cover of nightfall is integral to our departure as well. Those we rob of their money and valuables tonight will be far more hesitant to chase their money and a gang of armed bushrangers into the dead of night. I'm sure of it. It will buy us critical hours before the police are told.

Every minute will buy us time to ride hell-for-leather to Burrumbeet and to Steve. Sitting on the banks of the lake this afternoon, alone but for our horses and packs, I know he'll be watching the time tick past so slowly that he'll look to see if it's going in reverse. For Steve, the people he loves most in the world are in danger and no doubt his frustration will rise steadily throughout the day at being unable to help. What irritates him the most is the knowledge that he's unable to affect the outcome of today in any way. He had said this to me of course, but I'd assured him his role was an important one. Crucial, if we are going to make it out alive. We need the fresh horses ready to go. I'm not willing to trust an unknown with the job. It has to be one of us at the lake and I've made the decision it will be Steve.

Not one to let it go easy, he took up the argument again, but I cut him short.

'You're a brother Steve, to Ettie and to me, but so help me, if ye let me down and leave yer spot at the lake tomorrow, I'll hunt ye down. Do ye understand? That's how serious I am.' A reference to his arrival at the show, and he knew it. Nothing has come of his disobedience on that day. The success of my day at the show and at the dinner has meant Steve's showjumping adventure became a slightly amusing side-story to the day's events. But nothing ever goes unanswered. We are a gang of four— but there is no doubt who the leader is, and I won't have him make the same mistake again. Steve nods; no more arguments forthcoming.

I saw the fight go out of him and softened my voice. 'We're countin' on ye, Steve. Ettie's life is relyin' on it. But, if we don't get back, ye don't come lookin' for us. If it gets to the time before dawn and we aren't back, ye leave the horses and take off north, like ye planned. As fast as ye can bloody ride. We want ye away if things go badly. Do ye understand?' Steve had nodded. It was easy enough to say at the time, but now, sitting alone, getting cold under the shadow of gum trees with the breeze whipping across the lake, I imagine it will be a lot harder to do nothing than he'd thought it would be.

As if I've been having a conversation out loud, not just my own thoughts whizzing through my mind, Ettie turns to me, waving a fly from her face. It's painted with concern. She's been looking towards the lake. We can see the huge expanse of water in the distance from our carriage.

'It hurt him, ya know. To agree to stay away today. It's the first time, in a long time, that he's been away from the rest of ya. He'll be fightin' the loneliness of being without you all—his band of brothers.' She turns, no discussion, just a statement filled with the worry she has for her big brother. 'If we don't make it back, I hope he still will.' She sighs it—a final punctuation on a topic that doesn't need to be discussed.

Steve gave me his word. He'll wait near Burrumbeet, horses at the ready, until the darkness is broken by gunfire or by pre-dawn light. His eyes fixed on the dual mountains, Ercildoune and Misery, where the homestead sits. If we've not arrived by then, he'll leave without us and ride into his future alone. And Ettie knows as well as me, that it's this that terrifies him, almost as much as the threat of the noose.

My thoughts are drawn back by the bucking of the carriage beneath us. My eyes run over Ettie; she's stunning. She sits tall and composed, corseted within an inch of her life. But she looks as if this is a part of her every day life. Dan's told me before, he thinks me being with Ettie makes me softer. Said it makes him more unsure of our success, which smarted. My little brother thought I had a weakness which caused me not to think straight. That I might need him to be my protector. That was my job. I'd patted him on the back.

'Love does indeed make a man different, brother. I hope you know it too one day. It makes ye more aware of ye place in the world and what ye want from it.' I'd left my hand on his shoulder and squeezed it harder than needed.

'But ye needn't worry, brother. Don't mistake it for weakness. Ettie or not, I'll shoot a man point-blank, like I did before. If it's needed, I'll do it. You can count on that.' I had leaned in to tell him that, with the crackle of the fire beside us, so that Ettie couldn't hear me. He'd heard the steel in my voice.

The imposing entryway to Ercildoune appears before us in the distance. Iron gates and stone entryway guarded by giant oak trees each side, dressed in the new green of spring. Dan shifts his weight in front of me and I see him reach down, towards the hard shaft of the gun against his leg. He is ready for what might come. I know that he hopes he won't need it but, like me, he knows the steel in his pocket is likely to be his greatest friend today.

***

I feel confident and strong as Dan pulls up the driveway, curling its way from the main road around a thicket of trees. We're greeted by the imposing view of the two-storey homestead standing tall and proud; a stone monarch. Part is covered in lush, green creepers and overlooking a small lake. Swans float on the waters. It's so perfect, it feels unreal. I pick up Ettie's hand and squeeze it just to assure myself she exists. The homestead is a grey-stone beauty. I wish that my Ma could have lived in a house with such a profile, rather than the cramped little hut in which she raised her armful of babies. How I wish the same for Ettie. I know she would argue her needs are much simpler than the grand homestead that stands before us. She deserves that beauty.

Holding her hand as we bump along fills me with confidence. There aren't many who would stand by a wanted man. She's gone beyond that today, putting her own life and freedom on the line. There are plenty who would let you bed them, the trophy of a bushranger to talk about with their friends. But love and loyalty like Ettie's is something I've never expected. This girl fills my heart and I won't let her go. *Unless the noose makes me.*

Dan pulls the buggy to a stop close to the homestead. The sale yards are set up a distance away, nearer the shearing shed, but a steady stream of people make their way between the two. We've been lucky with the weather today. There are few clouds in the spring-blue sky and it's neither too warm nor too cold, which seems to have turned the day into a social outing for many. Quite a few women float around, so Ettie will not look out of place. Though Ercildoune is nestled in between hills, gusts of wind blow through, strong enough to make a man grab for his hat. This will play to our advantage. An excuse to have a hat pulled down and some dirt blowing around. People will keep their eyes down, meaning less scrutiny from the faces around us.

I jump from the buggy, reach a hand out to help Ettie down. I know my mind must be completely focused on the events of the day, but Ettie takes my breath away. She steps from the buggy without the slightest concern or self-consciousness, despite wearing some of the finest clothes that she's ever seen, and by far the finest that she's ever worn. She's a brave girl, young though she is. My heart tightens as she grips my arm until she steadies.

'Mrs Callaghan, you are a fine sight for a man. I'm a lucky one.' She smiles, mouth and eyes.

I look to Dan. He's alert and almost too rigid, even though the action is hours away. I keep my voice low, though there's no-one within hearing distance. 'Why don't ye pull the buggy up near a tree down there, Dan?' I point past the lake, where there are two other buggies and half a dozen horses tethered. 'Unhook the horse and give 'im a feed, but make sure he's ready to go after that. Then give yourself a rest while ye can. We won't need ye for a while yet. All goin' well, once the dinner starts, we'll need ye close and listenin' for a signal. You'll need to have three other horses ready to go. Joe and Harry'll have their own.'

He nods but hesitates. He's holding out on me. Wants to tell me something, but doubts himself.

'Spill it out, Daniel.' I tell him gruffly, 'I've no time for this—we need to get on.'

'That's it, Ned. This ain't the right time, but well, I won't be goin' to Ireland with ya, brother. I've decided.' He runs his words together. Looks relieved to get them out.

'What do ye mean you've decided?' I scoff at him. He's only a child, standing here trying to make life-changing decisions. He's right—this is not the time.

'Ireland's your dream, Ned. Not mine. Not Steve's. We'll not be there with ya, no matter how much ya might want it. I can't live in ya shadow forever. I can't be just Ned Kelly's brother.'

He looks so young sitting there, telling me his big plans, awaiting instructions and looking ready to jump at any loud noise. I need to let him know everything will be fine—no need for these nerves. I place my hand on his knee as he sits high on the buggy. 'I love ye brother, whatever happens today, I want ye to be sure of that. Ye'll do what ye need to.'

His gaze hits my own. His words are slow and full of meaning. 'I forgive ya, Ned. For all of this. I don't blame ya and neither does Steve. Ya can't blame yaself.' He flicks the reins and the horse moves off before I digest what he's said.

I must be gawping after Dan, because Ettie grabs my arm and steers me towards where people are gathering. I feel breathless, as if Dan has punched me in the guts, the only thing that makes me feel sick and short of breath like I do now. *He forgives me.* Ettie can sense my rising anger and puts on her best voice, the one with the rounded vowels that she's been practising for weeks.

'Breathe Ned. He didn't mean it the way that it sounded. I'm sure of it.' Her grasp is firm on my arm. I can feel the blood flooding my face.

'That little gobshite. Here I am pourin' me heart out to him and he turns around and blames me for dis bullshit.' The more I talk, the more I feel my cheeks warming and my heart rate quickening. 'As if he hasn't had a big bloody part in dis mess.'

Ettie's fingers dig painfully into my forearm as she turns her face to me and looks into my eyes. Her smile is wide as she looks up at me but her eyes are cold and anger flames behind them.

'You need to focus on the task at hand, dearest,' sarcasm smothers her voice. 'I need your full attention here. We need a good sale. We're dependin' on it, so you need to pull it together. For better or worse, you may never lay eyes on your brother again after this night. Let's not end it with ugly words.' Her voice is calm and steady. I know that to anyone walking past, they will suspect nothing more than a loving couple. She is right, of course, so I nod and she shakes herself to relax. Not for the first time, I count myself a lucky man for having her by my side.

We move closer to the yards that are set up away from the house and full of sturdy Merinos, the noise buzzing around us. Even the rams, each within their own little pen, are alert and trying to outdo each other with their bleats and stamps adding to the general noise and chaos. A large number of people mill about, inspecting the stock. We join them. Moving in and around the pens, I thrust my hand into their fleece, eyeing the quality stock on offer. The Duke seems to have been right.

Out the corner of my eye, I see the dark hair of a man that looks familiar. Black jacket and green neck tie. A little girl caught up in his arms looks at me. He turns and shuffles slightly. My heart catches. *It can't be him.* How can Curnow be here? Of all places? My breathing is rapid and I feel Ettie shake my arm. I look to her and open my mouth. I barely breathe it to her, 'You must leave—we're done for. That's Curnow,' I flick my head a little in his direction,

'From Glenrowan. He'll know me.' My words are a garbled mess and my eyes dart, searching for the quickest way to get Ettie away from here. Her eyes are round. Shock. I turn my head ever so slightly, trying to catch another glimpse, I'll need to show Ettie who we have to avoid.

He's gone. The green neck tie remains, as does the small child in her matching dress, now placed on the ground and grasping the man's hand. But it's not Thomas Curnow. How could I have mistaken him? My head spins as relief floods through me. Bile surges up my throat, but I swallow it down and focus on breathing. I grab Ettie's hand.

'Shit. It's okay. It's okay. It were just a mistake. It's not him. Thank God for dat.' The shock has sent my words back into my normal speech. She puts her hand over my own.

'It's alright, love. Breathe. We're gonna be fine.' She locks her eyes on my own. 'I will be fine. You've no need to worry.' *Yes, even without me, she will be fine.* I put her hand in the crook of my arm and turn to move back towards the pens. My heart slows as I realise the threat has passed. That it was never really there.

I notice Angus and Kate almost immediately, and lean my head to Ettie's ear. 'There they are. I hope that you're ready.' She smiles, the shock of the last minute pushed aside, and inclines her pretty head in assent, a steely resolve in her face.

This is the moment that holds our fate. I can feel it. We can turn and leave at this second, retrieve Dan and make our escape, to where I don't know, and with barely a penny to our name. But if we choose to keep walking towards Kate and Angus, our fate is sealed. We move towards them.

'Kate, Angus, it's good to see ye both again.' I try to be calmer than I feel. I don't want to bluster and speak too loudly. 'May I introduce my wife, Elsie Callaghan. Elsie, this is Angus and Kate McCulloch. They kindly took me under their wing at the dinner in Ballarat.'

I can tell that Ettie's dainty face and open, happy disposition charm them almost immediately. She's clearly young, but dressed up and as a 'married woman' she can pass for years older. She and Kate immediately bond over the topic of children. I listen in wonder as Ettie launches into an anecdote about one of our fictional children, and even I begin to think we may have some bairns at home, eagerly awaiting our return. She's been around young ones her whole life, as much as I have. Her words are convincing.

Angus is insistent we leave the women to their chatting and take a look over the rams before the sale begins. 'The real business of why we're here, Jack. Not this women's talk.' Kate tuts at him and grabs Ettie. They meander together back towards the house.

Angus and I head the opposite direction towards the rams and talk amiably of owning our own properties. We share stories about the difficulties of competing with the likes of Samuel Wilson and other dominant forces.

'Wait until you see inside the homestead, Jack! You'll not want to sit down for fear of dirtying something, I promise you.' I laugh at his self-deprecation. Angus McCulloch is a genuine, good man, and there are few enough of them around to be unique. In another situation, I'd be pleased to know him honestly, as Ned and Angus.

Though I'm sure, did he know our true circumstance, he may not be as keen about our acquaintance.

We take our time, looking over the many rams up for auction. I point out three I will bid on. Angus identifies two that've taken his eye. We have a gentleman's agreement not to bid on the other's picks. I, of course, am hoping to be out-bid on all of them, driving up the prices for the day. The more buyers, the more money there will be changing hands after dinner. We walk towards the homestead to meet Kate and Ettie, who we find settled on the veranda of the house, enjoying a cup of tea before the sale.

With chairs and tea service outside in the sunshine, the women look like they belong in London or Paris—or at least the London or Paris of my imaginings. I look to Angus before we reach the women. 'I want to thank you, for the kindnesses you and Kate have shown me.'

He waves my thanks away. 'Glad to help, Jack. We little men need to stick together. We're the unknowns in the world.' He gives an exaggerated sigh, followed by a chuckle and I join in, thinking how much that I hope to remain unknown for a little longer.

I stop and look to him. 'I want ye to know that I hold ye in great esteem. You're honourable and kind; scarce qualities in a man.' He doesn't know it yet, but this is my apology for what is about to happen. For dragging him and Kate into our mess, when they are two of the nicest people that I've had the pleasure to meet. Angus responds by looking at me as if I've gone slightly mad. He won't know until the guns are drawn, who I am. I only hope he remembers this conversation and the honesty he sees in my face. I hope he can reconcile who I am with what I need to do.

A wide smile breaks across my face and I slap his shoulder. 'Let's find our girls. They'll want to be in on the action when the biddin' starts.'

***

Mr. Gibson, of Fisken and Gibson, readies himself for the beginning of the sale. It's common knowledge that Sir Samuel has high hopes for today, despite fewer buyer numbers than originally expected. The pressure is on both of the auctioneers: Messrs Fisken and Gibson. Gibson shuffles papers around and clears his throat. He's nervous. He knows he must be at his best today to sell these lots, create a sense of urgency and competition. He's helped considerably by the fact that these are some of the finest rams he has ever been engaged to sell. Samuel Wilson might be one of the squattocracy, but the man knows his sheep, which is about the best and only compliment Gibson can land at his feet.

***

Lingering near the yards, waiting for the auctioneer's call, I see Harry arrive with his 'wife'.

'Not real bloody attractive!' Harry had laughed as we left Smeaton, watching Joe in his flouncy affair. We definitely gave the best of the dresses to Ettie. Harry and Joe had planned for their arrival to be just before the sale began. They timed it perfectly.

I watch them from the corner of my eye. They

make a show of walking around together on the periphery of the sale area, close enough to be in the vision of those around but far enough to have little contact with others. Joe then heads to the shade of a nearby tree. They have agreed on a feigned headache, which will allow Harry to go closer to the action on his own.

I watch Joe sit himself daintily under the shade of a gnarled gum tree, positioned with a perfect view of the sale yards and the homestead. Fan at the ready in case he's approached. I smile at the hilarity of it. It's both gutsy and ridiculous what we are doing—not how people will have pictured the Kelly Gang. This wasn't mass murder or robbing a bank at gunpoint. This requires nouse and balls, in equal measure, in its planning and execution. A thrill runs down my spine at the audacity.

Harry approaches the rams, one man amongst the bodies. The auctioneer yells and points as people in the small crowd raise their hands, bidding on their chosen stock. Harry locks eyes on me and Ettie in the crowd, but there's no acknowledgment, as we've agreed. He has scrubbed up best he can, though he still looks hardened. Not one of the men you would expect here. Harry smiles at people in return for the nods or small greetings that he receives but he doesn't interact otherwise. Instead, he watches those around us. He's to try and get a feel for who might be trouble later in the evening when the night's real events begin. Nobody seems to be carrying guns, which will mean less potential problems. There's the jovial feeling of a social outing in the air. Not unlike a day at the races. The familiarity is comforting. All seem to be enjoying the high spirits and sunshine in a town that's known for its cold and dreary weather.

In the days prior to the sale, Harry had confided in me that he was feeling young again, on this adventure with us. That's what he thought of it as—a grand adventure. I had told him it might go terribly wrong or give him the biggest excitement of his life. But he assured me he knows what he's getting into. 'I'm sick o' livin' like a hermit. Shut away from life. You lot 'ave made me come alive again. Ye ain't the only ones to live on the wrong side of the law, Ned. Nor the only ones to rob or threaten... or kill. I know what's comin'.'

As the auctioneer yells and takes the bids being thrown around, I see Harry's face taking in everything. I know that, like mine, the blood in his veins is rushing faster and harder and the time is flying as fast as the auctioneer's words.

***

No-one suspects a thing about us, I'm sure of it. Ettie agrees. The adrenaline that has surged through us as we arrived has subsided.

On my arm as my wife, we are respectable. The feeling is intoxicating, she leans in and confides to me in a quiet moment. Her whispering these words into my ear has done nothing for my concentration on the sale's proceedings. All I can think about is bedding her again, even in a situation as serious as the one we find ourselves in. I run my finger down the length of her arm and feel her shiver at my touch.

The sheep lots I'm interested in are a while away from being auctioned and we've managed to move ourselves to the back of the crowd.

'I dream of a life like this for us,' Ettie whispers into my ear. 'Just imagine … our own place, our own land. We're so close.' Her eyes gleam with hope, and trust … in me.

Her faith constricts my chest. Getting out of this alive, and with cash in our pockets, is all I can think about now.

***

Kate has been a vibrant source of much laughter for Ettie throughout the day. Clearly, the McCullochs have the same impact on Ettie as they have on me. She's genuinely warmed to the pair, and their friendship has given us a free pass into the crowd today. People have accepted their introduction of us. No-one's raised a question to either Jack or Elsie Callaghan, unknown though we may be, because we've been chatting and laughing with the McCullochs. Kate is well-known amongst these people. She's one of them. She has the same confidence and charisma as my own Kate back home. A coincidence or providence? I don't know.

The first dozen lots are through when Kate suddenly grabs Ettie's arm. 'We are leaving you to your smelly rams! Elsie and I have things to chat about. We plan on taking a walk around these charming gardens. Did you see the swans? What a lark!' Kate tells us with a flourish. The two move off and I spend the rest of the day shoulder-to-shoulder with Angus. The bidding is fast and furious, despite there being a smaller than expected crowd. The people that are here have money to spend, which bodes well.

Numbers dwindle as the sale nears an end. The hammer is banged for the last time and the crowd disperses from the stockyards to head towards the house and gardens of Ercildoune. The air cools as the sun lowers, but still holds the slightest spring warmth. The buyers have all stayed, with the business of the sale to be settled at the conclusion of the meal. The dinner is to be a celebration, with copious amounts of wine provided by our host, as a thank you for our many purchases.

The sun drops lower to the horizon, setting on the last day of my life in the Kelly Gang. Now that the time to act has almost arrived, the minutes speed past. Ettie must be feeling it too, because she's watching me closely. Distracted from her conversation, waiting and looking for cues. We've agreed to wait until the dinner is concluded. When their bellies will be full and senses dulled by the many glasses of wine that will have been drunk.

I feel no trepidation, no hesitation. Nothing but excitement about what lays ahead, and that includes the delicacies of the upcoming dinner. My memory of the dinner in Ballarat is fresh in my memory. I hope the fat old bastard, Samuel, will have us dining well tonight.

***

Ettie has drunk two glasses of champagne at Kate's insistence I notice, and looks giggly and carefree. I've watched her intently, trying to give her a silent warning—she can't be drunk, she'll be a liability, but it's out of my hands. I've sat holding the same glass of wine throughout the night, aware of the clear head that I must have. Dinner is served and savoured; good enough to be a man's last supper. God, I hope it's not though. The guests don't yet know it, but the real show is about to begin. Sir Samuel stands for a toast, his glass raised.

'Ladies and Gentlemen. Friends. I want to thank you all for your attendance today. It has been a grand success, thanks to you. I've enjoyed getting to know you on this wonderful day. Once again our ram sale will be known as one of the best in the country. You have acquired some fine stock today and I know that the Ercildoune bloodline will run strong in your own flocks over the coming years and decades.' His eyes scan across the seated group. Ettie's eyes flash to me as I move slightly in my chair. I'm preparing. This is the time I've been waiting for. She tenses, ready to move as planned.

My chair scrapes as I push it back to stand, my own glass lifted high in the air.

I've made sure to position myself on one side of the room, Harry on the opposite, with Wilson very easily in our sights. Not that I think he'll give us any trouble himself, but I want him to feel cornered, helpless. I give a cough as I stand, drawing myself up to my full height, taller than most in this room.

'Excuse my interruption, Sir.' Wilson looks at me, confusion on his face before his features lock into a look of disdain. 'Today has indeed been a grand success.' I let the polished accent that I've been carrying all day drop a little and my words roughen around the edges. 'But, I feel that it'll be tonight that's most memorable. For all of us.'

Some smile and nod, not yet catching on that this shouldn't be part of the night's proceedings, but others start to show concern. I can see the thoughts running across their faces. Who's this man interrupting proceedings? I lower the wine and replace it with my revolver, pulled from the inside of my jacket, where it's been hidden throughout the day in case of an emergency, and place it gently on the table in front of me. Not a word. It seems that the room itself is shocked into a state of petrified silence. Every move, quiet and menacing. Enjoying the theatrics of the moment, I string it out a little longer. 'Yes, ladies and gentlemen, this is to be an evenin' that lives in all of our memories for a very long time.'

Before anyone in the room can take in what is happening and react, Harry pushes back his plush chair and stands. He's opposite me, with Ettie to his right. He takes a step back so that everyone in the room is in front of him, and pulls out his own revolver, cocking it in one swift motion. The swivelling of heads is almost comical. From me, to Harry, and back again. Confusion quickly turns to fear. A flicker of recognition in some of their eyes as they start to look past my shaven face and expensive clothes. I can count the passing of time in breaths. There are only three.

The double doors to the left of me swing open with a flourish as Joe enters the room in his typically dramatic fashion, pistol also pointed. The theatrics are not required, considering that he is still dressed in women's attire, though he's sensibly removed his hat and gloves. It's very apparent to all now, he's a man dressed in women's clothing, which in itself is enough to cause a woman sitting two seats from Ettie to shriek and faint in her chair. No-one moves, not even her husband, who just waits and watches while her body slumps uncomfortably across the table.

Joe strides further into the room and throws a

cheeky wink at the toffee-nosed man next to him, who looks particularly shocked. More so when Joe goes on to blow a kiss in his direction. I'm shocked and it flashes through my mind that he's been drinking. Ettie smothers a giggle with her hand and all hell breaks loose in the room before she has time to lower it.

The object of Joe's mocking is furious, his face turns a brilliant red. Launching himself from the table towards Joe, he brings his dinner knife hard into the idiot's shoulder. The impact pulls a guttural cry from Joe's throat and he grabs hold of the man. A scuffle, standing arm-in-arm. A grotesque dance between the two. Until a shot rings out. People cover their ears and others duck to the floor. The shot has come from Joe.

I hold my pistol tighter, unsure of whether to employ it or not. Joe's attacker staggers back, grasping at his thigh, a red stain spreading through the fabric of his pants. The handle of the knife sticks from Joe's shoulder, most of the blade sunk into the flesh and muscle, but Joe stands straighter now that the man is off him. Ettie's gaze is drawn hypnotically to Joe's shoulder, fixated on it. I can see the rising panic on her face as she feels the energy in the room heighten—this isn't what we planned.

It has to be now. I send a second shot cracking through the room and a shower of plaster falls from the ceiling above our heads. My booming voice breaks through Ettie's glazed stare. 'Stand where ye are or I'll shoot ye like dogs!' I growl it, urging myself to be every inch the murderous bastard that they expect me to be. No-one who heard it could any longer doubt who I am. The moment hangs. Silence. Ettie's face watches my own, trying to read whether I'm calm or panicked at the situation in which we find ourselves. I breathe slowly, to look as cool-headed as I can. This is it—will there be uprising and battle from these wealthy men or will they submit? The shuffling around the room stops, eyes back on me, and I see Ettie release the breath that she's been holding.

'I'm Ned Kelly. Put down your weapons. Do not be reckless wit' yer lives.' A rustle of words pass around the room. Confirming their suspicions. I wait for stillness, to speak again. 'It's a pleasure to make your acquaintance, formally like.' All eyes are on me.

I glance at Angus, whose eyes are wide and his mouth slack. Not in his wildest dreams could he have suspected that the man that he's been speaking with all day, the man who he has invited into this circle, is Ned Kelly. Yet here I am, Edward Kelly—wanted bushranger, standing alongside him with my pistol drawn. His face brings me relief. There is no-one in the room who will believe Angus knew what was going on. He looks truly stunned.

The next moments happen quickly, my voice demanding. 'I'll need all the women to move through to the lounge. Joe will look after ye. This won't take long, I assure ye.' I wave my revolver towards Joe, but look at him hard. With the knife still sticking from his shoulder I'm debating whether he is capable of looking after the women on his own. Bending over, I take another, smaller revolver, from my boot and hold it out to Ettie. 'Accompany Joe. I'm sure the ladies'll be glad of yer company.'

I've never been prouder. Ettie doesn't miss a beat, stepping towards me to take the revolver. She strides confidently across the room towards Joe. A swell of whispers again. No-one knew there is a woman in the Kelly Gang. She's played the part of my wife convincingly, but perhaps they've assumed she was here by coercion rather than by active choice. There is no doubting her involvement now.

As Joe and Ettie move to shepherd the women next door, the doors where Joe stood moments before fling open wildly. Dan, dressed in rough clothes and armed, bursts in, breathing heavily. There's another audible intake of breath from the remaining men and I throw him a wry smile. ''Tis alright, Dan.' My voice is steady. I don't want to set anyone off again. The room is a tinderbox that only needs a spark to set it off. 'I've done the introductions, and everythin' is perfectly civilised in here.' Having heard the gunshots, he's left the horses and come barrelling in to help. Arguments or not, the boy is my brother, and clearly he'll give his life for me. Though I'm not sure it's a price I'm willing to pay. *But I may have no choice.*

'Yer timin' is good though, Dan, you'll be able to give us a hand. Go and round up the staff from the kitchens and make sure no-one's gettin' any silly ideas. Head them into the lounge with the women. In fact, you can help Joe. Ettie can stay here beside me.' She nods without a word and moves behind me. I'm acutely aware of making sure she's out of reach of anyone who might think her an easy target.

I indicate everyone should sit. Sir Samuel, quiet for the whole time, stiffens at the suggestion. He's stood watching the scene with red wine glass in hand and not a drop spilled. Now he puts it down and places both hands on the table.

'You may well be Ned Kelly, lad, but you are mistaken if you think that we are going to put up with your underhanded nonsense for a moment longer.' He puffs himself out and I'm shocked at his brazenness. As he opens his mouth to begin again, I cut him short, cold icing my voice.

'Oh, you'll do far more than put up wit' my nonsense tonight, Sir. Tonight I shall be takin' every coin and note that ye have on these premises, and any other valuables that I desire.' I look around the room. 'Ye've a fine house. I'm sure ye'll not miss what we take.'

My gaze falls upon Angus and I wait a few seconds before beginning, almost contemplating about whether to keep going. 'Angus, ye are a good man, a title that I'd not bestow upon many that I meet. I hope these men don't hold it against ye that I fooled meself into yer acquaintance. In fairness, I shall be robbin' ye of your belongings too. I hope ye understand.' Angus nods, dumbstruck. He looks more shocked again, to be singled out, as if I haven't spent the day alongside him, as if I have transformed completely.

'I'll need ye to help me tonight, Angus. Joe normally takes down me words but he's…indisposed like. Fetch a pen an' paper from the desk next door. Hurry back.' Angus moves from the table slowly and deliberately, hands raised in front of him, wanting to give me no cause to do something I'd regret. With Kate next door under the watchful and armed eyes of Joe and Dan, I'm sure he feels he has no choice but to do as requested. Pen in hand, he returns and seats himself back at the dining table. Pushing aside the remaining cutlery, he awaits instructions.

'I want ye to write what I say. *Exactly* what I say.

Dis is to be a letter for those who wish to know my thoughts. To know th' cause and th' purpose of the Kelly Gang.' I pull a chair from beside Angus into the middle of the room and sit. Ettie stands behind me, hands resting on the back of it.

My own emotions, reined in so tightly for the day, feel like they're running out of control as I sit staring at the faces in front. Perhaps my ideas of a republic and freedom from the British rule have waned, but I have a desperate need to be understood. This will be my last chance and I'll not let it slip away. I hate being seen as a criminal and thug, when I see what I've done, what we have all done, as being for a greater cause. I'm sure that Ettie will be furious at the grandstanding, but it's a risk I have to take.

'You are people. We are people. You of the upper classes can no longer ignore the poor of dis country.' I wait for Angus to catch up and only when the scribble of the pen ceases, do I continue. 'Our colony, our country even, may 'ave been bred from the shite of England. But we must become a country where a man is judged on his character and his willingness to work. Not judged by his birth. People like me, what chance do we 'ave? Pegged from the day we're born as no hopers and criminals. Yer givin' us no bloody chance.' That's the truth of it, isn't it? I was only a child when I was thrown into this life of crime. Jim and Dan too. 'My words at Jerilderie were stifled by those lyin', murderous bastards of the Victorian Police Force, but I'll not be silenced again. I didn't want the bloodshed at Stringybark, but we had no choice. Glenrowan was aimed only at the police and that bastard, Hare. We wanted no-one else to die on that day. Anyone with need to fear the Kelly Gang, be warned, throw down your arms and do not be reckless. Get away from the colony of Victoria at haste. Ye can no longer ignore the needs of your fellow men to simply fill your own pockets.'

With all of the passion and self-belief that I can muster, I continue on to every man that sits in the room. 'I am the son of an Irish convict and I was branded as such from th' day that I was born. But in the new country dat is bein' born here and now, there will be a fairer time for all. We've had enough of being treated like second-class citizens in our own country. The poor. The natives. We walk this place like ghosts. Not seen by you others. There'll not be peace in this colony until the corruption and injustice in the Police Force is removed. Until the men who live here can claim land as their own and be afforded every chance for success on that land, without bein' pushed out by the wealthy around them. Even when I'm gone, or I am dead, there will be thousands in line to take my place. To all those who stand ready, I tell ye, rise up until this injustice is gone. If injustice remains, you will live in fear of me, and my people, for all of your lives. I tell ye again, I am a widow's son, outlawed, and I must be obeyed.' Angus puts down the pen as he realises that my flow of words has come to an end. There is no more to be said.

I stand and Harry brings forward a hessian sack, which we fill with money and valuables from the men. Some spit on the floor as they hand over their belongings. I ignore the pathetic display. Let them spit. My blood is up and should they try anything else I'll blow them away. I know that Dan and Joe will be fleecing the women next door.

Bag full, Harry and I discuss the value of tying up

any of those who remain.

'It'd give me a great bloody thrill to tie up Wilson, but I can't see th' point.' Harry nods. 'Their fear'll 'ave to be enough to stop 'em venturing out after us.'

Joe and Dan come back into the room with the women and service staff and what had been a room with the wind taken from it, suddenly crackles with a nervous energy. We are almost out of here. As if sensing that the last chance for any action is here, the mood of the room shifts subtly. There are thoughts whizzing around, almost telepathically, eyes darting, silently urging each other on. Daring each other to be the hero. I'm waiting for it, but it takes a woman to break the inertia and make the first move. She steps away from the group behind Dan.

'You are a dastardly scoundrel, Ned Kelly. I hope that I see you hang for this.' She's small-framed but gutsy, stepping into my path, eyes blazing. The same look that my sister Maggie gets when she's got her dander up for a fight.

'Madam, I suggest ye calm yourself. Before ye incite a rebellion here.' I give a small laugh, wanting to diffuse the tension in the room, but I admire her courage and I want her to know it. 'Though I'll say you're the bravest man I've seen in dis room tonight.' There's a collective intake of breath, and a snigger from Dan behind me.

It's a stupid thing to say and the words taste bitter on my tongue. A red rag to the group of pressed and starched ninnies that surround me. One of the younger men, fuelled on by my insult, launches across the room and rams into my body. He knocks me hard in the side, shoulder-first. Nothing but an 'oof' escapes me, but it causes an enormous ruckus as the other boys jump in. Punches are thrown as Dan drags him from me.

Harry, sensible as always, stands back from the fray, pistols cocked, and bellows on top note, 'Halt, or I'll fell every one of ya!' From my place on the floor, I see the shuffling and movement of legs stop—eyes all on Harry. Dan has the reckless young buck stilled, one arm raised in tight behind his back. Almost to breaking. I stand, slowly, and run a hand across my mouth. The blood, bright red, is smeared on it. I taste the metallic sting of blood from inside my cheek and lip. We're lucky that Harry's quick thinking has stopped an all-in riot.

My eyes move to the boy—that's what he looks like pinned in position. 'Ye stupid bloody bastard, what are ye playing at? Do ye not know who I am? You're lucky ye haven't got yourself killed already.' The others in the room look decidedly uncomfortable at the heightened tension. As if on cue, Dan lifts the arm a little higher and a squeak escapes his captive.

I bring myself to standing proper and get some air back into my lungs. I take two large strides across to where Dan has the fella restrained, pull back my arm and smack him fair in the face with my fist. Blood pours from his nose, clearly broken, and his head lolls to the side, a limp marionette. With no-one holding his strings, the boy slumps heavy in Dan's arms, who holds him for only a second, before letting his weight collapse to the floor.

I look around at the others gathered. 'When he wakes up, ye can let him know that he's lucky I never put a fuckin' bullet in him.' To the faces I know, all I say is, 'Let's go.'

The woman that started the confrontation drops

to her knees alongside the felled boy. She's not done yet. 'I'll see you hang for this, Kelly.' She sounds so sure, her voice so clear and confident that it pulls me up short.

I stop and turn to face her. All I can say is, 'Well ma'am, maybe you will.'

***

The night air is frigid and it whistles past my ears as we gallop away from the homestead. Thunderous hoof beats crash around me, echo off the darkness engulfing us. That's the thing about night, it can feel like an enemy or friend, depending on your need. And tonight it is very much our friend. Ettie is beside me, dress flaring out behind her, and my breath catches for a moment watching her from the corner of my eye. That girl, leaning forward over her horse's neck, racing alongside me is a woman from my dreams. She is meant to be beside me; always.

We are safely away, all five of us, though Joe looks as if he's worse for wear. He rides in a way that shows he's sore. Still, it is a feat that I thought nigh-on impossible three hours ago. I had always thought that the money could be taken, but not with so little resistance. I guess when you have a lot, losing a little is not worth losing your life over. I hope they continue thinking that and stay put in the homestead.

Meeting the Kelly Gang will no-doubt make a good story for all those society types. Give them something to boast about for years to come. The young fella nursing a busted face will show his crooked nose proudly. Other than Joe ending up with a dinner knife protruding from his shoulder, the night has been smooth.

Perhaps him shooting a guest so early in the piece had been a stroke of good luck for us? Everyone had been a lot less willing to speak out against us when the man next to him had a bullet hole through his leg. We'd thought to remove the knife from Joe's flesh, but with the slowly spreading red stain on his shirt, I don't want to increase the bleeding until we're well gone.

Now that we are away, it's a race against time. We are gambling on the audacity and guts of the dinner guests. Surely no-one will go against the orders of Ned Kelly? Sir Samuel had blustered about as Harry and I collected the money from each of the men. Despite his protests though, no-one else had spoken up and he'd made no attempt to thwart us. Being that it was his own dinner party, I daresay the grandstanding was for the benefit of tomorrow's papers. The man with the gunshot hole through his leg had seemed enough to keep them quiet, though even he would be certain to live. I'd been the last to leave and given the warning for no-one to leave the house before daybreak.

'We've eyes and ears everywhere. Ye do not become a wanted man of my standin', without loyal supporters to assist ye 'long the way. I've trusted men lyin' in wait around these hills. They're warned not to harm anyone in this company. But, if ye leave before the sun is well-risen I cannot guarantee your safety.' I looked pointedly at the man with the injured leg. 'We wouldn't want any more unfortunate accidents now would we? No little *misunderstandings?*' I couldn't resist the final poke at Wilson as I'd looked back a final time.

I'm betting my life and Ettie's and those of all the boys, on the fact that the men in there, for the most part, are cowards. I hope that they won't risk losing their lives for a small chance at glory. A chance of capturing the Kellys. If they wait until daybreak, as we've planned, before heading into Ballarat, we'll have a good day's advance on the force that will be assembled. We'll need every minute of it.

The ride into the night, with the chill running through me and the success of the robbery, is exhilarating. I'm racing against the clock, towards my future and for the first time, I think I might be winning. Getting this far in our plan was never a given and I know that Dan and Joe have had serious reservations. But here we are sprinting through the bush together, blood beating in our ears and sacks full of riches, banging against the flanks of the horses. Money to buy us new lives. We are so close to freedom that I can taste it. Coming through the iron gates of Ercildoune, great oaks overhanging, it's a downhill ride to Burrumbeet. The moon glints on the water's surface—a beacon calling to us.

I know that Dan and Steve, along with Harry, will head north. Across the border at Echuca, was Harry's thought. Harry is charged with taking final letters and some of the money to the kids; they'll need some help getting started on their new land. I know that Jim and Kate will look after them until Ma is out, without Dan and me there. Jim has to stay on the straight and narrow path that I wasn't able to, to be the steady force for the family now. Better himself. Harry volunteered himself for the job. We knew that he would be the least suspicious and recognisable of all of us. It's lifted a weight from my shoulders, that this last message will get through to my family. My last words to them from Australia's sandy shores. Perhaps my last words ever.

Joe is the unknown quantity amongst us. Ettie and I have agreed to keep our heads down before we try to board a ship to Ireland. It's a risky move, but it will give us time to find the right ship. Time for the dust to settle and for the police to follow an imagined lead…hopefully away from us.

Joe is still unsure. As we gallop through the gateway, Dan yells to him, 'Next stop, Queensland!' But he shakes his head. Losing Aaron, and now us, I imagine his mind is swimming with confusion. But now I fear it's too late to help my friend, my brother, get out of his own head and find himself a future. There are no hours to discuss plans and weigh up options. Now, there is only time for action. I've reassured myself for weeks that when the time comes he will come with me. I've been delusional. In the darkness of this ride, with the light of our future on the horizon, I know he won't.

The ride to Burrumbeet is swift. The frosty night air hasn't touched me. In what seems barely a blink, we are almost at the lake's edge to find Steve and a change of horses in the bush. He emerges from the shadows, exactly where we've planned to meet, on the western banks of Burrumbeet. Our steady horses and packs ready. Steve's joy and relief at our arrival, all essentially intact, is obvious.

Ettie pulls her horse to a stop, barely, and jumps from it to throw herself into Steve's embrace. I watch them as they shut out the rest of the world, in this circle of sibling affection and pleasure that each other still lives and breathes. Any annoyance towards Steve is gone. Whether this ends badly or well for us, this will likely be the last time Ettie and Steve see each other in this life. With her insistence to join her destiny with mine, she's cut her own life from any kin she has ever known. The inevitability hits her now, in this moment of night, as she clings to Steve.

The others pull up beside us, with barely a word spoken between them, and set about seeing to their regular horses; animal and man greeting each other as old friends. The ones who have carried us here are unsaddled and left grazing nearby. A quick pat on the neck as a thank you for their part in tonight. Success gives way to resignation. Everything is coming to an end. *Hasn't it come to an end already?*

Though it's dark, past midnight, a kookaburra is disturbed and sets to its laugh on a branch in a nearby tree. Its cackle breaks through the silence of the bush around us, scolding us for disrupting an otherwise peaceful night. The laugh has an edge to it, as if nature itself is laughing at me. *You can't all get out of here, you know that already.* It taunts me. I hold my breath until it stops. The feeling isn't as quick to leave.

Our packs lie amongst the undergrowth; bare necessities only. Though we own little but our names. The others shuffle around, readying themselves for the moment that rushes towards us; that has been coming since the train derailed at Glenrowan all those months ago. The end of the Kelly Gang.

The younger boys and Harry are the first to get away, after dividing up our take. There are embraces all around. How quickly they are done. The decision to leave is Steve's. 'Well, we'll be away then,' is all he says. Ettie is inconsolable as she clings to his neck and I feel like crying myself as I watch her pain and tears. All of us know that this moment is inevitable, but the threat of it had seemed so unreal. To part ways had seemed out of reach. The chance to actually say goodbye has been so remote, that we've ignored it.

Ettie kisses the stubbly cheek of her older brother and he tells her to be safe.

'Live a good life, Ettie. Be happy,' he shoots me a quick grin, 'And look after this great lump for us will ya?' Again, he's the Steve I know. Our troubles laid to rest. He puts his hand in mine, a shake that becomes an embrace.

'She's ya only job now. Nothin' else matters but gettin' her safe and away.' I nod. This is his blessing to us. Would he have given it so freely if we were to meet again? I'll never know.

I hand Harry the letters for Jim and the girls, and he grabs my hand.

'The day you came knockin' lad, was a good one. You take that girl of yours and make a life.' There is an embrace for both of us. There is much that we owe this man, but the time for words has come and gone. It is only goodbye that's left.

Dan stands to the side, the brother who has walked in my shadow. He steps forward and embraces me. 'You've made th' decision, Daniel. Don't hide away. Ye are your own master now. Take every day you've been given.' I grab him and he holds on tight. It's hard to break away. I worry he doesn't know how to live outside of our loud, overwhelming family of brothers, always telling him what to do. He'll have free will for the first time in his life. I worry he'll be too afraid to use it. The three mount up and give a final wave. They set off into the bush at a trot, a kick then a canter. None look back. Ettie stands, hand raised, until Steve is swallowed by the darkness. I hear only one sob escape her. She catches herself and wipes her eyes, looking to me. 'They're really gone.' *They're really gone.*

Only Joe remains. She moves to him despite their clashes. Ettie holds him for this final time, her last link to the life we know.

'Let me look at ya shoulder, Joe. I can wrap it.' He shrugs her hand off. 'Nah. I'm headin' to a camp. The Chinese there'll have medicines. They'll fix me up right.' His decision is made. Ettie moves away and I lean in to hug his good side—my other brother. My chosen brother. The embrace is long and heartfelt, and he returns it. Leaving Joe is difficult. Made more so by my feelings that I've let him down, this man that I love. But there's no time for me to convince him anew, which is why, maybe, he's done it this way.

'Be safe, brother.' There are no more words. No more time. He pulls himself into the saddle, wincing as he grabs the reins. He nods at me one more time, a smile on his face. One which doesn't reach his eyes. I hear him whistle a tune as his horse moves away. I wonder if he does that to ease my mind, or whether his heart is truly as light as that tune?

***

I can feel the wet tracks down my cheek, but I can't wipe them away. I try and struggle, but nothing moves. My hands, my arms are limp and unmoving. The tears fall, one, and another, each following the trail of its brother before it.

I couldn't save him.

Even in my dreams, I couldn't save him.

***

Of course he is dead.

My friend. The man who I counted as a brother: dead. And I can't believe it. I read the tiny, black print, along with the rest of the country. I'm only one of many to find out he has died in the dark, smoky hovel of an opium den, in Ararat. No doubt the same one. Those inky, printed words are enough to send a crack through my very being. Ettie takes the paper from my hands. It is a week old. Found lying as rubbish in the road—it is sheer dumb luck that we know our friend is dead. Her eyes scan the words, but my voice breaks.

'It says they hung his body on a doorway. Dead. For everyone to come and gawk at. Even takin' bloody photographs with it. Who does that to a man? He weren't no fuckin' animal.' I can't hold the sobs in any longer and I can feel the tears and snot running down my face. Ettie puts her arms around me and we stay like that until my sobs quiet. My eyes feel raw, as does my heart. I sit on the dirt, camped beside the road between Ballarat and Adelaide, not far from the township of Nhill. We'd been through there the night before, avoiding the Cobb and Co. coach and scavenging for food and news. We had found both. She begins again to read the newspaper. Capturing a member of the Kelly Gang has made front page news. Her voice breaks the silence around us. 'Police have credited Thomas Curnow, a school teacher from Glenrowan, with assisting them. The teacher, who was also held captive by the Kellys at the Glenrowan Inn earlier in the year, gave them the lead to capture the killer. Police have revealed that Mr. Curnow reported seeing Ned Kelly himself departing a Ballarat train, which he believed had travelled from Ararat. This knowledge only came to light after Mr. Curnow read of the gang's callous robbery near the town, weeks later.'

I interrupt her. 'Thomas fuckin' Curnow. It was him.' *It's always him.*

Ettie looks at me with query in her eyes and her voice tender, 'Ya didn't tell me ya'd seen 'im at the station.'

All I can do is shake my head. 'I don't know what's real anymore. I've seen 'im so often. Jesus, Joe. Why the hell couldn't ye just ride away wit' th' others?'

Ettie's hand runs back and forth across the page as she reads the details of his death. She stops and places the paper to her chest. 'Oh, thank Christ.' She wipes her eye with her hand. 'He were already dead, Ned. When the coppers got there, he were already dead. It weren't the coppers, it was the poppy.' My head in my hands, it's a small relief that I feel for my friend who had needed to escape so desperately.

The last line of the article is almost as large as the headline and it sends a gallop of fear running through me. WHERE IS THE REST OF THE KELLY GANG?

***

I dreamed of Joe last night, after I read his body had been hung from a doorway for one and all to gape at. I had been trying to reach him, to take him down. To carry him. The dream jolted me back to consciousness, a cold sweat covering my body and my heart drumming a rapid beat in my chest. I woke feeling sick with the grief and the knowledge that I had not done enough. I woke with the smell of rotting flesh and sweet poppy in my nose, as if I'd been standing right beside him.

The piece in the newspaper left me questioning. What more I could have done? Would he have come with Ettie and me if I'd pressed him harder? I doubt it. But now I will never know. On a night, not so long ago, wrapped in her arms in Smeaton, Ettie had asked me to put her first. That's what I'd done. But at what cost? In life there was never an easy option. Never a choice without a consequence. And hasn't that been my life? A long list of choices and consequences.

Joe had told us little of his plans. What he had said, he had lied about. And, if I was honest with myself, I had known that it was a lie. And I still did nothing. He is one more body which I can add to the count of people that I've killed. As surely as if I had shot him, I've killed Joe Byrne.

I wonder whether he had always planned to stop at Ararat, needing to escape from himself again. Was it the knowledge that no-one was waiting for him, or encouraging him to get to safety, that pushed him over the edge? At another time, Aaron would have been there—his counter-point. Aaron had been the one who had known Joe from when he was a boy, who had shared his adventures and his dreams. But Joe had ended him, so now there was no-one. I'd left him. Dan and Steve too. That kind of hopelessness and emptiness must eat away at your soul.

I can only hope that on that night, in the arms of the poppy, that the pretty girl with the dead eyes had convinced him to embrace her as well. That he had gratefully accepted her body as solace against a world that had become too hard. And that my friend had found some sense of peace from her, the pipe, and the knowledge that he would see Aaron again. *I love you, brother.*

***

Even news of Joe can't stop us. Ettie and I must keep moving. *Yes, this must end soon.* The days and the nights meld into one another as we inch ourselves closer to Adelaide. We move at night. The days we spend hidden, trying to get some rest. It's in these waking hours that we talk of the boys. That Ettie talks of Steve. Whispered words of love and worry.

'He always loved to watch the sun set, my Steve. Even as a boy. Ma always said that. He'd take off and find a place on his own to sit in the quiet and watch the colours bein' painted 'cross the sky. I hope he's seein' 'em now.' I assure her that the flat, red expanses of dirt that he calls home now, will bring quiet, beautiful sunsets. It brings a small smile to her face. Each morning, the rising sun will signify that he is both alive and living, which are two very distinct things. Things that we'd all thought we wouldn't have.

'He won't waste it, ya know. Steve'll do more than just survive. He'll watch those sunsets and he'll know how lucky we are.'

'I just hope that his dreams of that tightenin' noose, will leave him be. I hope his sleep is settled and safe. Even if he's on his own.' She tightens her own grasp on me as she says it.

I hope, as she does, that as Steve has galloped away from Dan, and away from the life of bushranging that has stained their early years, that the two felt their future lay in their own hands for the first time. Maybe they hope one day we will all be together again. That we will be able to tell each other of our dreams and the sunsets that we have seen in the years since we said our farewells.

Ettie is desperate for news about Steve. She scans any paper that we come across. But I convince her any news we see of Steve will only be bad for him. Better to see nothing at all. I know that part of her heart broke that night at Burrumbeet, with the knowledge that she would never see her brother again. He had been her last connection to home and family. Her pain as we rode away from the lake had been as great as if he'd died a bloody death on the dirt floor of Glenrowan Inn the night we'd taken down the train.

We know north is the safest place for them. That the red earth will stretch itself endlessly in front of them, to what will seem to be the edge of the earth. It will become a landscape of safety, with no-one nearby, no threats of being seen, being shot, being captured. The weeks that they will take to travel north will be happy ones, with these two friends starting a new life.

She's a realist though; her upbringing has made it so.

As much as she dreams of their happiness, she has imagined their final farewell, when the two friends will stop being the cruel, wanted men of their reputations and return instead to being the cocky-but-unsure boys that they are at heart. Agreeing to go their separate ways is the smarter option. The safer option. It's what they had decided. For Steve, she imagines that the goodbye with Dan will be even more difficult than their own. Would the two embrace? Would they linger? She lets her questions hang in the air to me, as if hoping for someone to answer them. Would Steve leave first? She wishes that she knew, but I can tell her nothing.

Only nothing.

***

Our days have merged into weeks.

It has been weeks since we arrived in Adelaide. Weeks since we found ourselves a ship to Ireland. Weeks filled with me watching this endless, rolling ocean. My initial feelings of being trapped aboard this floating cork, being worried about any person who might notice us, have given way to a feeling of incredible freedom. Ettie radiates happiness and a peace of mind which I've only ever imagined in her. The vastness that surrounds us is agreeing with us both.

Our trip overland from Burrumbeet was an uncomfortable and hungry one. The seventeen days of hard and careful riding to get to the Port of Adelaide, where we could find passage on a ship to Ireland, was tough. I think Ettie would call them cruel. We'd slept rough, avoided anyone, stayed bush as much as possible. My fear for Ettie was overwhelming at times. I worried about what I was putting her through. Much of the food we'd packed was gone within a week. Though we'd spent time in each other's arms under the shade of eucalyptus trees, or talked for hours on end, the overwhelming feeling was worry and dread. By the time we'd arrived at the port, we'd been exhausted. I watched her become a ghost of a woman as every day passed, as her hunger grew, then ceased. On our arrival, I'd gone at once to secure us passage. And luck was again on our side.

There's been no sign that anyone on the ship has any suspicion of who we really are. We are just Mr. and Mrs. O'Brien, heading back to our homeland. I'm clean shaven, my wife on my arm and a long way removed from the rough and dirty bushranger whose face has been on the wanted posters and the newspapers for the past two years, terrorising the colony of Victoria.

This isn't a passenger ship that we're on, which suits us well, the less people on board the better for us. A story of being stranded, a family disaster, and a sum handed over quietly to the Captain was all it took for us to secure a berth. We are just another type of cargo being delivered. We make sure to keep our heads down, which suits all on board.

The two of us aren't married yet, but I've sworn to Ettie that we will be in the weeks ahead, as soon as we land in Dublin. She nods, knowing that I've always been a man of my word. She's shown the courage to leave her family and homeland. Given up everything she's ever known, the only place she's ever walked, to be with me. I will be her only family, and I don't take her sacrifice for granted.

I can see with every day we get further from the shores of Australia, her despair at saying goodbye to Steve has slowly given way to hope. We are starting to believe that we may really have gotten away with our lives. Escaped with our freedom.

She looks over the bow of the ship, her back to me. She is almost untouchable, she is so beautiful. Peaceful, contentment etched on her face. I come up behind her and she doesn't flinch as I snake my hand around her waist.

'I'm glad to see that ye sickness is gone, my girl. Ye seem happier now.' She only nods at me, a small smile creeping onto her face. 'I mean, look at ye here. You're a proper sea dog now that you've found ye legs.'

I feel the same sense of peace. I find that I'm even losing track of days and dates.

Maybe a life on the sea would have suited me. A thought I'd had on more than one occasion during our voyage. I haven't needed to gain my sea legs, it seems I've been born with them. I've begun to relax and enjoy the empty openness of the sea. It is a balm to my strung nerves.

A life is something that I haven't counted on having for a very long time. Especially not one shared with Ettie. She is someone who I love completely; a different love to the one that I saw my ma endure with my father. For me, our partnership is made all the sweeter in this new life, where I will never be Edward Kelly again, that she will know me wholly. There will be no lies between us. At night, when the faces of the men I have killed arrive in my nightmares, I won't have to make excuses to her about them. When I cry for Joe, she will know. I will be able to draw strength from her.

Parting from Australia means leaving my life as a Kelly, parting from my ma, my brothers and sisters, which is sorrowful. I feel gut-wrenching sadness and guilt at deserting them. I feared that these feelings would consume me. But the further from my homeland that this boat travels, the lighter I feel. I've made the right choice.

She turns to me, that smile still there. Without a

word she takes my hand and places it onto her belly, low, where I feel the smallest of bumps beneath her dress.

'Yes, we're very happy to be out on the open seas now,' she says.

The shores which bound me to Australia were my shackles, of birth and of misguided choices. I find that they are set free through my escape from my country. The men on board our ship say that we shall be in sight of Ireland in the next few weeks. My first look at the green hills of my father's childhood, and of his father before him, for thousands of years. Never did I think that Ireland would fall under my feet. I won't be a Kelly by name, but this land will know me. Its air runs in my veins. I am sure of it. This Ireland feels like I am returning home, and she is giving me the gift of life. For me and Ettie and my children after me. And such a life it will be.

***

The rocking is relentless. To and fro, to and fro. It's not what I expected.

I had imagined the ship to be gentler, not this endless jolting that won't stop.

Then it does. The movement halts and a singular thought reaches my mind. This isn't a ship.

Nothingness surrounds me—and I know that this is the last time that I will be able to forget.

I cannot escape any longer.

A light cracks through. Blinding. I look ahead. It's time to look now.

Ned, you have to look.

PART 3

THE FINAL JOURNEY

I have no memory of the trip from Glenrowan. Of my arrival in Melbourne. Only the movement. The jolting and constant whir of the wheels and the darkness. There is no rocking boat. No Ireland.

They tell me I was transported in a police cart; a blue wooden box with barred windows and drawn by two horses down the highway to Melbourne. Ironic really—it may as well have been a casket. It seems it's all to end in a wooden box for me in the near future. Why bother with the middle man?

The lurching trip to Melbourne has been filled with hallucinations. Hundreds of miles of jouncing giving

my tired, injured mind a way to escape from the reality that
is my life. They were such beautiful delusions. I wanted it
so badly to be real. But none of it was. The moment I
opened my eyes, my life and dreams slipped away.

I'm barely clinging on to life, that is the truth.
More than 25 wounds mark my body from the Glenrowan
guns. So she tells me. My left hand is ruined, not that I'll
be having need of it for too much longer. My right foot
was so badly injured that my boot was cut from it. The
great bustling woman who nurses me told me all this with
a smile on her face; she's very proud of the patch-up job
that she's done.

'I thank ye, ma'am. I'll be headin' to the gallows in
th' finest of health, I can assure ye.' I don't mean it as a
compliment, but she nods and smiles at me anyway. She is
real. This life I'm in is real.

Glenrowan is a blur. Flashing back, little-by-little,
each day that I sit in this cell looking at bare walls. Nothing
is clear, just sparks of memory; a sound, a smell. I
remember hearing the train in the distance. The noise of
the wheels on the track echoing through the night air. I
had given the call to the boys once we heard the train.
There was a blur of bodies. I was looking for Dan.

I remember knowing that everything was going
wrong. I knew the train was stopping before it reached the
town. We were scrambling—people everywhere in the inn.
And then the panic when we realised we were surrounded.
Dan was crying. He and Steve hugged each other and cried
like the boys they were. I stood there firing. I remember
thinking that we were all dead.

And they are. Joe and Steve. My brother. All dead.
And I the only one to still breathe, though only for a

moment longer. It was my fault. I let Curnow go. Thomas bloody Curnow. I was an arrogant bastard about the limping teacher. I let him go, not believing he'd go against us. But defy me, he did. He flagged the train with the scarf from his sister's neck on the outskirts of the town. I haven't been able to forget it. Even in my delusions he's haunted me. His face taunting me.

Other faces taunt me too. My fractured mind mourns the loss of Ettie and Harry. Harry, nothing more than a fragment of my mind. How can that be? How can I mourn what has never even been? He has been the father I've yearned for. A man I can rely on. But he's only been born of my desires.

Ettie is here, of course, but not the Ettie that has lain in my arms and shared my dreams. She's not the woman who is carrying my child—the one who will share my life. She is all but a stranger, a girl I barely know. Ettie is still my love, but only one that could have been. She waited for me, as we had agreed, but I let her down. I never came to her from Glenrowan. I'll never know how we could have loved, or how she might have changed me. No Angus. No Kate. No escape. My life is nothing but unrealised possibilities.

I wish I'd died in the first wooden box that they'd carried me in. I'd rather that than be stuck in this bare cell—hard and cold. I'd at least be saved this waiting and thinking, which is tormenting me, not just killing me. I miss the freedom of the bush and being the master of my own movement. Here I can't even take a shit without someone making comment on it.

'I'm better off hangin' than spendin' the next thirty years locked away in dis hell hole.' I tell anyone who'll listen. But I can't help but wonder. What will the world be like in 1910? I do think of it—but I know the truth of it is that I'll never know. No matter how much I might want to live, I have no choice in it.

In this frigid cell, I miss the comfort and companionship of the boys. My brothers, all of them. They're gone and the thought of it is the only thing that can bring me to tears, though I close my eyes to hide it. Tuck my head into my shirt and let my sorrow spill onto my chest. I should be dead with them. Why would I be the only one? It's a cruelty beyond belief.

The Ettie of my imaginings would tell me that I'm brooding, that I shouldn't give up hope yet, but I don't know what else there is to think of but my impending death. I see no reason for hope. I am icy. It seeps into my bones from the stone that surrounds me: walls, floor, ceiling. Though the bed is wooden slats, with the thinnest of bedrolls, it is dry and relatively comfortable given how I've been living these past months. But I'm isolated, away from any other prisoners. There is no noise, no light, save the small amount that creeps through the barred windows, into my cell. It's like being stuck in the darkest parts of my mind—locked in, with nothing but regrets and memories. Maybe this is how Joe felt after Aaron? Trapped. Isolated. No way to escape the horror of his memories. Because that was real. Joe went to his death at Glenrowan mourning his friend, tormented by the life he had seen drain from his eyes.

The exercise yard I see each day is little better than my cell. If I look up I can see a small rectangle of sky, beyond the tower of hard walls. A sliver of blue in a mass of grey. There is nothing but laps of dirt. I get to tramp around that bare expanse for an entire hour each day. I am never out there when the sun might be above me, shining directly onto my body to warm me. Wouldn't want a prisoner like Ned Kelly to feel warmth or comfort—oh no!

It's not only the walls which send the cold through me. Sitting in these cells, pacing the tiny confines, I hear whispers. Murmurings that Aaron wasn't the bastard traitor I thought he was, or at least not to Joe. Could I blame Aaron for wanting to save his mate, at my own expense? Maybe he was a smarter man than I, and could see our destiny was a doomed one. His betrayal of us had a price: Joe's life. He had tried to protect his brother in the only way he knew how. I'm grateful Joe didn't know. It would have sent him into madness.

The only things that warm my heart now are the letters of hope that Ettie and my family send me, in their words and their wishes. And the thought that the boys will be there to greet me, at the end, and I'll embrace them again. I hope that they're pleased to see me.

***

My note told her not to visit, that she shouldn't entwine her name with mine anymore than it already was. I am concerned for her life and her reputation, but that's not my only reason for telling her to keep her distance. I don't want her to see me locked away; confined, hopeless and helpless. I'm less of a man in here, and I don't want her to witness it. But she ignores my words and my warnings. Maybe the Ettie I've known in my mind is not so far removed from the girl I love in the flesh.

She enters under a cloak, pulled high around her, and speaks my name quietly to the gaoler on duty. She hasn't given them her real name, instead coming in as a Kelly, as Kate and Maggie have told her to. I imagine in ten years, twenty years, fifty years, when they speak of my capture, someone may look at these ledgers and all they will see is the name of another Kelly visiting my cell. There'll be no understanding that my Ettie has come to console me and love me while she can. Why should I care what they think? I will know.

I watch her, restrained, as she enters dressed all in black. Black dress, black woollen shawl knitted by her own hand. What other colour could she wear, given the circumstances?

'You came.' It seems the only thing to say. I thought this moment wouldn't arrive after my note had been sent from the gaol.

'Did ya really think that I wouldn't come?' She shakes her head at me. 'You forget that I loved ya 'afore you were anythin' other than Ned.' She puts a hand on mine, still chained to the other, as she quiets her voice. 'Do ya forget that I would have loved ya forever, gone away together, if this had only gone a different way.' Her face is grey in here, her eyes smudged with sleepless nights. Her sweet face marked with sadness makes my heart creak in my chest.

'I've missed you.' A dull cry to the hopelessness of our situation. I grasp her small hand in mine.

'You're as captured and chained as I am, me girl. I'm sorry. More than you'll ever know.'

The gaoler on duty is decent and allows us some privacy. He turns his back to us in the cell and stands just outside, albeit with the door wide open, and my hands chained. She runs her fingers over my hands, as if trying to store away in her mind every bump and scar that covers my gnarly fingers.

I can't quite believe that she's here in the flesh and talking to me. My tortured mind is having trouble deciphering the real from the imagined. We have a familiarity between us. But the life that I imagined, the moments that we've shared, and the way I've touched her and held her, have been all my own delusions. There is a closeness between us, a yearning, but we're divided by a distance that we've never broached—and now we never will. Her body will always be a dream to me, and I to her. I don't know which is worse, to have lost what we were, or to never have had it in the first place.

She is more reserved in reality, here in this cell, faced with what is happening in the now. Less the carefree girl I have loved in my dreams, and more my brother's sister. But she holds my hand. It hangs there, as does the silence, as thick as the confessionals of my childhood.

'I waited for ya. Like I said I would.' Her mouth turns upwards, though there is sadness behind her eyes. 'I waited all night, and the next day. I would have come, ya know. I didn't sleep til I heard it was lost.'

I nod. She meets my eyes and I try to stay light but my voice is strangled. 'Maybe it's better dis way. I've killed Steve. I couldn't bear to take ye too. And that's what happens to th' people I love. People who love me.' The silence is heavy. 'All of these people, dey think I'm a monster. A killer. Someone who doesn't feel. I've let 'em believe it in a way. Actin' bigger than I am.' I know that I am burdening this slip of a girl that I've loved, and love still. But there is no-one else who can hear my secrets. I don't want a priest to hold them. But this girl, my girl, she can hold onto my secrets for me. Until we meet again.

'You're no monster.' She whispers it.

'No. I'm not. I'm a fool. A bloody fool, whose belief in th' good of people is goin' to get me hanged. Damn Curnow to hell. Did you know that I let him go?' She says nothing. Just listens. 'I let him and his wife go from the hotel. Last thing I told him was, 'Go quietly to bed, and don't dream too loud.' What an arrogant fuckin' thing to say.' My voice chokes, caught in my throat. 'Serves me right. It should be me dead in the ground. Not Steve or Joe. Not Dan.' My voice catches on my baby brother's name.

We hear the man on the other side of the door cough. He sounds as distant as he will ever be from the two of us. She leans into me, moving into the space that I created trying to bring the physical distance between us that I don't feel in my heart. I tense when she breaches the boundary but she squeezes my hand and moves in close, until her lips are almost pressed against my ear.

'Dan is alive.' Her hand squeezes even tighter and she moves back slightly so that she can look into my eyes, checking that I've heard. She leans in again. 'He made it out of the inn—it wasn't his body they found. He's made it to Queensland, ya Maggie's had word.' As she pulls away, I grab her against me with a rattle of chains. My head pushes into her neck and I let out a sharp sob against her. I cling to her like a man holding onto life itself. Relief floods through me. He's alive. I lean in to kiss her, cupping her face in my tied hands, my eyes tracing her face in the same way that hers have run over my hands only moments before. I kiss her. Gentle, consoling; not the hungry kisses I've thought of. But the fire is there, as I knew it would be.

She is still close, but moves her face a little to speak to me. 'Some of the boys brought the bodies, well, Steve's and Joe's anyway, to Mrs. Skillion's hut and they was given a proper wake and we buried 'em both.' There is silence except for the creaks and moans of the gaol around us. She hesitates, looks as if she's weighing something up, unsure whether to share it with me or not.

'Go on, girl. Now's not th' time to worry 'bout what you're goin' to tell me.' She nods.

'Dick had words with the coppers at Glenrowan—at McDonell's. He told 'em if they interfered with the boys' funerals they'd have another fight on their hands.' I shake my head, eyes downcast.

'You tell Dick he's no' to get himself caught up in dis mess. You've already lost one brother, ye need not lose another one.' I take in a big breath. 'The fight is lost— that's on my head. I lost us our chance.' I breathe in huge gulps of air.

She waits for me to compose myself. I sit, still holding her hand before she sits beside me on my cot. 'Hope is not lost yet, my love. There are protests happenin', petitions are bein' signed with thousands of signatures—tens of thousands—from all across the Colony. Surely they have to take notice of that!' Her eyes are warm, speaking from the heart as she is. I shrug in response.

'Have ya given up, Ned?' She touches the stubble of my chin. Gently. 'I see the light fallin' away from your eyes. Have ya lost all hope?'

Another shrug, but my head drops low, to rest on her hands that I clasp together. My left hand is weak and can barely hold hers. If I was to ever leave this gaol, I would be little better than a cripple with my hand the way it is. I breathe in the smell of her hands, feeling their softness beneath my cheek. Unsure what is worse, to live as a cripple without her. Or to not live at all.

'I've not given up, but I'm resigned. Resigned to the future, to me fate.' I stare at her directly. 'I'm resigned to the fact that I'll never see ye, or hold ye again. That I've never been able to hold ye like I want to.' She draws in a breath. I hold her gaze and can see that she is struggling to take air into her lungs, is forcing her airways to open, as the realisation of our future comes to her with the force that has buffeted me for weeks. This is our only moment.

***

I have sat in this court for days, watching man after man come to the stand and swear an oath, then proceed to spill lies and hate in my direction. A seemingly endless stream of witnesses to my crimes. There is always two sides to a story. But to them there is only one. No-one around me has been able to see it for the lies that they are. The Judge sits, pompous and arrogant, on his chair at the front of the court and nods solemnly at each witness statement. Each one another nail in my coffin—or more likely another knot in the noose. For I know that it's the hangman's rope that awaits me.

I sit passively. Something I've never been good at in this short life of mine. I've had my own character testimonials come forward of course, but the judge has waved them away or shaken his head. Has let his eyes glaze over and roam the courtroom, often assailing upon me and trying to stare the truth from me. There is nothing anyone can say to prove him otherwise. I am a Kelly, so I'm guilty. I'm a dead man.

And so, the trial comes to an end.

Judge Barry turns his body to me to ask if I have any statement to make. At this point, with my fate evidently sealed, I see no reason to show respect or manners where none is due.

'Well, it's rather too late for me to speak now.' I see the Judge sit up a little in his high-back chair. I knew the imperious prig wasn't expecting any sort of reply. 'I had thought of speakin' this mornin' and all day, but there was little use, and there is little use in blamin' anyone now. Nobody knew about my case except myself, and I wish I had insisted on bein' allowed to examine the witnesses myself.' I throw a withering glance at the pathetic excuse for council that I've been afforded. 'If I had examined them, I am confident I would have thrown a different light on the case.' I haven't though. I've known as well as any, that there will only be one conclusion to this trial.

There is a rumble of discord around the courtroom, some exclamations of disbelief that I dare speak in such a manner to someone as high-and-bloody-mighty as Judge Redmond Barry. The gavel smacks down twice to bring the rabble to order. I hear the undercurrent and whispers that surround me and I cut their suppositions short. 'It is not that I fear death. I fear death as little as to drink a cup o' tea.' It is the knowledge of Dan's escape that fuels my words. At this moment, I feel as invincible as I did standing beside the railway tracks at

Glenrowan, waiting for the train to arrive, when we had been on the cusp of greatness. I feel the same moment arriving now. This moment where I know I'm about to become more than a wanted man. A mouthpiece for the downtrodden. These words are the ones that might follow me into history, when my worm-riddled body is gone to the ground.

I push on. 'On the evidence that has been given, no juryman could give any other verdict. That is my opinion. If I had examined the witnesses I would have shown matters in a different light, because no man understands the case as I do myself. I do not blame anybody—neither Mr. Bindon nor Mr. Gaunson. But Mr. Bindon knew nothing about my case. I lay blame on myself that I did not get up yesterday and examine the witnesses, but I thought that if I did so it would look like bravado and flashness.'

The crowd in the court erupts and there is yelling on top note to bring order to the court. Barry's face is red from the exertion, the downward tilt to his mouth exacerbated by his distaste for my words. I can see that he wants to argue me down, this learned man in his robes. He has all the power of the court and yet he still rallies to cause ultimate humiliation to me and my family. And I decide, here and now, that I will not have it. The words will spill out of me in this court, my last chance that I have to bring about any justice in this life of mine. I will have my say.

'A day will come at a bigger court than this, when we shall see which is right and which is wrong. No matter how long a man lives, he is bound to come to judgment somewhere, and as well here as anywhere.' I still for a moment. I know how to hold a crowd. It's been one of my greatest gifts. I can capture a man's interest and his trust. I see that I have the court hanging on my every word. In a different world, a fairer one, I might have used these talents on the other side of the law or even as a man in government. Only a dream for a rebel Kelly like me.

'It will be different the next time they have a Kelly trial, for they are not all killed.' I look around and see them taking measure of my statement. Court reporters scribble madly. These words recorded forever. The image of Dan flashes into my mind; my little brother who may well be reading these words in a matter of days. I don't want to uncover his miracle escape but I want him to know, as I swing from the rope, I know he is safe. That I know he made it out, and he has my blessing. This is the gift that I can give Dan, to live the rest of his days.

The Judge's words interrupt my thoughts. He is looking stern and with my wind up, I'm finding it difficult to latch on to what he is saying. He is telling me that mine is an aggravated crime, taking up arms against society.

I address him with directness. 'That is the way the evidence came out here. It appeared that I deliberately took up arms of my own accord and induced the other three men to join me for the purpose of doing nothing but shooting down the police.' There is a levity to my voice; a mocking, accusatory tone. Those in the seats surrounding me snort and laugh at the comment. Their laughter is one of nervousness and incredulity that I would dare to speak this way to the man who holds my life in his hands. But Barry and I both know that there is only one ending to today's proceedings, despite whatever I may say to him in his court. He squares me up. He will have his say as much as I.

His chest puffs out. 'In new communities, where the bonds of society are not so well linked together as in older countries, there is unfortunately a class which disregards the evil consequences of crime. Foolish, inconsiderate, ill-conducted, unprincipled youths unfortunately abound.' At this his eyes roam the court with its many sympathisers sitting watch on proceedings. 'And unless they are made to consider the consequences of crime they are led to imitate notorious felons, whom they regard as self-made heroes. It is right, therefore, that they should be asked to consider and reflect upon what the life of a felon is. A felon who has cut himself off from all the decencies, all the affections, charities, and all the obligations of society is as helpless and degraded as a wild beast of the field. He has nowhere to lay his head. He has no-one to prepare for him the comforts of life. He suspects his friends, he dreads his enemies, he is in constant alarm lest his pursuers should reach him. And his only hope is that he might use his life in what he considers a glorious struggle for existence. That is the life of the outlaw or felon.' He stops and casts an eye around at the young men before him. 'And it would be well for those young men who are so foolish to consider that it is brave of a man to sacrifice the lives of his fellow creatures in carrying out his own wild ideas, to see that it is a life to be avoided by every possible means, and to reflect that the unfortunate termination of your life is a miserable death.' His lips purse as he looks at me and I focus on the deep lines etched around his mouth. This man, whose words speak of death and misery, knows nothing of the life of an outlaw, nor of my reasons to take up arms against the Victorian Police Force. He knows only what has been written in the papers, what he has been told by the constabulary. I think he's about to stop and pass sentence but he looks at me harshly and shakes his head, ever so slightly, before going on.

'New South Wales joined with Victoria in providing ample inducement to persons to assist in having you and your companions apprehended. But by some spell, which I cannot understand—a spell which exists in all lawless communities more or less—which may be attributed either to a sympathy for the outlaws, or a dread of the consequences which would result from the performance of their duty—no persons were found who would be tempted by the reward.'

I nod my head, which he may have thought was my agreeance with him that there was no-one who would turn us in, but in fact I was thinking of the many informers that I know who had given information about us to the police, willingly or coerced. Most of all I was thinking of Aaron, who was almost our brother. He was only a step away from being in the Glenrowan Inn with us on that night; instead choosing to go against us in the worst of ways. Barry is working into his speech, his face reddening with the exertion of his words. Spittle flies from his lips. 'The love of country, the love of order, the love of obedience to law, have been set aside for reasons difficult to explain, and there is something extremely wrong in a country where a lawless band of men are able to live for 18 months, disturbing society.' His finger stabs at me as he speaks.

We continue on, back and forth, debating what I

have said and haven't said. I can feel he's tiring and my moment in this stand, this court, and in fact this life, is coming to an end. He slows his speech and looks me in the eye, ignoring all others in his court. 'Your unfortunate and miserable companions have died a death which probably you might rather envy, but you are not afforded the opportunity.'

I cut him off, mad as hell that this self important arsehole would dare to speak about the boys, who I love more than most in this world. My boys that were murdered by the Victorian Police Force, if not at Glenrowan, then by their actions in our youth that led us to Glenrowan.

'I don't think that there is much evidence that they did die that death.' I didn't envy Joe's death. His dead body propped up for photographs to be taken and printed on the front pages of all the papers. As I didn't envy Steve's death, huddled in the inn, shitting himself at the hopelessness of the situation and driven to putting a bullet in his own brain before he was burnt to a charred stump. No, I didn't envy them, as I'm sure that they wouldn't envy me swinging from the end of a rope. Death was death, no matter the way it came to you.

'May the Lord have mercy on your soul.' He looks solemn as he delivers the final words, usual with the pronouncement of the death sentence. But I refuse to let the pompous arse have the last say. If these will be my last words on record, they'll be remembered. I stare hard at him. 'I will go a little further than that and say I will see you there where I go.' The crowd in the court erupts and I'm dragged from the stand and out the back door.

PETITION for REPRIEVE

To His Excellency the Governor-in-Council,—
Your humble PETITIONERS (having carefully considered the circumstances of the case) respectfully pray that the Life of the CONDEMNED man, EDWARD KELLY, may be spared.

N.B.—This List to be sent to Mr. David Gaunson, M.L.A., Solicitor for the Prisoner, so as to reach Melbourne on Monday morning next, 8th November, 1880.

NAMES.   RESIDENCE.

***

I'm not sorry for much of what has gone down in these last years, but there are moments that run through my dreams, sounds that ring in my ears even when I'm awake and moving. One of these is Annie Jones pleading to us—to me—to let her take Janey and John away from the inn, out of harm's way as things went awry at Glenrowan. He was no more than a boy. I'd watched him stand tall and sing sweetly on that night. Just a boy, shot by one of the bullets sent flying into the hotel. The coppers have blood on their hands, even though they chalk his death up to me. Not that it matters to Annie or John, which bastard gun that bullet erupted from.

She'd held him in her arms, shot and pale, bleeding out onto the dirt floor, mixing with the piss that escaped him. Her voice loving and strong—a mother's voice. Reassuring. But before that, to me, at the front of the hotel, she'd screamed that she must leave, she must take her children with her. That shriek leaves me cold. It was the call of a woman dying inside, crazed with her inability to save the ones she loved most in the world. A caged cry of desperation. I yelled back for her to go. Under the hand of a white handkerchief, frantically thrown about, she left. It was the last time I saw her, Ann Jones, the woman who I had counted as a friend—or at the very least, not an enemy.

I heard afterwards that John died and the knowledge sat heavy in my guts. I didn't blame her for the words she'd told the coroner and the court and the newspaper. It was her pain spilling out and she had to aim it at someone. I heard she'd been told to say I'd killed the lad. If she did, her application for a part of the reward would get forwarded on. I don't know if it's true. The coppers deny it, but I wouldn't put it past the bastards.

The hurt inflicted on Ann, the loss of a child, the same pain that I am about to inflict on my mother, eats away at me in my dank cell of stone. Ma had been allowed to come and see me, released from her own cell for a short time. She hadn't cried as Ann had cried. But she had touched my face. Told me she loved me. Her lip barely quivered as they'd returned her hands to irons as she was leaving and told me, 'Mind you die like a Kelly, son.'

I hear her cry, even when my eyes are open and moving around the walls surrounding me, I feel like I could be losing a little more of my humanity. Maybe it is my mind that is lost.

***

Melbourne Gaol, 11 November, 1880

THEY'VE spent the last weeks watching me every minute of every day. God forbid that I find a way to take my own life and deprive them of their show, now that it's scheduled. The door has stayed open, a gaoler outside at all times, watching and waiting. I'm allowed outside in the yard to walk around for exercise, but even that is done under the watchful eye of two guards. I might overpower just one of them, with my leg irons riveted around my ankles, chaffing them raw.

Time is coming quickly to a close for me. I've spent the past days dictating letters and contemplating what lies ahead. They want me to apologise, to fall at their feet and cry why I shouldn't have done what I did. But what they don't understand is that I'm not sorry—I did what I did because I had to, there was no choice.

They send me Father Donaghy, hoping that I'll repent my sins. I feel them watching from outside my cell, rubbing their hands together, that I may 'break' and ask for forgiveness. They'll be disappointed. I won't give them the satisfaction.

On the walk to the condemned cell, where I'll spend my final night on this earth, we have to pass through the gaol garden which surrounds the hospital ward. I turn my head to avoid seeing the wooden handcart that I know my body is to be dragged out upon. Broken. It's easy to turn my attention away as I look at the bright pink of one of the roses in the garden. Perfectly shaped and the most vibrant of colours. The warmth of sun on my back, which I haven't felt without the shadow of a wall for so long, along with the buzzing of the bees amongst the flowers, sends a flood of warmth through me and I breathe in the scent of the garden. I am trying to appreciate the last thing of beauty that I might ever see.

'To find such beauty in this shit hole.' I tell the

gaoler leading me along, but all he does is grunt and ignore the comment. For the first time since the Judge announced my sentence as death, my heart feels light.

I barely slept last night, tossing and turning. I was caught between wanting to slip into oblivion where I wouldn't have to think about what is coming today. But then I would be jolted by the idea that I would be spending the rest of eternity in that oblivion so then not wanting to close my eyes. Exhaustion won out in the end—but only for a few hours.

This morning I dropped to my knees and prayed for the first time in many years. I must be a good Catholic-boy at heart because it all came flooding back. I don't even know if I believe in an afterlife, even if I did deserve one, but I figured praying couldn't hurt. I prayed to God and told him that I hope heaven looks and feels like the garden that I passed through. And now I sit here, waiting for them to arrive and take me away. There is nothing else to do.

At the gallows they try to tie my hands and I object. 'There is no need for tyin' me up!' I'm not going anywhere with the hundreds of people crammed in here, unarmed as I am. But I am forced to submit and they bind my arms above the elbows with a leather strap. My shoulders cry out at this pressure and muscles cramp. It's the first time that I've wanted to cry out. But I hold it. I push back my shoulders against the pain and just feel it.

I look down at the people surrounding me—all of them waiting excitedly or apprehensively, for the drop of my body through the trapdoor. My stomach lurches at the thought and I feel light-headed. I catch a face that I know, and I lock eyes on him. I want the last face I see not to be one of a gawking stranger, or a face of hate. The face I find is of Father O'Hea: I know him. He's the man who baptised me 25 years ago. The man that promised my soul an eternal life. I can only hope that he knew what he was talking about. I can't make physical contact with him, but locking eyes with him is enough. He's come today for me. Edward Kelly. The boy I was and the man that I am. I'm grateful.

I had planned on giving them a final speech, urging them to fight on against the corruption of the bastard classes, but I fear that my voice may struggle or that I may piss my pants with the fear that runs through me. So I lift my head and with all the strength that I can muster, tell the waiting crowd, "Ah, well, I suppose it has come to this." It is all I can say.

It isn't the green hills of Ireland that dance before my eyes. It is a white bag, shoved forcefully over my head, making it difficult to breathe. I will never see my Ireland. The land that I may have seen, with Ettie at my side, had I not made so simple a choice as to let Curnow out that night. I know that my body will rot in the grounds of this God-forsaken gaol and my head will be exhibited and investigated in the name of science. It will be on display to any who want to gawk at the face of a killer.

Joe and Steve are dead. The Glenrowan stand claimed them. My mother cries for her two boys. I told her, that last time I saw her, I had gone back for Dan, when I was already out of the fight. I strode out of the hotel, armour on and battle ready, knowing that I had to protect my brothers. I'd managed to get behind the gunfire in the haze of dawn and smoke. But when I should have left, I went back into the hotel to try and get my baby brother. She'd told me that she was proud of me for that. I wonder how many times she's been proud of me.

It was that limping teacher, Curnow, who'd flagged the train and called it to a stop before it hit the upended tracks. I had ignored my feelings about him on the night. I thought that a man like that would not have the spine to go against us. If I wasn't about to swing for it, I might actually admire him for what he did; a bloody stupid act that could have got his brains blown from his head. I wouldn't have hesitated to pull the trigger. People will remember his name and his family will share in the spoils of my capture. One small mistake, on my head, changed my life, and that of all the people that I love.

I shall never see my Ettie again. I know that she cries for me, and I feel sick about her heartbreak. We both knew the chances were small, but we had hoped for a life. A blessing and a curse of youth, I suppose. I have sent her word that I love her, but she is not to waste her life mourning me. She knew what I was. If we were honest with ourselves, we both knew this was always the way it would go.

I wince slightly at the first touch of the rough bag to my face, though I recover myself and lift my head a little to better allow the faceless hangman to position the rope. It feels heavy around my throat. My heart beats an erratic rhythm in my chest and I think for a moment that I may vomit, my final humiliation. I try and calm myself and think of the faces of my boys: my brothers. The loss of them rips into my soul. I know they will be waiting for me. How I long to laugh and ride with them again. Will they let me? Will I have their forgiveness—that which I cannot give to myself?

I hear the creak of the floor beneath me, and refuse to think of what will be next. I see the vision of the green, Irish hills of my dream.

And I reach out to touch them.

ABOUT THE AUTHOR

By day, Nicole Kelly works as a primary school teacher, instilling a love of reading and writing in her small charges. The in between hours are filled with her own stories and writing. Nicole has short stories published in the anthologies, *Close to Heaven* and *Just Alice*. She lives in rural Victoria with her husband and two young children. Lament is her debut novel.

Lament shortlisted in the Hawkeye Publishing Manuscript Development Prize 2020.

www.hawkeyebooks.com.au/nicole-kelly/

To follow Nicole and hear about her upcoming book releases, register for the newsletter at
www.hawkeyebooks.com.au
or follow her on Twitter @ruralvicwriter.

ACKNOWLEDGMENTS

Thank you for picking up this book and reading through to the end! Without you, the reader, there is no story. Together we've created it—each bringing something to it, which has made it the story that it is.

I have long dreamed of telling this story. I've loved the story of the Kelly Gang for as long as I can remember and it's by sheer luck that I married a Kelly. For a time growing up, I lived in Glenrowan and would drive past the big Ned Kelly statue every day. I am sure this story has sat in me for 20 years, waiting to be written!

The first part of the book is based on what happened at Glenrowan, up until Ned let Thomas Curnow go. The rest is purely fiction, based around real events. The Duke of Manchester did visit the Ballarat Agricultural Show in 1880, while Ned was awaiting execution. The Ercildoune ram sale did really happen only a couple of months later. Rumours of a love between Ned and Ettie Hart persist as well as the romantic notion that Dan escaped to Queensland. I love these ideas, and though not proven, I love to imagine they may be true.

There is a danger in writing about real people. I have endeavoured to treat those people with respect and redeeming features. Though I used newspaper accounts of people where possible, their characters are purely fictional creation.

I have not written this book on my own. There have been kind words and encouragement, constructive criticism and questions from countless people over many years. I ask your indulgence to thank some of them here.

To 'the girls'—Jen, Nat, Lani and Suzanne. Your support and friendship has been unwavering and it has given me the courage to put myself out there. To Karin, thank you for your encouraging words, and your round tuit. I put it to good use! Melissa Cornell-Smith, when I was ready to put this story into a bottom drawer, you read it and cheered it on. The coffee and conversation that we shared, your enthusiasm and reassurance, were the reasons I kept going. Sometimes the keeping going is the hardest part.

Thank you to Alison Arnold who worked with me first and gave me the courage to rip and re-write. To Carolyn Martinez for seeing the rough diamond in my words and helping me to polish them into a story I love.

To Brad Webb, whose feedback helped me to get my Ned more on point. To Bren MacDibble and John Harms, for your kind words, feedback and encouragement. The time you gave me was appreciated and I will pay it forward. Thank you to Greg Tobin for his inspired words when I asked for them.

Most of all, thanks to my family. Mum and Dad, thank you for being my first readers and champions. To my husband, Damien, who takes all my crazy ideas in his stride and says yes when others would say no. And finally, to Jack and Elsie. You two are my whole heart. This book proves you can achieve your dreams, because I have achieved mine. I love you.

Nicole Kelly

BOOK CLUB DISCUSSION QUESTIONS

1. What role does the image of Thomas Curnow play in *Lament*?
2. Ettie was the love that Ned Kelly desired. How did his love for her change him?
3. What does the armour that they wore at Glenrowan represent for the Gang and for Ned?
4. How is the theme of lamentation explored throughout the story?
5. Why does Ned Kelly continue to be spoken of and explored through art and literature 140 years after his death?
6. In what ways is the portrayal of Ned in *Lament* realistic rather than idealised?
7. Though *Lament* is a work of fiction, it is based on real events and real people. How is historical fiction able to provide its reader with both truth and fiction?
8. Does Ned have an awareness of the choices that he has made in his life and their consequences or does he see himself as a victim of circumstance?
9. Ned's love of his family is central to the story. Is this the quality that defines him?
10. Ned and Joe Byrne had a relationship as close as brothers. Discuss.

A FAVOUR

Can I ask for your help?

I love writing and I aim to entertain you. If you liked what you read today, could I ask you to leave a positive review or tell your friends about this book?

Book reviews can make or break a book.

Lament is available at www.hawkeyebooks.com.au and all good bookstores and libraries.

INTERESTED IN MORE NED KELLY?

www.ironoutlaw.com contains history, tourism, links to books and merchandise for sale.

REVIEWS

'*Lament* is clever, wicked, action-packed, thought provoking and satisfying. This book took me on a journey packed with emotions and delightfully bittersweet moments where I couldn't help but root for the success of Ned Kelly. If you want a story that connects you mind, body and soul then this is a definite read. And what have I learned by reviewing *Lament* as part of my final year university internship? – the wonderful experience of broadening knowledge by reading outside our usual genres. A whole new world awaits. An epic story that connects you mind, body and soul. Highly recommended,' *Catie Leigh*.

'It's pure happenstance that author, Nicole Kelly, shares the same surname as Australia's most enduring legend. However, it could reasonably be argued that 2020 Kelly has done a better job of getting inside the head of 1880 Kelly than so many others who have tried to capture the man whom we still – 140 years on – regard as our greatest rebel. Indeed, Lament is a better fit than Ned's famous helmet,' *Greg Tobin*.

'Nicole Kelly writes with such engaging olde world charm, you'll be immediately pulled into discovering the person Ned Kelly might have been. If you've ever wondered what might have happened if the Kelly gang lived on, this is the heartbreaking read for you,' *Bren MacDibble*.

www.ingramcontent.com/pod-product-compliance
Lightning Source LLC
Chambersburg PA
CBHW050203120726
47903CB00002B/736